12-9-09

Adriana —

I hope you en...
the stories ...
book ...
You will ...
slami from you ...
Cheer + ... in Mexico.

Lots of love,

B. Blahuta

Reluctant Journey

by
Gilbert Andres Archuleta

authorHOUSE®

AuthorHouse™
1663 Liberty Drive, Suite 200
Bloomington, IN 47403
www.authorhouse.com
Phone: 1-800-839-8640

First published by AuthorHouse 1/21/2009

ISBN: 978-1-4389-2581-3 (sc)

*Printed in the United States of America
Bloomington, Indiana*

This book is printed on acid-free paper.

Table of Contents

Dedication

This book is dedicated to ENOCH, a mentor who believes in the worth of others and who inspired me to write.

Gilbert Andres Archuleta

Preface

In the isolation of the northern-most mountain valleys of northern New Mexico are a breed of people whose ancestors settled and survived in a remote and harsh environment. These earliest of European immigrants into the northern limits of the Spanish empire in the new world of 1598 were also from a unique religious legacy. They were a people whose faith is now all but forgotten and remains only in the memory of some of their descendants whose "stories" went beyond the overt manifestations described in the occasional books that attempt at describing religious practices from the cold objectivity of recorded facts.

<u>Reluctant Journey</u> in some of its stories takes us through the cultural memory of decendants describing the legacy of the Penitentes from the point of view of these second generation adherants to the faith as well as sons and grandsons of those early practicioners of the faith. It describes the passion of the practicing Penitentes

and the emotional and deep rooted commitment to what they believed was a covenant with God and the teaching of Jesus Christ.

Reluctant Journey is also a story about a young Hispanic boy growing up in the midst of a group of people who were born in this new land which was distant from a larger cultural community and other larger populations of people. Gibo Herrera grew up in the relative isolation of a mountain valley in which the only available communication was word of mouth and the wisdom that lingered in these remnants of a historical legacy.

Gibo's story is that of the discovery of self and his surroundings, the natural beauty of the mountain valleys, a family loyalty and young love. The reluctant journey in which Gibo Herrera embarks upon is more of a commitment to promises made and the yearnings for home and loved ones, than it is of distance. It is a journey of discovery and the meeting of other people like himself who also have their own sense of belonging.

Gilbert Andres Archuleta

On The Last Valley of the Cordilleras

Embargo, my birth place, is now an ancient land where the ghosts of a time that used to be, now live. Settled in the high mountain valleys of the Sangre de Cristo Cordillera, its name means *seizure of property.* I prefer the *sin-embargo* that in Spanish is more like a casual after-thought or a transition in mid sentence to mean, "on-the-other hand," as in, *Este lugar no sera El lugar ideal, sin embargo, aqui nos quedamos* (This place may not be the ideal place, on the other hand, it's here that we'll stay).

Embargo is a deep valley in New Mexico, nestled between huge mountains lumbering south from the Colorado Rockies. Technically it is not really a valley because, through its two-mile swath, it is bounded by meadowland on the north side, a river bisecting the center from east to west with an alluvial fan which creates a hillside running along its length on the south side. The river, with a length of about three miles through the valley, is a fast-moving stream of cold, clear water originating in the snow banks of the high mountains and the seeps and springs of the watershed. This is no meandering river. Its waters fall at a rate of three hundred feet per mile. Its banks are rock-strewn beaches (*playas*) with almost perfectly rounded rocks hewn by its rapidly tumbling effect.

The migrants who settled these mountain valleys were looking for large *praderas* (grasslands) for their livestock: goats, sheep, cattle, horses and donkeys. Embargo had little akin to these dreams. These early settlers were, in spirit and ilk, risk-taking adventurers whose faith in a suffering Christ and their 14th century stoicism made them perfect for this minimal land. Embargo may not have been much, but these pioneers were accustomed to not having very much. The early settlers, which included my great, great grandfathers, were not easily deterred by the severe cold which lasted six months of the year, the limited variety of food and at best, a barter economy. These hardy folk had gone so far north from the rest of the colony that they were isolated in the keenest sense of the term. La Villa, the closest town, was located south and one to two hours away in good weather, unreachable in snowy weather.

For my brother and me, life seemed to start in the spring of each year (*la primavera*) when we were children. The twentieth day of May signaled freedom for us since this was the last day of school and soon we'd be able to peel the shirts off our backs and rush into the mountain sun. We dared the cold waters of the the Red, a river that ran behind our house and one that would not be a small river for long. Snow melt in the high mountains would cause it to swell and for a few weeks it would rampage its way on its journey to the big river. At night, we could hear the rumbling noise   made by the rolling rocks carried by the angry river.

My brother, our friends and I awaited the *veinte-y-cuatro de junio* (24th of June), *El dia de San Juan* (the Day of St. John). This was the first official day for swimming; any sooner and you could be "bit" in the bones by the freezing waters. This is what we were told by our parents and we had evidence of this bone-chill that happened any time we lingered in the river.

By mid May, we'd already seen several of the neighbors plant their *habas* and peas. We knew that sooner or later these fields would come under our discreet supervision and at the right time we would be the first to savor the fruits of our neighbors' labor and the taste of summer. After the long winter, spring brought on a profusion of newness, a renewal of life, and all the discomforts of winter were forgotten and forgiven. The cottonwood trees in the *bosque* (woods) were bursting with young deep green leaves and their shoots, now growing along the rock playas of the river, began to reach up as if in adulation of the sun. In years past, the rock playa had been bare of any growth, partly due to the devastation of the high spring waters of the Red, and partly as a result of the denuding effects of the goat herds belonging to the villagers during my father's youth. During the springs of my childhood however, the trees having waited silently through "the quiet time" of winter now mushroomed with a frenzy to grow in what appeared a desperate attempt to escape the violence of the river and the omnivorous appetites of decades of hungry goats.

La primavera, exploding with life, brought forth a plethora of birds, many returning from their winter migrations as well as others like the crow and the owl who had never left. They showed their presence with animated fervor of nest building, serious hunting for food and filling the bosque with chatter. The owls continued their haunting hoots throughout the summer nights. Red-top woodpeckers with their white apron fronts and black bodies and the red-speckled woodpeckers, who flew in dips and rises, again came to telegraph their presence in the depth of the bosque. My father aptly named the woodpeckers, *carpinteros* or carpenters. Blue birds, the ubiquitous robins and wrens built their nests and busied themselves chasing insects. A sky full of green-winged swallows settled in on the mud cliffs of the south side of the valley. At dusk they skimmed the course of the river to swoop up the insect flyers that made their life on the waves of the noisy waters.

My brother and I never failed to note the fervor of the life around us. We too, were part of that *joi-de-vivre*. We looked with anticipation to the fishing that awaited us as soon as the season opened. We looked to eat the cottonwood seed bunches, *tetones*, that lingered for a short time before these tiny green grapes burst forth with the cotton seed that flew in the wind to spread that tree of life, *El alamo*. We internalized the sounds of the spring and summer and could name the sources of each, except one that started at dusk. The sound varied between a fast flutter of wings and a midnight wailing cry. These sounds we ascribed to *El pajaro chinchonte* (the bird chinchonte). For us this was a mystery bird.

In late April, this strange bird-noise would come from a lone grove of cottonwoods about a quarter mile from our house on the north side of the narrow valley. Because we had heard that sound for so many years and never knew what it was, and because we could not find traces of any birds living in the cottonwood grove, we decided to call it *Chinchonte*. The name for the bird came to us after watching a Mexican movie that had come to town, in which a love-struck Mayan told his intended bride that she was as lovely as the song of the pajaro *Chinchonte*. Our questions about this mystery bird were never answered to our satisfaction. My father dismissed our curiosity about the mystery bird, with its strange loud flapping of wings and plaintive cry usually heard in the early hours of the morning. The closest he came to a satisfactory answer was, "*Son dormilones* (sleepers). These birds sleep during the day and hunt for food at night, " he said.

I had seen the night hawks flitting high through the early evening sky. I admired their lithe bodies and the white horizontal bars on their under-wings, but I never equated them with our mystery bird.

One late-summer evening at dusk, as I returned home from fishing in the box canyon, I had a strange experience. Light from the last rays of the sun still lingered on the high canyon walls and the sky was still quite visible from my shaded vantage point. Some cows which walked ahead of me on the same powdered trail out of the canyon had kicked up a haze of dust. In this place between shadow and waning light, I felt a sense of expectation and a strange, atavistic dread.

Presently, I heard a cry in shrill bursts right over my head. I heard a flutter of wings and the cry came louder and closer. A small bird fell from the sky, onto the path right in front of me. On the ground it flapped its wings and emitted a cry of pain that made me cringe. On its chest was a large beetle, one-fourth the size of the bird itself, which had dug his pincers into the chest of the bird and was holding on in mortal combat. I knew I had to remove the beetle from the chest of the bird to stop its pain.

The bird was unlike any that I had ever seen. It was of a brownish-gray color and had a remarkably large mouth. Its mouth, it seemed to me, was larger than its head as it opened wide in its agony. Using the tip of my fishing rod, I pried the beetle off the suffering bird. I deduced that this strange flyer might be a night hawk which, while scooping insects from the sky, had made a miscalculation, and "bitten off more than he could chew." After extracting the insect from the injured bird, I looked for the telltale wing marking of the night hawk that I had so admired, but it did not have these markings. *This bird was*, I thought, *a stray flyer visiting these canyon walls.* I tried to encourage it to rise and fly away, but it was too weak from the struggle. I left it there, subdued on the dusty trail.

"*No seria un Chinchonte*," my younger brother suggested after I told him the story.

"Not unless he too, is *un dormilon*, a nocturnal hunter," I said, "But, anyway I don't want to believe that he is our mystery bird."

Much later, when I became an adult, I found pictures of a whip-poor-will, a nocturnal insect-feeder characterized as a bird whose sound and wings were like that of our mystery bird. The book said it made its home on the deciduous forests of the midwest. I was puzzled by this fact but since ours was truly a mystery bird, I realized it had wandered into these mountain valleys long ago and its descendants had made Embargo their adopted home. I had finally identified our mystery bird, the one that had come to haunt my summers. To this day, when I return to visit Embargo, I can hear the flapping wings and the sad cry of our transplanted Whip-poor-will.

Summer of Language

Days were now a routine of activities. We swam in the cold, clear waters of the river, fished in the evenings close to dusk and caught cutthroat minnows by hand in the rivulets that ran parallel to the river. We caught the little green frogs that made their home in the still waters of the spring-fed ponds of the lower valley and once in a while had frog legs for dinner. The sun got steadily hotter. After shedding our skins, our bodies got darker and our feet formed calluses from running on the river rocks. On the swampy, spongy grounds of the north meadows, red winged blackbirds trilled their summer song. The horse flies aggressively bit the horses and boys alike. We were in a rhythm of our own and that of the world around us.

At night my uncles and cousins would gather on our grandmother Maria's porch, the adults to smoke, *tabaco mexicano* and the rest to hear the stories that my uncles told of sheep shearing in the early spring in places like *la ceja.* This *was* a place of sheltering trees or canyon lands in the eastern plains of New Mexico and Colorado. The storied Ceja was a name that was often repeated as being located in Huerfano County Colorado, but it was ranchland away from there where my uncles would hire out to those owners with sheep herds numbering in the thousands. I would listen intently to the pride of my uncles as they related the number of sheep each would shear in one day. The task of *tresquilandor* (sheepshearer) was a respected profession and one that brought home the money needed to run the households. My father, the youngest of the brothers, never developed the skill of shearing sheep, nor that of sheep herding, which his own father had done most of his life. As we sat on the porch facing the mountains to the east of us, I would see a flicker of rose-colored light that silhouetted the mountain for two or three seconds. Throughout the summer we saw this reddish light far, far away. I never imagined that one day I would again witness this thunder-less lightening overhead in the flat plains of Kansas.

The events of the day, the week, or season, were told and retold at these gatherings. My Tio Adon who was the storyteller of the family always sat with his chair slanted against the wall of the porch resting on the chair's back legs. He was a couple of years older than my father, and he claimed the prerogatives of the older sibling. His opinion prevailed in the conversations and he took it upon himself to be the first adult to lead the storytelling.

He challenged the youngsters with riddles and *dichos*. He would ask, *"cuantas estrellas hay en El cielo?"* (how many stars are in the sky). *"Sin cuenta,"* he would answer himself. Sin Cuenta means without count, which sounds exactly like *cincuenta* (fifty). The riddle drew the same sounds of amazement after hearing it twenty times as when Tio Adon first told it. After these openers and after getting the attention of my brother, sister and me, as well as that of my cousins, he started his storytelling in earnest.

We heard about the seven-headed dragon that laid waste to the countryside and how the young peasant offered to kill it in exchange for the hand of the king's daughter. Tio told of the king's eager acceptance of this arrangement, as he wanted to get rid of the dragon.

"Meanwhile," Tio told us, as if confiding a secret, "The young peasant and the king's daughter were in love and had been seeing each other secretly."

We followed a story that took as long as it took the stars in the firmament to move across the sky. It ended only when the young peasant had killed the dragon, but was now betrayed by the King who refused to give his daughter in marriage now that the dragon had been dispatched. We cried when the young peasant was sent off to war in far off lands and the king's daughter died of sadness as she pined away for her lost love and promised husband.

My Uncle Adon regaled us with many stories that often ended in a happily-ever-after. These stories about weddings or other celebrations, invariably featured my Uncle Adon as a first-hand witness to his tales of wonder. His role however, was that of a humble waiter at the long tables in these celebrations.

My Tio Adon never lacked for stories. They were the road on which we found our dreams, by which we traveled to distant lands, and met kings, liars and thieves. Through them, most of us in the valley were introduced to what we would later come to know as literature. Tio Adon's stories were all told in Spanish because neither he nor any of us spoke English.

I was the oldest of a family of four. Everybody called me Gibo. My sister Flo was two years younger than I, and my little brother Vivian was enlisted as my fishing buddy. One day my mother took sick and yelled at me from her bedroom to fetch my Grandmother Maria. When we returned, there was a little red baby crying on the floor. I was ushered out of the room by my grandmother but I'd seen something that I would never forget; It was the birth of my baby sister Jo.

My brother Vivian was the closest friend that I had. I treated him as both my little brother whom I loved and protected and my personal slave. He was my Sancho Panza, a character from my Tio Adon's stories. Vivian was the food taster of a plant or fruit which neither of us had previously tasted. He was the one who found out whether or not a certain bee or insect would sting or bite. He served as my guinea pig in fifth grade when I was given the assignment of proving that the pupil of the eyes open in the dark in order to receive more light and closes up in too much light.

I called my brother Vivian into the room that we shared with our two sisters and in the dark shined a flashlight into his eyes. When the light hit his eyes in the dark, the pupil quickly closed. I had proven by my experiment that the pupil of the eye is open wide while in the dark and close when subject to the light. When I explained the process of my experiment to my teacher he was amused, but I am sure that he didn't think too kindly of me for using my little third-grade brother in my experiments.

The most outrageous abuse of my brother Vivian, however, came on the afternoon when a bird chased a chipmunk into our kitchen. When the chipmunk rushed into the kitchen through the open door, we followed and cornered it and I ordered my brother to grab it. He refused and I insisted. He then grabbed the animal, who immediately clamped its teeth down on Vivian's little finger. My brother cried out in pain. I grabbed the chipmunk around the belly, squeezed hard and he turned loose. Meanwhile my brother's finger was bleeding profusely. I took the sugar bowl from the cupboard and poured the sugar on his bleeding finger. I'd heard from my cousins that you could stop the bleeding from a cut this way. I felt terrible about the incident and hoped my parents wouldn't find out. Meanwhile, the chipmunk scurried out the kitchen door. My big brother oppression of Vivian slowed down after this, but it did not stop until he grew up big enough to take me on.

All of the information that my curious mind gathered in those days was either from listening in on adults' conversations or from my Tio Adon's fascinating stories. I also listened to my father read from the Spanish language newspaper, El Crepusculo (The Dawning), which we got about once a month from La Villa, or whenever he managed to find an outdated copy.

I noticed very soon that books were nowhere to be found. The school had books but they were textbooks for studying. Books with stories like those my Tio Adon told did not exist in the entire valley not even in school.

One day when I visited my Tia Juanita I came upon a book tucked away in a niche in her kitchen wall. I was curious to find it there because I knew of no other house in the valley with a book of any kind! I picked it up and leafed through it. It was a strange book with strange stories. I could read in English by then and I soon discovered that the stories in this book were not straightforward but were, rather confusing. They were about a rabbit prancing around with a pocket watch and another rabbit called a hare, sitting on a table and drinking out of a cup, together with a man in a large hat. The story was entitled the "Mad Hatter's Tea Party." "Mad" to me had always meant angry. I'd never heard of a rabbit called a hare and the characters seemed to come from a dream. When my Tia Juanita saw me with the book, she said, as she came up.

"You can look at that book all you want whenever you come here, but you can never take the book out. You must put it back in the niche after you look at it."

My discovery at my Tia Juanita's house became a treasure to me. I had found the book that would open my eyes to literature, to a world of characters that were both impossible and zany, to a rhythm in language that I had never found in the English which I learned in school, not even in the stories told by my Tio Adon. More importantly, I could read the stories again and again, sometimes until I knew them by heart. This book written by Lewis Carroll was *Alice In Wonderland* and *Through The*

Looking Glass. It contained strange, improbable creatures like the Griffin with the head and wings of an eagle and the body of a lion, and the tortoise, walking on its hind legs. There was that pair of deceivers, the Walrus and the Carpenter, who invited a bunch of oysters for a walk, only to betray them by eating them, all the while holding an interesting conversation with them.

Then there was the most frightful monster of them all, The Jabberwock, in a poem that Alice had to read by placing the book on a mirror as the poem had been written in reverse. The poem not only appeared nonsensical, but the language seemed unintelligible. When, later in the book, Humpty Dumpty (of all characters), interpreted the introduction, I was facinated.

I too, took to substitute words that made sense in setting the mood of this adventure poem:

"'Tis brillig and the slithy toves, Did gyre and gimble in the Wabe, All mimsey were the borogroves, And the momrath, outgabe."

Since my Tia Juanita had forbidden me to take the book from the niche in her kitchen, I memorized those parts of the book I liked. I wrote the above introduction of The Jabberwocky from memory during language arts class in fifth grade and successfully deciphered its mystery by assigning parts of speech to the nonsense words: *Slithy* was an adjective, because it describes *toves*, which is a noun. *Gyre* and *gimble* must be verbs, because they seem to describe what the *toves* did and *Wabe* was a noun because it follows *the*. I was pretty impressed with myself and imprinted the stories from the book into my head, so much that I could not sleep for hours at night from the poems and songs that kept going round and round in my head.

The knowledge in the book was so overwhelming to me that I tried some of the poems on my brother and sister, as well as on my school friends. My brother and sister were mesmerized. With my classmates at school however, it was a different matter. I had to stop sharing my stories when some of the girls laughed at me and the boys avoided me.

When I mentioned this to my mother, she said, "If the kids and your teachers don't like you being smart, then act dumb. You know, no one likes a show off." And she laughed.

But I never relinquished the power of that book nor the language which it instilled in me.

The Raggedy Man

On a cold day in January my father woke me up to remind me that it was my birthday and to tell me that he had a surprise for me. He had made breakfast for both of us. It consisted of a blue corn flour mush we called *atole.* I waited for him to surprise me with a gift but no gift seemed forthcoming. I was seven that year and no big affair had ever been made of birthdays but because my father woke me up before any other member of the family, I knew something special was going to happen today.

After this sparse breakfast, he asked me to dress up in my heavy winter clothes and to put on an extra pair of socks. Soon we were outside where he had saddled our mare, Canela (cinammon roan). He climbed onto the saddle, pulled me up behind him, and we were on our way, heading west toward the box canyon.

"Where are we going?"

"We're going to visit El Zordito," he said.

19

Even at that early age I knew that Zordito (deaf-mute) was a handyman, an all-purpose servant, a man to do the work no one else wanted to do, and my father's friend.

We rode about a mile and a half and we came to an adobe house with blue smoke coming out of the chimney. As we approached we saw Zordito with an armload of wood, heading inside. When he saw us, he dropped the wood, waved his hand high in the air to greet us and with a barely audible voice, said, "*lleguen, lleguen*" (come in, come in).

"*Buenos dias Zordito*," my father said in a soft voice. Both men's breath turned a visible vapor in the cold of the morning. My father let me down from the horse and then he dismounted. The two adults shook hands, Zordito picked up the wood and we all went inside.

The place where Zordito lived had an earthen floor, the walls were still un-plastered with the adobe bricks still showing. There was a wooden stove in the kitchen and the house was warm, especially for me, coming in from the cold. The house had a bedroom and a room to the back that was used to store meat and other food.

Zordito helped me take off my heavy coat and he took it along with father's into the next room. He bent down to me and said in his mangled voice, "*Feliz Cumpeaños, cuate*," (happy birthday, pal) and handed me a very small paper-wrapped item. My father then handed me a brand new Prince Albert tobacco pocket-can, and said, "You too, tell him *cumpleaños*, it's his birthday too." I handed Zordito his present and everybody laughed.

I couldn't wait, so I opened my present. It was a large button with a string through the two holes. Zordito took it from me and began to wind the button on the string. He then pulled both ends of the string and the button came to life. It spun forward on one pull and backwards on another. The strings seemed to sing as Zordito handed it to me. After a few tries, I too had the button humming. I loved my birthday present.

The men sat down to smoke and I noticed that food was cooking on the stove. There was a wonderful aroma coming from the steaming pots. Shortly, Zordito got up, walked to the back room and returned with two white flour sacks. From one, he pulled out pieces of *carne seca* (dried beef jerky) and from another he pulled some half a dozen dried green chile peppers. He pounded the jerky on the heavy wooden table with a hammer and placed the chiles in a pot of boiling water. The smell coming from the pots was from whole peeled potatoes with onions cut in half. Meanwhile, Zordito would occasionally stop his pounding to speak to my father. They each spoke in a soft voice, neither intending to be heard, mainly conversing by reading each other's lips. As I played with my *trompo* (spinning button) I could understand my father's side of the conversation but could not make out the broken words coming from Zordito.

Zordito told a story of a deer that had fallen through the ice in the old adobe dig close to where he lived. Through gestures and an occasional word, which my father could understand, he told of a deer that had wandered into the meadow and tried to crawl through a hole on the fence next to the dig. This dig, my father told me later, was a large hole dug out of the earth where people extracted clay for making adobe bricks. Zordito told us, in big heroic gestures, how the animal fell through the ice. He told us how Maclovio, his neighbor, came one morning in December and loudly knocked on the door and awakened him. Maclovio told him to come help him get a deer. Maclovio, he gestured, first roped the trapped deer and asked Zordito to hold the rope while he shot it. There was no mistaking those gestures showing the roping and shooting of the hapless deer. He finished his story with an air of triumph. I wondered whether it was the deer meat which was now the jerky that Zordito was pounding to make ready to toss into the pot.

The meal that Zordito prepared in the couple of hours after we had arrived, was stupendous. He made the different ingredients into a meat, potatoes and green chile stew. He made some thick flour tortillas and a pot of pintos, with smoked corn (chicos). After we ate this delicious food the men sat back and smoked again. The little kitchen where we ate was full of slowly undulating clouds of smoke suspended just above our heads as the men talked.

After a while, Zordito sprang out of his chair, and with a big theatrical gesture, said, "Now for the surprise!"

What was this? I asked myself. He emerged from the cold store room with a big bowl of red quivering jelly-like substance. He showed us the bowl and set three small bowls on the table together with clean spoons. He poured three spoonfuls of this gelatinous material into each of our bowls. I had never seen this food before. He took a bite and asked me to eat. It was a food that could not stay on the spoon if I waited to put it into my mouth. He called it Jell-0 and showed my father the box with a picture from which it came. I enjoyed my birthday surprise, this mystery food.

My father's friend and my birthday pal had treated us to a wonderful birthday meal. I had seen Zordito at my house and other houses in the village, working, helping, giving his all to people that did not always value his work or presence. He was one of many men and women who seemed to live on the edge of society, sometimes ridiculed, sometimes shunned, sometimes belittled. Zordito's curse was that he had been born deaf and mute.

Years later, when I was a fifth grader, our teacher

read a poem to us entitled *The Raggedy Man* by James W. Riley. I thought, as he read it, that it was about just such people as Zordito. In the poem was celebrated a man who was perhaps marginal, but whose heart was full of gold:

> O' The Raggedy Man, He works for Pa
> And He is the goodest man, you ever saw
> He comes to my house everyday
> He waters the horses and feeds them hay
> He milks the cows for Lizbeth Ann
> Ain't he an awful good Raggedy Man?

It was then that Zordito stopped being the lesser human being as others had cast him. He became for me *The Raggedy Man.*

The Rifle

After my grandmother passed away, we lived in her old house. One summer evening, we'd finished supper and were heading to the porch when my mother's younger brother Al and a friend of his drove up to the house. His friend was from La Riata, a small town in Colorado, known for its local ruffians. They were quite excited and asked my father into the kitchen, where I heard them describe a fight that they'd just had at the bar belonging to Benigno Pacheco, in La Cueva two miles away. Not fifteen minutes passed when another car arrived. It belonged to Eusebio Rangel. A passenger with him was holding a gun out the car window.

My Uncle Al knew instantly what this was about. He jumped from the porch to the driveway so fast that the gun-wielding passenger had no time to aim. My father followed and a scuffle ensued. Al grabbed the gun with one hand and punched the assailant with the other. I heard the passenger, whom I later learned was El

Chupilote (the buzzard), yelling out, *"te mato, cabron,"* and then I heard a gun shot. Al would not turn the gun loose as he continued to pummel Chupilote. My father grabbed the gun barrel and soon they extracted the weapon from the shooter.

Al and my father struggled for the gun. Al wanted to use it against the visitors, my father was trying to keep him from doing exactly that. Meanwhile, Eusebio in a panic reversed the car and sped away, down the driveway toward the rock-strewn road along the playa. In his panic however, Eusebio turned left too soon, fearing that the guys now holding the gun would use it against them. He missed the road and drove right onto a thick cedar post on the neighboring fence line. The car bounced back on impact, like the funny shorts in a movie cartoon. With smoke and dust clouding the lights of Eusebio's car, the two assailants turned tail and ran.

Caught up in the excitement I hadn't noticed that my father had punched my Uncle on the nose and extracted the gun from his hands. This prevented my Uncle Al from shooting the trespassers or following them as he and his friend Henry had asserted they would have done.

My father calmed down the high excitement of the moment and jokingly assured Uncle Al and Henry that there was no further need to pursue the issue.

"You beat them twice tonight." he told them. He

quietly secured the gun in one of the back rooms in order that the weapon not be an issue again this night. Al complained.

"If you hadn't hit me, *cuñado,* (brother-in-law) I would have killed that *san-a-gan.*"

"El Chupilote shot the gun," someone said and they all went out to the porch to see if there was a bullet impact somewhere on the wall. Sure enough, slightly to the right of the kitchen door, at about a man's height, they found a small caliber bullet hole dug into the whitened adobe wall. My father did not pursue the incident with the authorities and Al and his friend returned to more frequent encounters like this one in La Riata.

With this incident seemingly forgotten, I returned to the back room a few days later to look for the gun. I found it in a closet in my parents' room. The gun was a 22 caliber long rifle with a short clip that held six cartridges. I took the gun out when no one was looking and found that the clip still had five bullets left. My father who never kept a gun in the house, had not even checked for ammunition. I knew that the Chupilote had come to use the gun against Al, but I fell in love with it and vowed to shoot it.

The next day I took it out into the bosque. I was not up to killing any animal with it, I just wanted to fire it. It was an exhilarating feeling to hear the noise, feel the recoil on my shoulder and smell the smoke from the burning gun powder. I ejected the casing from the breech and kept it as a souvenir. I shot it again but decided that I couldn't afford to use up the remaining bullets.

 I wanted to consult with my Cuate Leve, my father's old friend who had shown me how to shoot a gun and taught me a few things about the safe handling of a rifle. When I did a few days later I didn't tell him about the gun that we had at home, but he knew I had something on my mind.

"Cuate, are you shooting the gun that you took from El Chupilote?"

Evidently the people throughout Embargo had heard about the incident at my house and Cuate knew that it wouldn't be long before I'd get my hands on the gun.

"Has Benito Ortiz talked to my Cuate Andy about the gun?" he asked.

 "Why would he ask my father about the gun?"

"I understand it belongs to him," he said, "I understand that Chupilote had borrowed the gun to shoot some prairie dogs behind his house in El Llano."

"Too bad," I said, "that gun belongs to me now!" I feigned courage brought on by my fear that I would lose the gun.

"El Chupilote tried to kill my Uncle Al with that gun and we are not going to return it to him or to Benito

Ortiz."

"Be careful, Cuate."

He figured he had upset me and he was now referring to my careless use of the gun. Cuate, after all, was a gentle soul who had been a family friend ever since I could remember. His nickname, Cuate, meant, pal, or good friend.

Benito Ortiz waited about two months before he had the courage to ask, or rather, plead with my father for the return of his gun. My father did not really want to keep the gun but he wanted to put some fear into anyone associated with the incident at our house that summer evening. He had some stern words for Benito, who happened to be related to my Tio Miguel, husband to my Tia Juanita. My father told Benito that he'd think about his request and said that he might get some advise from *la ley* (the law). In this part of the county, State Patrolman Douglas was the sole dispenser of law and order and was feared by all potential law breakers. Benito agreed to wait. But I did not.

It was the 27th day of September and about six inches of snow had fallen on the ground. The rocks on the playa were covered with white and the cottonwoods were coated with powder. School was in session but I chose not to go. My plans were to take the gun and go hunting. I had two bullets left in the gun clip and I envisioned myself, as I did my maternal grandfather, as a great hunter, a good shooter and an excellent stalker of game. My grandfather had, some years earlier, imbued me with that vision.

When I was seven years old, my Uncle Pino, on my father's side, had a goat that was troublesome and would not stay in the corral nor stay tethered. One morning, about eight o'clock, Uncle Pino came down from his house on the hill to our house. He was looking for me. I was just a boy but he asked me to walk to my grandfather's and ask my grandpa to shoot the goat which had run off and threatened to run away. He pointed to the piñon forests that bordered the valley on the south side. By the time I got to my grandfather's house I could see that the goat had already crossed the river and was standing on a hilltop about one-quarter of a mile away. I told my grandfather what my Uncle Pino wanted him to do.

My grandfather Lafevre was a descendant of French trappers and was known in the valley as a good hunter himself. He had no problem with the request. I pointed to the goat on the hill and he went into his house to get his 30-30 caliber long gun. I ran back home and as I approached the house, I looked up at the goat still on the hill and then I saw it fall. Seconds later, I heard the report of the gun, since that was as long as it took the sound to reach where my uncle and I stood.

With this vivid picture in my mind, I now entered

the young forest of cottonwoods. Soon enough I saw the fresh track of a rabbit and followed it. I walked slowly, my heart pounding with excitement as I followed the tracks. I noticed that the tracks led to a bush and stopped abruptly. I waited quietly while my heart slowed. I remembered my grandfather's comment to me once, when I asked how he could spot the deer that he shot up in the mountain. He said that if you stand quietly and look straight ahead, that even if deer were not in your frontal vision, you could see them out the sides of your eyes. Sure enough, I detected a movement to my right. It was a rabbit. I turned slowly, lifting the gun to my shoulder, aimed and slowly squeezed the trigger. The rabbit seemed to jump when I shot, but he lay still after that. I approached slowly, my heart racing again, and whispered a silent prayer, *God I hope I hit him*. I had. I experienced the euphoria of a kill, and I knew then that I would someday become a hunter like my grandpa.

After that experience in the cottonwood bosque, I resigned myself to let the gun go. I knew that my father would not keep somebody else's property but I put on a show of determination to keep it, since he knew by now that I had been using the gun. I started looking in the Montgomery Ward's catalog and found a replica of the gun belonging to Benito Ortiz. I told my father that I had no problem with returning Benito's gun if he would buy the gun for me that Christmas and that the gun only cost twenty-six dollars. I also offered to help him pay for it the following summer. That year I had just reached my fourteenth birthday but I'd be fifteen in January. I added that I'd be willing to wait. I did not get my new gun in December, but on my fifteenth birthday it showed up at the post office and my father and I went to town to get it.

My father made me promise not to shoot anything except rabbits and I obliged him. Once, however, when I disobeyed him and shot a porcupine off the top branch of a yellow pine, I experienced the pangs of conscience. It so happened that I shot the branch instead of the porcupine. The porcupine fell from the height of the tree, hit a branch, fell and bounced off the pine needles at the foot of the tree. His moans were so sad and pathetic that I hated myself for having brought him down. Then I remembered my father's admonition and I felt the shame and guilt of a moment I have chosen not to repeat. With all my skills as a hunter and all the subsequent guns that I have acquired since those days, I have kept to my promise to shoot only rabbits, jackrabbit and prairie dogs

Juez de Paz

During the early years of my childhood, around the age of ten or eleven and up until I was fourteen, my father was the Justice of the Peace for Embargo and La Cueva. He was given the post by petition from the citizens of the valley because, I suppose, he was an honest man, fair and above all, a pacifier. He was a reconciliator in situations involving disputes between his neighbors and among couples needing marital counseling. He was reluctant to take on this job because he knew that a lot of people would be coming to him for answers to problems which he knew really had no solutions. I remember his deliberations before making what was to him a monumental decision. For a couple of nights I could hear him quietly discussing the matter with my mother. I heard my mother say, at one point, "Why not take it, all you have to do is read them the law and collect the five dollars." My mother was much tougher and more direct about her decisions. My father finally decided to take the job.

My father was, at the same time both extremely competent and ill fitted for the job as the keeper-of-peace. His personal skills in internalizing the problems of others and his empathy toward their needs, together with his literate skills in both English and Spanish made him a natural for the job. His dislike for conflict and his dismay at dealing with the envy and greed of human beings disarmed him. This was true especially when he came face to face with conflict involving these very human traits. By the time he decided to become Justice, he was fully aware of his strengths and his weaknesses. I think that the people in Embargo and La Cueva, as well as the Anglo enclave of Retriever, knew my father and hoped that if they should come before him he would at least be fair. He was known as Andy to the Anglo folks, as Guero (blondie) to his male neighbors, *El Andres* to the women folk and *Andresito* to the old people who had seen him grow up among them.

My first experience in my father's court was that of a case brought about by an Anglo citizen for property trespass against a *mexicano* (a local Hispanic) whose cattle had trampled on the plaintiff's garden. As I understood the case, on a morning about two weeks before, two cows belonging to Donisio Martinez broke down the fence on the property belonging to Mr. Anderson. They got into his garden, ate most of the vegetables and trampled the rest. Mr. Anderson recognized the cows as belonging to "Donizsio," he said and he was angry that Donisio denied that they were his cattle. Mr. Anderson had the brand drawn on a paper and he presented this as evidence to the court.

Donisio Martinez, on the other hand, had retained a "lawyer" (his cousin, Amargo Mares) who fancied himself a real lawyer. After Mr. Anderson, a good guy known to my father as Okie Anderson completed his presentation, Amargo went on the defense. He gave a long speech: He talked about the history of the Martinez family in Embargo, about his cousin Donisio and his hard-working sons, and he talked about some treaty that gave the *mexicanos* the right to pasture their livestock in the commons of La Cueva. As he gave his oration, he repeatedly swung up and down on his toes. He talked for a good forty-five minutes and confused everyone in the court room.

When it was Okie Anderson's turn, he did not address the court but rather looked straight at Amargo, who was now seated and said, "Amargo, that was a pretty good speech you made, but I don't believe you."

From where I stood, against the wall of our kitchen, I could see my father's face draw a faint smile. I knew then, that he too saw through Amargo and the weak defense that he had offered on behalf of his cousin Donisio.

My father asked Mr. Anderson what he thought were the damages to his crops. When a dollar amount was proposed, my father, in his mediator's voice, then urged the two neighbors to get along. He told them that being good neighbors was far more important than a minor disagreement over cows and crops. He asked Donisio to pay Mr. Anderson the small amount that he was asking and instructed them to shake hands. He told them that in the interest of their friendship, he would forgo the court costs.

My father was busy discharging his duties as JP. He married couples off, especially those coming across the state line to avoid Colorado requirements. He tried and succeeded in resolving conflicts and issues before they got to a formal hearing. Those which could not be handled by the goodwill of the justice, and which were clearly violations of the law, he dealt with as he should. The case of *State vs. Gil Montoya* (alias Take-it-Easy) was such a case.

Tommy Holder, the game warden for the area, had apprehended and arrested Gil Montoya for fishing out-of-season. The violator was brought before the Judge the same day of the violation. Gil (or Take-it-Easy) had been very successful on his fishing venture. He had caught twelve nice rainbow trout. Tommy carried the fish with him on a stringer as he and Gil came into court. There was no doubt that Gil had broken the law, and although my father would have preferred to send him home with his catch, Tommy was there to see that the man was prosecuted. Poor Take-it-Easy, my father was helpless to assist him. He was fined for his crime and his fish taken away from him. After the trial (involving the three adults, and me eavesdropping on the proceedings) Gil was sent home minus his fish. Tommy Holder thanked my father and started towards the car with Gil Montoya's fish, then he turned around and handed the fish to my father.

"Since this case is resolved, I guess you get to keep the fish."

My mother, the realist, very naturally took the fish, cleaned them, fried them and we enjoyed a hearty fish fry, thanks to the evidence.

The Justice of the Peace performed his duties with a combination of peace-making, conflict resolution and common sense. He applied the law in situations that needed it as well as when there was no other recourse.

One day he got a case that tested his mettle, both as a Judge and a neighbor. He was given the case that might have been handled by King Solomon himself, except that my Father was not Solomon and his options were limited, if non-existent.

The case involved young Jaime, seven years old, who had been adopted by a mixed couple who lived less than a half mile from us, and who were now being called upon to give up the son that they had raised since the child's birth. The natural parents, egged on by an aggressive relative, now wanted the child back. In their favor was the fact that they had never given the child up formally, that is, no papers were written up to effect the adoption. Mr. and Mrs Mills, the adoptive parents, were devastated. Mr. Mills, an Anglo, and Cordie a Hispano had no biological children and had raised little Jaime as their own. The Trujillos, Jaime's natural parents, had many children, but now wanted Jaime back.

At first my father tried the mediator tack. He recounted the happiness of the Mills, he recounted how, during last Christmas, Mr. Mills, as Santa Claus had brought together the families of the valley. He described the apparent bond the Mills had made with Jaime. He congratulated the Trujillos for having shared one of their many children with the Mills and spoke of how young Jaime was growing up to be a well-provided-for and happy child. The Trujillos, under the prodding of the relative, would have none of that. They demanded from my father that he force the Mills to return the child, threatening to follow up with a higher court if he did not do so. The grief on the part of the adoptive mother was evident. She cried, she pleaded, and my father was clearly (at least as he could be, legally) on her side, wishing for a peaceful resolution to the conflict.

But the natural parents would not yield. The relative had incited the Trujillos to the point that "Mano" Frank Trujillo, who was a shy, quiet man jumped up at one point and flung himself at Mr. Mills. My father had to come out from behind a table that he used as his official bench to stop the aggression.

It was a clear-cut case legally. The Mills knew it, my father knew it and the meddlesome relative of the Trujillos knew it. She made fun of the court's attempt to stop the inevitable. Her anger, her vituperance and her jealousy became apparent and my father knew that, as he said to my mother later, "Esta Doña Cuca has other fish to fry." To which my mother responded:

"*El que da pan a perro ajeno, pierde El pan y pierde al perro*" (He who gives bread to a stray dog will lose the bread and lose the dog).

My mother was a cynic when it came to placing too much faith in people's kindness.

The case ended poorly, even when my father decided in favor of the natural parents. The crying and desperation on the part of Cordie Mills and Mr. Mill's efforts to console his wife only emboldened Doña Cuca to gloat in front of everyone.

"*Yo te dijia, Felipa, que yo te ganaria a tu hijo*"

(I told you, Felipa, that I would win your son back).

The trauma was yet to come for young Jaime who, at seven years of age, suspected something drastic was happening. His mother Cordie had tried to keep the court battles a secret from him. The day after the court hearing, Doña Cuca, Felipa and Mano Trujillo, escorted by Patrolman Douglas, drove up to the Mills' house and asked to take Jaime away. Cordie erupted into a high pitched cry that could be heard as far as my father's court room (an improvised room with a table and chairs). Jaime was totally surprised and he too started to cry. He was scared. Clearly he had never even met his natural parents. Mano Trujillo, now back to his timid, quiet demeanor, cowered behind his wife while Doña Cuca raised her voice and ordered Jaime to get his clothes and come with his "tia" Cuca. The deed was done, the pain was all over the valley that morning. Jaime was taken away, and my father was never the same again. He mistrusted his instincts of good will and he blamed himself for not having done more to save the Mills family and to repel the evil of Doña Cuca. Less than a year later, my father resigned his post of Juez de Paz.

After my father abdicated his position as Justice for Embargo, I concluded that just like Superman from the comics, who was defeated by Kryptonite, my father was defeated by the evil of those in his own neighborhood.

From time to time we would hear that little Jaime was

trying to adjust to a household which was considerably different from his home with the Mills. I had glimpses of him at school and his head was always down and his face was without a smile. Once we heard that he had tried to run away and his blood parents, together with the law, brought him back. After a few years of living in Embargo, the bitter defeat of the Mills was too much and we heard that they moved to a place, somewhere in Texas. Much, much later, when Jaime was a young man of sixteen, he ran away and was reported to be living with the Mills some place where the law of the state and the old court of the Justice of the Peace could not reach them.

Nor could the evil of Doña Cuca.

Ochre, At The End of the Trail

In late July every year, and perhaps as they had for a millennium, the Tiwas came. They came on horseback, in groups of three or four. They were young boys, about ten through twelve years old. They were flanked by an occasional adult, and they came trekking in from early in the morning and throughout the day. They were the Pueblos or sedate Indians from the multi-leveled homes some forty miles to the south. The people from Embargo and their ancestors were quite familiar with this yearly pilgrimage. As if by prearranged agreement the giant cumulus clouds, also arrived. Clouds, white, cotton-like and brooding, slowly settled on the fringe of the mountain and flashed a pale pink light that came from within. They contrasted with the pristine blue skies and seemed to herald an ancient ritual.

The Tiwas march on. They stay to the south side of the Red and to the east of the Cabresto, never venturing across either river except to head east or to cross the Red toward the Almagre. The predicable behavior of this path becomes apparent to those that have seen it for several generations or have been told by locals. They follow a route prescribed perhaps by ancient instructions or promises and pacts made long ago with other indigenous people of the area. By tradition or plan they have delineated the northern-most boundary of their spiritual territory and thus have defined for the people of Embargo, La Cueva and Cieneguilla the *last valley of the cordilleras.*

The Tiwas are coming to comply with a sacred tradition of instruction of the young recruits on learning the limits of their spiritual and temporal territory. They are coming to reaffirm pacts made eons ago with other peoples and to collect the red earth, *almagre,* that will serve them as badges of manhood in the years to come.

They are anticipating the quiet time, a season of tranquil repose where nature is given a chance to renew itself, for fulfilling promises made to the animals and trees and the fish in the streams and lake, of rest and restitution. The end of the trail for the Tiwas comes at the bottom of a huge scrape on the earth where either through glacial movement at a time even before the Tiwas, exposed the earth to sun and wind or where the spirits created for its people a cavern with a cache of Almagre.

The canyons enveloping the rivers or rivulets of the valley show the ancient writing (pictographs and petroglyphs) in abundance, but only on their southern sides. Clearly the Tiwa authors of these ancient writings did not venture beyond the watery demarcation of the Red and the Cabresto. On the extreme western side of the Red, where the rushing waters of the combined rivers empty into the Rio Grande, a massive bear paw is etched on a nondescript rock at the water's edge. The bear paw and bear claw have, even to this day, been recognized as the totem, the insignia, the talisman of the Bear Clan of the Tiwas. Was this the point of spiritual and spatial demarcation, the sign-post of an ancient people announcing to the northern tribes: the Utes, the Kiowas and even alien horse-mounted Comanches that from this point south is the domain of the formidable Tiwas? Were they honoring the land "belonging" to the northern tribes and are serving notice of the Tiwas' own borders?

Surely, the rivers to the south of Embargo, like the Arroyo de los Hongos, have a plethora of rock writing on both sides of their canyons. The Pueblo and Rio Chiquito also have their mute stories on both side of their canyons. But on the Red and Cabresto only the south and eastern sides have these messages.

The petroglyphs remain a riddle to present-day humans and perhaps even to the forbears of the ancient Tiwas. Some of these glyphs on the rocks easily provoke the imagination, as it did on the ancient residents of

Embargo, since they too, seemed to sense that this valley and no further, becomes the last valley to settle. The stories on the rocks depict men fishing with a line. Fish, resembling the native trout and pictures of mountain goats, deer and sometimes, monstrous sized wapiti, (ancient elk) are clearly depicted. Were these pictures static representation of animals that these hunters saw, or were these etchings part of a ritual necessary to sanctify or demonize the chosen animal before the kill? The mist of lost memory of the Tiwas might not be certain, but the ethos of culture can deduce some ancient meaning.

The Tiwas, guided by the billowing cotton clouds with fire in their bellies come in on one day, extract the red almagre from inside the cavern, conduct their most efficacious totem and are gone before day-break the next morning. Who knows their motives in their spiritual and human ruminations? Who knows what is sacred and what is taboo? We know, for certain, that at the end of July under fluffy clouds, the Tiwa come to an almagre pit in the bowels of the earth and return with young men who have perhaps, been given the opportunity to witness another view of their future as adult Tiwas.

Fishing As a Way of Life

In the pools and eddies of the river lived the fish of my brother's and my dreams. They were lithe forms in the water, facing the current. Some were light brown and others were greenish, their tails undulating in the water. If we got too close and they saw us they would dart with such speed that we lost sight of them in an instant. Our first fishing teacher was a magical bird sitting on a bare branch on an old cottonwood. My brother and I would sit quietly by a pond that had been dammed in the middle of the river, constructed by beaver and later enlarged by the boys of the valley. We would watch a King Fisher dive from a high point in that tree and disappear under water. His catch ratio was at least four catches to one miss. He was formidable, he was a great fisherman and a *will-o-the-wisp*. He was magic. The King Fish was on duty early in the morning and was gone by late afternoon. We didn't know where his nest was but we guessed he had someone or some ones to feed because he carted away a lot of fish. His choice were fish about six inches long. It was incredible how he could see from that height, dive bomb his prey, account for the movement of the fish, yet nail them almost every time.

"Did you see him?" my brother would ask every time the bird took a fish. My brother was fixated on the precise time the bird hit the water and when he speared the fish. We could often see exactly where the fish were schooled. Soon we grabbed our own poles made from willows and long enough to reach the hiding places of the larger Browns and yellowish Browns which a family friend, Cuate Leve, called "Loch Laven."

Our fishing jaunts were leisurely. The clock stopped and nothing in the world mattered except the excitement of the catch. I often walked ahead to take advantage of being first at the pools. Because older brothers often pull rank as was the unwritten law among the boys: *de mayor a menor* (from older to younger) my brother had to devise other techniques to be able to catch fish. He developed a tenacity that soon made up for my forced advantage. His increased fishing skills and his knowledge about just where the fish were, or so it seemed, made me wonder if going ahead was really the advantage. Whether behind me on the river or ahead of me my brother's catch was always bigger than mine.

He soon started striking out on his own and one day

he returned with several trout that I knew were not from the Red. They were a dark grey, almost black with faint red and orange spots on their sides. They were beautiful and not unlike the Browns that we often caught in that part of the river running though the box canyon.

"Horale! Where did you catch these?"

"I got them at the Lagunita."

"*Hijole, Carnal* you know what the *cuates* (twins) would do to you if they found you fishing in their property?"

"They didn't see me," He said, and walked away to place the fish in an old refrigerator, with coiled tubes on its top that my father had bought from old Bill Noggles.

My brother Vivian, was now a pre-teen and his fishing had become an obsession. He had now ventured into a deep, clear-water drainage that belonged to the family Cadena. The Lagunita, was not a lake at all, but several channels of crystalline water with water cress choking the troughs. In these waterways lurked huge trout that had mutated into a black coloration because they were always shaded by the submarine water cress. The *cuates* were twin brothers whose father, Mano Pepe and his wife, my father's first cousin, Crecencia, had inherited property belonging to the family Herrera. My cousin, Polo, had often argued that our fishing in las Lagunitas was only fair since the property had really belonged to our Grandma Maria's family. The Cuates were the self-appointed guardians of las Lagunitas. One of them was a gentle, amiable and shy person and would overlook the occasional boys fishing on his land. The other was aggressive, proud and disliked by most of the boys of the valley including his cousins, Tano and Eliseo. The *cuates* were about five years older than my cousin Polo and me.

My brother Vivian had now set his sights on the fast flowing troughs of the Lagunita and nothing would dissuade him from fishing there. He would invite me to join him but my discomfort in coming upon the twins inclined me to refuse. One day however, I was convinced by Vivian that the fishing would be great if I would only join him. He said that he had invented a "gizmo," as we had heard our Cuate Leve describe any new contraption that he created. And, in the spirit of the "gizmo," we walked to the Lagunitas for our day of fishing for the Brooky, or mutated Brown, whatever they were. These fish hid under the logs that once had been live trees but now had rotted and flopped into the water channels.

Vivian had in effect made a crude net out of chicken wire, a rare commodity in Embargo but which he had "rescued" from some abandoned chicken coop or fence. The excitement of trying out the net with the determination of a gambler, led me to brazenly cross the fence into the flat meadows of the Lagunita.

At first, poking the underside of the submerged logs yielded a fish or two but then Vivian rolled up his pants and took off his brown Converse tennis shoes and signaled me to bring the net. He quietly slipped into the water and whispered for me to set the net on the downstream side of the log. He was up to his thighs in water and his stealth was amazing. Slowly, he put both his hands with fingers extended, into the upstream side of the log and made a pushing motion. Immediately I felt the weight and violence of something in the net. I immediately pulled it up and in it was a fourteen-inch fish. Vivian smiled when he saw me with my eyes opened wide. We repeated the netting several times and every time the make-shift net yielded a beautiful spotted black trout. At about the fifth dip of the net and with my brother's stealth herding the fish into the "gizmo," Vivian had an unpleasant surprise. He was groping under the log this time, just as we had done in catching the cutthoat minnows in the rivulet by our house, when his brow furrowed and he whispered, "I got something." He abruptly yanked his catch out of the water. Instead of a trout, however, he pulled out a snake about three feet long. He instantly dropped the reptile and ran out of the water channel, yelling, "*hijo de la chingada*, he almost bit me."

We gathered our catch, he put on his tennis shoes

and we walked out of las Lagunitas.

During our conversation, on our way home, I tried to calm down the atavistic dread from his recent experience. I related an experience to him that I had when I was only six years old.

My father, Mr. Lange and I had traveled up into the Moreno Valley to seine for minnows. I had never accompanied my father on such a trip but he told me that Mr. Lange himself had asked that I come along. When we got to a tiny creek meandering through this high mountain draw, I knew why. I was, like my brother had been, the person required to drive the fish into the nets. In the case of the minnows it was a net with very close netting and it was called a seine.

"Just like the net that you invented," I told Vivian, "This one was placed on the downward side of the stream. I was told by my father to take my shoes off and walk downstream, and like you," I said, "I had to scare the little minnows into the net. It was wonderful and at the same time terrible, for among the minnows in the net were many different little animals: ugly, crawly things. Since I was asked to scoop them into a bucket, while my father held the seine from one side and Mr. Lange from the other, I recoiled. Mr. Lange did not want to scare me and so he scooped two or three cupped hand-fuls and sat down with me on the grassy bank to show me that the beasties among the minnows were harmless. He introduced me to the hellgrammite, a water nymph that would later become a flying insect; he showed me the tiny clams he called crustesea. He showed me tiny ghost shrimps and tiny white worms that most often slid through the holes in the seine. Mr. Lange had a laconic speech but this morning he gave me a lesson in marine life that opened my eyes and mind to another world that lives underwater," I told my brother.

I told my brother that for Mr. Lange, it also calmed down his helper and my father knew that I had absorbed the lesson of the morning. If my father had only known how this experience fired up my imagination and desire to fish forever, he would have been pleased. We returned to the minnow catch and I proudly walked the sandy bottoms of the creek for Mr. Lange.

Vivian laughed at my story and asked me why I hadn't told him this story before. Calm and collected Vivian hid the make-shift net under a fallen cottonwood and we made our way home with our fish.

Early that evening, as the sun dipped low just skimming the top of the Guadalupita Canyon, "the box," a hazy ambience enveloped Embargo. The swallows were out on their pre-dusk hunt. There were so many that they looked like swarms of mosquitoes at a distance. Already the night hawks dipped their wings as they sped along with open mouths to splash the insect morsels into their palates. Bats would soon emerge from caves and crevices on the canyon walls and at deep dusk would venture even close to the house, where a bare electric bulb lighted our porch, and where they would fly along the fringes of the light scooping the moths that drifted in the air as in a stupor.

When it came time to prepare supper, mother called Vivian and me to the kitchen and asked, "Where did you get these ugly fish? Are they those horse-flesh-eating fish from the hatchery?"

"No, we got them in a secret place," I said.

"You and your secret places," she addressed me.

"You'd better not be going into that property belonging to the Cadenas. *Ya saben como son esos* (you know how those 'people' are)."

How did my mother know about the Lagunitas? My guess was that her brothers, my uncles, Toby and Al had probably been chased off that place in recent years.

My father came in late from work at his new job with the mine. After he put down his lunch pail and took off his hat, he asked mother if *los muchachos* had fed the pigs and brought in the wood to cook supper. Before my mother answered, he continued.

"Do you remember *El Douglas*, you know, the State Policeman?" My mother, looking down at her cooking feigned a lapse of memory. She had often voiced her dislike for the policeman, ever since her two brothers had gotten into trouble for breaking the law and Douglas had dealt with them.

"Yes, What about him?"

"Well," my father said, and he looked out to where we were, so that we would not listen in on the conversation.

"He was found dead this morning at his home in La Villa."

"Que le paso?" (what happened to him) she asked and before giving my father a chance to answer, she said, *"Ya era tiempo"* (about time). I thought that she had used the term,*"ya era su tiempo"* which meant "it was his time to die," but she had not. And I knew then how much it had hurt her to have her brothers humiliated before a judge. She blamed the policeman for her brothers' transgressions, and now the deal between them had been squared.

"No digas eso, mujer" (don't say that woman) my father added. *"Se suicidio,"* (he committed suicide). My mother responded with an "Umph!" and continued her work over the stove.

Next day my brother and I walked down the box canyon and decided to fish close to the first and second water-falls where huge boulders had fallen off the canyon walls and had blocked enough water in the river to create two large waterfalls. Here is where we had seen the big Browns fly up the rapids and over the waterfall during the last days of summer. Here too lived a water spirit, called, *"gallinita del agua."* (water-hen). It was a small water bird with springs on its legs. It was a Dipper, we learned from Mr. Lange, whom I considered my water denizens' encyclopedia.

The Dipper lived on the water all the time that we had seen it. It walked on the top of rocks, which were submerged as deep as the size of the bird itself. It did not linger on the rock but dove or rather walked on the rocks, ducking its body underwater to permit it to hunt while submerged. It speared the tiny cigar shaped hydras, less than an inch long and any water bug that might be living on or under the submerged rocks. The constantly dipping, genuflecting body would brave the currents that were swift and, at least for us, treacherous. The rocks themselves were slippery and the water was icy-cold, especially in the shaded, narrow canyon. The Dipper was a will-o-the-wisp. He would fly to the far shore sometimes and we would often see his nest on the lower levels of the cliffs that came up to the water's edge. He was there from the first days that I walked into the box and he never failed to provoke my imagination and sense of wonder.

The End of the World

The day started normal enough for me. My brother, sister and our friends who played with us along the rocky playa now gathered at a warm-water pond between the cotton woods and the river.

That morning we again heard the hoof beats of the palomino ridden by Cecilio or "Cowboy Cilo" and we knew him and the palomino well. Cilo always rode his horse at a gallop. He rode that horse from la Cieneguilla, where he lived, to his Aunt Raquel's in Embargo, about two miles distance. That he rode the palomino at full gallop didn't bother him. He rode the horse over the wooden bridge, and the noise from the hoofbeats on the planks could be heard all the way to the pond where we were swimming. The older boys admired Cowboy Cilo because, of all the guys in Embargo, he was the only one who owned a palomino that looked just like Trigger, Roy Rogers' horse. Cowboy Cilo, thought of himself as that cowboy which he had seen in the films brought to La Cueva by the itinerant movie guy.

The youngsters from the neighborhood thought of him differently. They would yell out to him, as he rode over the rock-strewn road:

"*Cowboy Cilo, del agua salada, tira El lasso y laza cagada* (Cowboy Cilo, your aim is spit, you try to lasso, but you lasso shit)."

This morning the warm sun beckoned us to swim, wade and simply waddle in a spring-water-fed pool where fat, multi-colored minnows swam. The sky was clear and from the dense cottonwood bosque came the telegraphing of the Flickers on the dead trees and the scolding of the ubiquitous crows. The grasshoppers had by now sprouted wings and were rasping their flight-hum and were now almost too fast for us to catch. The insect and bird chatter was only rivaled by the babble of the youngsters in the pond. We splashed and swam and sent the white, gold and blue minnows scurrying away as we took possession of the pond. We swam till the afternoon and when the sun was past the halfway point in the vault of the sky, we began to detect a faint smell of wood- burning smoke in the air.

And then it happened. The sun started getting opaque. At first no one wondered what was happening, but soon the sun took on a yellow hue. Quickly after that it was fully covered. We could only see the white orb, like the moon, behind the clouded sky.

"*Miren*," MaCat said, "*Se esta acabando El mundo* (Look, the world is coming to an end). Everybody panicked, and we scattered in confusion as if MaCat's words were true. I experienced a fear of dread, for I too had listened to the preachers in the Assembly of God church proclaim "the end of the world." I knew what MaCat was declaring. I ran home and pointing to the eclipsed sun, told my mother to look. My mother was, like her family, somewhat superstitious. She simply gathered her children, closed the door and the curtains and began to pray. My heart was pounding and I feared for the worst. I feared that I was too young to die and I wanted to have my father there to help me make some sense of all this. Once, in an early evening when I thought that all the stars were falling from the sky, he had calmly said that it was a meteor shower. He had allayed my fears. I hoped he could do that today too.

I indulged my mother and her prayers (of the moment) for she was not too religious and only went into fervent prayer during the night's thunder and lightening storms of the summer. I began to reason, like my father would have.

What would my father say now? How would he explain what is happening? If it were the end of the earth, wouldn't

59

it have already happened?"

I walked out of the house and I saw some of our neighbors looking at the sky and talking. I ran over to where Tio Pino was standing by his wood pile.

"Did you see the sun Tio?"

"Yes," he said, "*Es una quemazon cerca de Guadalupita* (It's a fire close to Guadalupita)." I feigned calm for fear of being ridiculed. I returned home and told my mother that uncle Pino had said it was probably a fire west of the Guadalupe Canyon. Later that night, with the valley covered with the blue haze of wood fires, we learned that a whole mountainside, across the Rio Grande had burned down to the stumps.

After a few days, we realized that the end-of-the world had been delayed and we returned to our swimming, but never again to the pond where the multi-colored minnows swam, for we associated the minnow pond with an omen of the dreadful eclipsing of the sun.

When I saw MaCat again, I admonished him for having scared the daylight out of me. He rebutted:

"God so loved the world that he gave his only begotten son; John: ten-free (10:3)."

"Free?" I laughed and he pointed his finger at me.

"*No te reias* (don't laugh)" he said. "It will happen one of these days," as if he was sorry it hadn't really happened.

Long Days of Summer

We returned to the mundane things of the gang. MaCat showed off his skills in being able to walk the rails of the long wooden bridge that spanned the Red and it's rock-strewn flood plain. The bridge was a whole one hundred feet long. MaCat gingerly strode the rail as if walking on a narrow path. The swift waters of the river and the thousands of rocks along the bank invited him to fall. I shivered because I knew that a fall from that height would surely mean death. The water was too shallow to take a person's fall and the rocks would have ended it all for Mac. I was the oldest of the boys and I called to MaCat to get off the rail but he would not get off.

"*Mira Mac, tu eres El Tarzan del Embargo* (you're the Tarzan from Embargo) and if you climb down I'll give you a comic."

"*De veras?* (really)" He stopped to ask.

"*Si pendejo*," (yes fool) I said and he feigned falling off the rail, but clearly into the bridge. We laughed.

Tarzan "chapters," were the obsession of the population of boys that lived in La Cueva, Embargo and Cieneguilla. For us, Tarzan was to be emulated, as I think MaCat was doing this morning on the bridge.

The movies, at the sala de Mano Juan Rel were a weekly must-see for us. We gathered our money, however we could and saved for the dime that it would cost us to see the "show" provided by an itinerant movie host nick-named "raccoon." The movies were held every Friday night and featured movies in series we fondly called chapters. First it was, *Hop-Along Cassidy*, then *The Durango Kid, Buster Crab, Roy Rogers*, and later, *Tarzan*. They were movies that totally captivated us. *If school had been like this*, I thought, *we would all have gotten "A's."* After each episode we walked home in the star or moon-lit night and recounted every part of the film that we had seen and I knew that each one of us was Tarzan that night.

The boys from La Cueva were close to their homes and they never lingered around the sala. The boys from Cieneguilla often had horses tied to different spots around the sala and immediately mounted-double in most cases and bareback. Most of the time they rode home right after the movie. The boys from Embargo started running as they rushed out of the hall and soon met down the street of La Cueva near a car garage that had been built into the hillside. Once, when we got out of the movie, a group from El Llano was waiting outside the hall and confronted us. With invectives hurled at us they'd say, "*Horale, Tusas,* (Hey, prairie dogs)." We knew that they were referring to the large prairie dog colony on the west end of Embargo. We tried to ignore their insults.

"Hey, you guys think you're good because you have money for the movies, eh?" We knew then that they had not been able to see the movie and now were taking it out on us. Andy, the larger of us boys, and my Tia Juanita's son wanted to challenge them. I wanted to run, my brother Vivian had already picked up a rock and MaCat was the cool one. He pretended not to have heard the conflict-laden remarks so he calmly turned to them and said, Hey *vatos*, you like fishing? The Llaneros were taken aback. Mac continued, "If you guys come down to El Embargo tomorrow I'll let you fish in my pond." Mac and his older brothers had constructed a pond at the bottom of a the hill where they lived. They had connected a pipe to a spring on the hillside and planted the fish that they had caught in the river.

"You know Jovie," he addressed one of them. "You know we have a pond full of fish."

"You know this guy?" One of the Llaneros asked Jovie.

"Si," Jovie said timidly. "He is my cousin's son."

"Ah, shit," the leader of the boys from El Llano said. "Let's go."

"No, really," Mac insisted, but the gang walked away.

"Why did you promise them that?" Andy scolded MaCat.

"Hey, they left us alone, didn't they?" Mac answered. The incident spoiled our experience with Tarzan but from that night forward, we ran south to the safety of our home in Embargo after a movie in La Cueva

Pidome Esa Palomita

The languid days of summer had arrived. The pace of the valley had slowed, the dogs weren't as quick to jump at passing cats and even the flies seemed lazy in their flight. The days were warmer, but where a slight breeze came to touch the dry earth, it often created "dust devils" that ran off in their willy-nilly ways. Dragon flies skimmed the warm waters of the ponds and settled on those plants that pierced the surface of the water. This was the time of summer where you would hear my Grandmother Maria say, "*Donde estan esos chileros, ya tardan.*" (where are those chileros, they're late). The chileros were itinerant fruit and vegetable peddlers who came north from Embudo and Velarde, and farms in the upper Rio Grande valley. They were the merchants that had provided produce of all kinds to the people in the northern settlements. They were the bearers of "news" from all the villages which they had visited. Their visits were anticipated like the changing of the seasons.

Today however, no chileros arrived but the Trailways bus stopped at the Lange's place to let off a passenger. Although we didn't know who came off the bus at the stop a half mile away, we soon saw a lone figure in a suit and a dress hat walking up carrying a small tin suitcase. He looked haggard and he had a dejected look. He made his way toward the house in the lower valley where My Tio Pino and his wife were now living. In their house also lived Mana Cleofas, Tio Pino's mother-in-law and a young girl, Marita. My mother looked out the window and declared, *"Mira quien es, Rafel"* (look at who that is, it's, Rafel)." The man was Mana Cleofas' former son-in-law. When Rafel came to the door he was greeted by Mana Cleofas, who did not invite him in, but rather, stood at the entrance of the house talking and explaining something to Rafel. No one had seen Rafel in over a year. He had been married to Ofelia, Mana Cleofas' daughter. Rafel and Ofelia had a daughter but the daughter was with Ofelia who, we all knew had gone off to Denver to *"rehacer mi vida"* (start my life anew) she'd said. Marita was Ofelia's daughter from a previous union but had been given away to the grandmother, Mana Cleofas.

Because I was curious I approached the house and I could hear Rafel plead.

"Pero yo la quiero todavia" (but I still love her) Mana Cleofas. *Digame donde esta* (tell me where she is)."

At that point Simosea, my uncle's wife, came to the door and invited Rafel in. The door had been left open and I could see Rafel inside the house now, trying to gain the confidence of the two ladies. Mana Cleofas stood by the stove and was immovable. After some time Rafel walked out.

"*Es El desamor Rafel, entiendelo* (there is no more love there, please understand)." When Mana Cleofas ventured, "*Ella te queria tambien, lo sabes* (she loved you too, you know that)," Rafel fell to his knees and started to cry. He said nothing now, but I knew without being told, that I had seen a man with a broken heart. Rafel got up, wiped the tears with the back of his hand and turned and walked away. Dejected, he hunched his back and walked up the rocky path from where he'd come. Rafel looked as sad as I had ever seen anyone and his tin suitcase made a clicking sound with every step.

Going home I saw a butterfly flutter to a stop on a holly-hock that grew near the gate to my Uncle's. And because we always said this, and because I wanted to shake off the sad sight of Rafel, I invoked my usual pact with the butterfly: "*Pidome esa palomita, pa' la hora de mi muerte, amen* (Today I choose this butterfly to be with me the day I die, amen)."

I asked myself, *Can a person die of love?* and I hoped that if Rafel died of love tonight, that he had at least invited the butterflies to his funeral.

The Cookes

On the hill on the opposite side of the river, *la otra banda,* lived Cuate Leve, his mother, La Mimi, his sister Carol and Mr. Cooke. The family had come down from a place up in the mountains called, "*Las Manzanitas*" (the site of the apples). The Cookes had lived in a mud-chinked cabin with two rooms. Cuate Leve was slated to return home from the war in Europe and Mr.Cooke had been running the only other grocery store in Embargo. It was the store preferred by the Hispanic ladies of the valley. The other store that carried groceries belonged to the Langes.

Mr. Cooke's store had been open for about five years now and his dealings with his customers had always been fair. He made friends with the children too. For me he always had kind words and at the end of my purchase I got a piece of candy or a stick-sucker. Mr. Cooke always asked about my parents, particularly about my father.

"Has your father found any more wild bees?"

"No," and I would add that my father now worked at the mine and not for Bill Noggles, the bee-keeper.

Mr. Cooke was from Kentucky, or so it was said. He had married Mimi, a Hispanic. They now had three children. We knew Cuate and Carol but not Tom, the oldest, "...still in Europe" as Mr. Cooke would add, when someone asked.

"The boys are at war with the Germans but they'll soon be coming home. I'm going to marry Carol off as soon as I can and turn the store over to Lee or Tom when they come home."

He'd say this to tease Carol, who was now into her late twenties and still single. To tease her further, he said one day:

"I guess Carol is waiting for you to grow up so she can marry you," he told me, a ten-year old. Carol laughed and punched the jovial Mr. Cooke on the arm. They were good friends besides being father and daughter. Carol then looked at me and said.

"You're my boyfriend, huh Gibo, and we're not sharing our secrets with this old goat, are we?" I said nothing, but once, at a birthday party that my parents had held at our house, I saw Carol go off into one of our bedrooms and was laying on top of the bed with Fred Maxwell, a friend of my father's. Fred had just moved to the Mine camp and *he could play the guitar "like a cowboy,"* I thought. I guessed that Carol had not told Mr. Cooke about Fred Maxwell. I'd seen them again, walking together, crossing the wooden bridge that spanned the Red. Maxwell was walking on the heels of his cowboy boots and Carol was giggling and flirting with him. The summer passed, Fred Maxwell quit his job and left. Carol told no one how she felt after Fred left but the whispering around was that Fred Maxwell had a wife in Clayton, wherever that was.

That winter I visited the Cooke's store many times. My mother had given me the responsibility to buy the few things that we needed. I asked Mr. Cooke for sugar and oatmeal, but he said that these items were rationed because of the war. I didn't understand what that meant but my father said that a lot of things were rationed or rather, that these and many other items were being sent to the soldiers fighting the war. I then remembered that I'd heard my Uncle Toby tell me, with mischief in his smile, that Virgilio Barela, our cousin, would take the gasoline stamps given to his mother by the "government" for her washing machine and would sell them to Turibio Cordova for his old car. For my part, I now bought wheatina instead of oatmeal, Karo syrup instead of sugar and other substitutes that Mr. Cooke had suggested. As time went on we developed a taste for wheatina with syrup and it was a while before we used sugar again. The milk and meat were also rationed but we got our milk from Elsie, our milk cow, and pork, cueritos and chicarrones from the pigs which my father and Tio Adon butchered.

That same winter, when the bluish smoke from the piñon wood in the stoves created a permanent haze in the air, we often took a sleigh ride to my grandparents' house in Cieneguilla, a couple of miles away. The snow was often so deep that it made for an easy ride in our sled, a large two-seater, big enough for the whole family. The cold caused the river to freeze almost completely and no bridge was necessary in crossing the river at Cieneguilla.

Winters were a time to take advantage of another aspect of living in this high valley, and that was to enjoy the snow and ice and the closeness of family. We could actually walk to my Tio Tone, living "*en la otra banda*," over the ice, without it breaking. These nights at my uncle's were times of story-telling, gossip among the adults and bonding.

The nights in the dead of winter were so cold that I remember by father saying to me one night, "*Mira,*" pointing to the sky, "*està tan frio, que las estrellas estàn llorando."* (Look, it is so cold that the stars are crying). And sure enough, I could see the entire firmament full of stars winking their eyes from a billion miles away.

More and more these days the Cooke store was run by Carol. Mr. Cooke took ill that winter and never seemed to get well. Carol never spoke of Fred Maxwell and when spring came, we finally saw Mr. Cooke again. He was the same happy and kind man that he had always been but he now looked older and smaller than we remembered him.

A man that showed up that spring, as he had done every spring, was Ed Rigler, the hermit who lived in a cave down in the canyon of the Rio Grande. We saw him walk up the valley from the west. He walked along the river in Embargo and followed the rock-strewn road of the playa. He was a hunched man with a huge white sack on his back and a skin cap on his head. He was making his way to the Cooke store on his bi-annual trip to buy supplies for the summer. The Cooke's store was the only placc he ever visited outside his haunts in the Rio Grande Canyon. He carried beaver pelts which he exchanged for salt, sugar (or molasses), tobacco, some hard candy, coffee and a few other necessities that would hold him over the long periods of time living in the Rio.

Ed Rigler was a mysterious man. No one knew much about him. He had confided to Mr. Cooke once, that he had a daughter in Illinois (and I wondered where that was) but he had no visitors in his home in the Canyon; a makeshift cabin in the spring and summer and a cave in the winter. The hermit was a quiet man and once when I went to the store and he was there, he sat in a chair in a corner drinking a coke which had been given to him by Mr. Cooke. I don't remember ever hearing his voice and I was sure that by force-of-habit, he spoke very little. Mr. Cooke told Mimi and she later related to my father that Ed Rigler was obsessed with guns. Mimi said that the central question during his limited conversation was, "When Lee comes back from the war, will he bring his gun with him?" or he'd ask, "I wonder what Lee's gun looks like?"

Those of us that wondered out loud about the life of the hermit concluded that he did not own a gun and that perhaps all the hunting that he did was by trapping. He must have also fished because, *what was the use of living in the best fishing spot in the area if you aren't going to fish.* What no one ever talked about was how terribly lonely the man must be, especially in those nights when the stars are crying.

I saw Ed Rigler come up from his cave about three more times and then I never saw him again. It appears as if a fisherman who'd ventured to explore the cabin site, assuming it was abandoned, found his body between two huge rocks a few feet from his cave. Ed Rigler was no more and we talked of his migration that would be no more nor by anyone else coming up that trail.

In late summer I again went to the store but found it closed. I walked around to the back of the house where the front entrance to the kitchen was located. Strangely enough I was greeted by the howling of Bones, the family dog. Bones was a greyhound, gaunt and long and of a gray color. He had the habit of howling a mournful cry on Sundays when the family went to church in La Cueva. But today was not Sunday. I turned the corner towards the kitchen. The door was open and I was ushered in. On the eyes of the family members, Mimi, Carol and an older daughter of Mimi's from a previous marriage, was a look of resignation and a sadness that told it all. In a bed in the next room, separated from the kitchen by a bed sheet on a clothes line, lay Mr. Cooke. His eyes were closed and he struggled to breathe. Estela, the older daughter, and who had less of a stake in this matter, volunteered to wipe his brow with holy water that Mimi produced from a shelf in the kitchen.

What am I doing here? I asked myself. But because everyone in the family considered me kin I became a witness to the death of a kind man who had been a constant in our lives. His troubled breathing was audible, and his chest was heaving. Estela declared what he was going through: *Està en la agonìa de la muerte* (He's in the throes of death)." I decided to leave and Carol let me out. Outside the house Bones continued to howl and I got an eerie feeling, I decided that Bones knew that Mr. Cooke was dying or perhaps the crying of the women had moved Bones to howling, and he too was mourning.

Two days later, the village gathered at the Cookes' to pay their last respects to *"El viejito Cooke,"* (old-man Cooke) which was actually the name we used when referring to Mr. Cooke.

There were lots of strangers present: a few Anglos, other friends of the family and some people I'd never seen before. There were relatives of Mimi's from Arroyo del Hongo and from Valdez, a place where Mimi had been born and which had been founded by her great grandfather, Pedro Valdez. There were the big wide-brim hats of the ladies and the hats in-hand of the men.

My father and I attended the viewing. My father stopped to talk to some men that he knew and I walked out to Mimi's flower garden. The flowers in this garden this afternoon were like the flowers of the meadows: There were purple iris, white marigolds, yellow, pink and white daisies, purple petunias, holly hocks and blood roses. Among the flowers were, what seemed, hundreds of butterflies. Some were yellow, others were white, still others were black and an occasional large monarch. I was mesmerized, shocked and enraptured with the scene and with the firmness of a conviction that I hold to this day; I was convinced that Mr. Cooke was like me, a *collector* of butterflies. And I could see Mr. Cooke as a child, speaking in English and saying:

"Today I choose this butterfly, to be with me the day I die (*Pidome esta palomita, para la hora de mi muerte, amen*)," for hundreds of butterflies chose this day to visit the Cookes' garden and to accompany Mr. Thomas J. Cooke on the day that he left Embargo, forever.

Los Americanos

Early on in my childhood the *chuga-chuga, chuga-chuga* sound of a machine broke the silence of Embargo. It came from the Lange's place, a short half mile distance from where we lived. And although we suspected something strange was about to happen at the Langes' we had no idea what that would be. This sound would start early in the evenings and stop around ten o'clock at night. The people in the valley had not had to contend with too many alien noises and except for the rooster's crow, the bawling of cows and the barking of dogs, the sounds in the valley had been predictable. The *chuga-chuga* was now constant and would not go away. Another thing that accompanied the "*ruido*" (annoying noise), as my Grandma Maria would say, was a bright light coming from the same place as the noise. Upon investigation we found that it was the first of many surprises that Mr. Lange had in store for the inhabitants of Embargo.

Mr. Lange had installed what he called a gasoline

motor which, when started, made light. This was not any ordinary light. The light inside a little glass was as bright as the sun and would hurt your eyes when you looked at it. It should not have surprised us because we had seen light like that in the headlights of Mr. Lange's pickup. The engine, as he called it, was a large machine nailed to two huge square logs on the ground. It had a large wheel that turned at the same time that an arm he called a piston dove in and out of a pan full of black oil. If you got too close to the engine you were splashed with droplets of that black stuff. The light was bewitching. The moths flew around it and one night even a *"dormilon,"* (nighthawk) slapped the little glass with its wings. It was a splendid sight for us since our experiences had only been with our lamps of Kerosene and our recently acquired, gas-lamps.

We naturally celebrated the coming of this machine and marveled when Mr. Lange put a large belt around the wheel on his machine on one end, and on the other end, a large plate with teeth, just like my father's hand saws that he used for cutting down trees. The new contraption, Mr. Lange told us, was a cross-cut saw. He showed it off one day and he could cut a log as thick as a fence post in less than a minute. *A miracle,* I thought. From there on, other miracles appeared. The Langes had a radio that played loud music all day (because Mrs. Lange preferred it that way) and a washing machine that ran on a motor.

Mr. Lange, my friends and I decided, was "Machine Man." Just like Superman or Aquaman, he truly was Machine Man. When Mr. Lange was able to pump water to a shower, we knew that he had outdone himself and best of all, he allowed us boys to use the shower once in a while. The water was hot and I pretended, with a great deal of seriousness, that I must get used to the hot water because, surely, Tarzan must endure the hot rain that one would find in the jungle.

Mr. Lange was a new breed of men coming to the long sleepy valley of Embargo. He brought contraptions with him, or maybe even invented them all on the spot. Mr. Lange had nets that caught little fish and big fish. He had a fishing pole with a long line in a spool, like my mother had in her sewing box and he had little hooks that looked like flies which he used to catch fish. Mr. Lange, "Machine Man," was amused by our captivated sense of wonder.

"What do you think of this, Jurnior?" He'd ask when I followed him as he tried out some new contraption.

"You think it's going to work?"

"Oh, yah, yah," I'd say with an enthusiasm that I think he enjoyed. And the wonders would never end. His pickup, for example had a picture on the front that looked like a small ship with sails.

"This is a Plymouth," he said and "that is a picture of the Mayflower." This time the whole thing went over my head and I was content with checking out his marvelous machines.

A few years later, when my father had bought a Maytag gasoline washing machine for my mother, I was finally convinced that Mr. Lange was indeed the Machine Man that we had claimed.

My mother discovered, on the day she was going to do her washing, that the ringers on her machine were not working. She walked around the house agitated because of her problem with the machine. She came out of the house and told me that she wanted me to do her a favor.

"Walk over to Mr. Lange's and ask him to come and see what's wrong with this machine."

The Langes had by this time moved across the river and up on the hill. I showed some reluctance and asked, "Why don't you wait until my father gets home?" I didn't really want to walk the distance to the Lange's and I thought it somewhat unfair to involve Mr. Lange in my mother's minor problem. We argued momentarily.

"Listen," taking me by the shoulders, "I want you to go to Mr. Lange's and ask him to come and fix my machine. You know that Americanos invented the machines and therefore, they can fix them."

After that assertion, I walked to Mr. Lange's and

delivered my mother's message. We drove back down the hill to my house. He got off his pick-up, now an International Harvester. He looked at the ringers on the machine and then went back to his pick up. He brought back what he called a cotter pin, inserted it into a place in the rollers and fixed the machine. My mother was effusive, she asked Mr. Lange what it was she owed him.

"Nothing Della, but do say Hi to Andy for me."

My mother waited until he had made the turn up the road and into the cottonwoods before she turned to me and with her head held high said, as she walked away into the house,

"*Que te dije* (what did I tell you)?"

I knew then, that we had just had an encounter with MACHINE MAN.

Another Americano now living in the valley was Mr. Mills, who drove around in an open-top car which he called his "Model T." Mr. Mills had learned two words during all the years he lived in Embargo, "*Star-Buener*" (meaning to him, It's Ok), a phrase that I'm sure he'd learned trying to pacify Cordie, his native Embargo wife. Mr. Mills was the only Americano who ever attempted to speak even one word in Spanish.

There were Old Slim McComb and Bud Parr who could fix any car or truck in the valley but who spent most of their time fishing. Bud and Slim were the champion fishermen of the Rio Grande. They had some fishing contraptions that Slim would say, "These'll git 'em evertime."

The Hurds, another family of Americanos, evoked the word "money," the moment they showed up at their new two-story house on the hill. Before he worked at the mine my father had worked for the Hurds, helping to build that house. Some locals from La Cueva called the place "Gringo Hill."

The Hurds were Texans, and they wanted everyone to know it. They spoke "funny", we thought and were different from Mr. Lange and Mr. Mills. My father once said, and perhaps after I'd asked him about this difference: "The Hurds are Tejanos and the Langes are Okies." The Hurds had running water that they piped in from a natural spring a short distance up the mountain and the house was a series of rooms. They called them guest rooms. There was an enclosed patio with a fireplace, floors with hardwood or flat rock and big heavy tables and chairs. Each member of the family had a car. D. J. Hurd, the father, had a Cadillac, so did his wife. Their son Buster, who was "*repugnante*" (hateful), my mother had said after meeting him at the Hurds' once, had a jeep. Guests that often came up to stay during the summers, were Baxter and his wife Nellie and friends of the family.

The *Tejanos* were nice enough, but they were used to ordering people around. They were always in a hurry and always seemed tense, or at least I sensed their restlessness. One day Buster drove his Jeep off the road and onto an embankment near the Cookes' store. He was very angry when he came out of the car. Dust was flying all over from the collision with a mud bank. He cursed and yelled and kicked his Jeep. He grabbed his cowboy hat from behind the seat where it had fallen and then he pulled a pistol from under the seat and shot his car five times. He then put his gun under his belt, said "Sonbitch," and walked to the house a few yards away.

The Hurds had a cook named Guadalupe. They called her, "Lupy." She was a short dark-skinned woman who said that she too was a Texan. Lupy spoke a different Spanish from what we spoke. Guadalupe said to my father when they were introduced to each other, *"Mucho gusto Señor Andy, aquì tiene a su humilde servidora, para lo que se le ofresca"* (very happy, Sr. Andy, I'm your humble servant to do your bidding). I had never heard anyone make such a long first greeting and especially one that offered themselves to do anything. Her accent was different. She said to me once when I went there, and when the Hurds were out.

"Andale joven," in a sing-song voice, *"llama a los morritos a compartir contigo estas golocinas,"*

"*Que?*"

"*Tus amigitos, Jur frens,*" she said "to come to eat the sangwish."

After that I asked my father why it was that she talked so funny. I told him that I understood the words, but not the combinations in which she used them.

"*Asina, hablan los de Mejico*" (that's the way they speak in Mexico) he said. We started to know Guadalupe better despite our differences.

"Did you hear about Buster, that he put five bullets into his Jeep?" I wanted to know.

"*Oh, jes. He do that all the time in Midland. He jus ah spoil, American boy.*" Buster was twenty one years old.

The Hurds were strange, to my way of thinking, and the only person that I thought they spoke to with respect, was my father. It didn't take me long to know that the Hurds knew who was more or less important in the valley. Shortly, after building their home on "Gringo Hill," the Hurds nailed signs all around their fence line. The signs read, "Private Property, No Trespassing." They were similar to signs that I had seen nailed on trees in parts of the Forest Service. I blamed Baxter for having put them up and I got to know what that meant one summer when Andy, my cousin, MaCat and I walked up to some wild apple trees, a short distance from the Hurds' place. We were in a carefree mood, picking and eating the wild, sour apples, when we heard someone coming and yelling.

"Hey, kids, get the hell off those trees, can't you read the signs?" It was the summer guest, Baxter. He started running after us and we bolted, running up the cañada (draw) and disappearing among the piñon trees. I heard my name called and I knew that he had seen me and identified me as one of the "trespassers." We had never seen signs like these in Embargo or anywhere in the valley. I told my father about the incident and when he asked the Hurds whether or not we had damaged anything in the property, Baxter laughed, somewhat embarrassed, and said,

"I was just funnin with the kids." But I knew what those signs meant. From that day on, and as more of these signs showed up in different places in the valley, I knew that *los Americanos* had a "thing" about their properties.

I continued to visit the Hurds and talk briefly with Guadalupe, but I was never at ease in that house.

I was often surprised and sometimes amazed at the antics of the Americanos, as my Grandmother called them. I asked my Grandmother once,

"If they are Americanos, what are we?"

"*Yo soy mexicana*" (I am Mexican) she said. I told her that I'd overheard a boy and his friends from La Cueva, call themselves, "*Chicanos.*" My grandmother was very smart and she laughed.

"Maybe they are *mechicanos*," and left it at that.

The Americanos, I finally realized, had come to Embargo for the plentiful fishing in Cabresto, The Red, the Rio Grande, El Rito and the "Nine Lakes," located high on the mountains to the north and east. The newcomers were all fishermen. Mr. Lange too, was a fisherman, even though he spent most of his time working at home. He sold minnows, fishing supplies that he called tackle and rented cabins to fishermen. The only other Americano that was not always a fisherman was Mr. L.D. Jones. He bought some property in La Cueva, on the sunny side of the hill and opened up a sawmill across the river in Embargo near the forest service property.

Mr. Jones always spoke with his teeth clenched, or so it seemed. He'd also come from Texas but he was different from the Hurds, perhaps because they had money and he didn't. Mr. Jones and his small family had lived down in the Rio Grande canyon during a time the adults called the "depression" and had learned to fish out of necessity. I don't think that he had ever met Ed Rigler, the hermit, but in either case, they had little in common. Mr. Jones' little sawmill was a busy place. My Uncle Tone worked there for a short time and so did my Tio Adon. But when Mr. Jones could not pay them in cash and instead paid them with lumber, which neither one of them needed, they quit. Other men from La Cueva took their places soon enough and Mr. Jones continued to cut rough lumber, slabs and slats, in his busy little mill.

Mr. Jones was a tall, good natured man and he liked to say, with clenched teeth.

"There'ze only two seasons in La Cueva, July and Winter." Then he'd laugh, with a sort of, "see, see, see," through his clenched teeth.

During one of the years when my father was Justice of the Peace, he was called by State Policeman Douglas, Tommy Holder, the game warden and some men from the county seat to the scene of a boating accident near El Chiflo in the Rio Grande. My father told me the story that a man had launched a small wooden boat south of Los Sauces in Colorado and had attempted to float, row or simply ride it down towards Pilar about twenty five miles away. He had been unaccounted for over a month. A search team came upon the shattered boat but the body was not found. When it was found, and my father and the coroner's party were called, the body was all but unrecognizable. My father said that all his parts were missing and said that the body had been petrified. I asked, "What parts were missing?" He said that his ears, one arm, a leg and other *things* were missing.

"What other things?"

"Well his, you know what, including his *tanates*

(slang for testicles)." I knew what he meant by "other things" and simply wanted an explanation on how this had come about.

"You know that when he wrecked he was probably slammed from rock to rock by the current. This is what probably did it. The pertrified condition was probably due to the amount of sand that his body had absorbed from being in the water all this time."

I mulled over the details of the accident and wondered out loud. "Who was he and what would cause him to try to ride the rapids of the Rio?" His name had some Anglo name that I failed to keep in my memory.

"*Estan locos estos Gueros,* don't you think dad?"

"I don't know if they're crazy, *pero son atrevidos.*" I thought that "*Atrevidos,*" were men like my Tio Pino who would ride a wild horse or Legubre Gonzales, who chased them until he caught them.

That Americanos had strange habits I now had no doubts. No *mexicano* from the valley or La Cueva would think of swimming across the Rio Grande, much less try to float a wooden boat on it.

What would make a guy ride a boat on a fast river strewn with big rocks, unless he was crazy?

Another Americano, or as far as we knew, a German, who was not a fisherman, nor did he have anything to do in Embargo, yet, there he was, Dr. Bolita. He bought a small piece of property a quarter mile west of the Cookes' store and had built a house on it. The man was of medium build with a balding head. He had a huge bulge on his right cheek, the size and shape of a native plum, or "*cirguela de Indio*," and smaller than an egg. Because of this strange appendage on his cheek we nicknamed him, *El Doctor Bolita*, (Doctor Ball). Dr. Bolita was called a doctor, but I never saw him treat anyone. He kept to himself but on Christmas day, when the kids would go "asking" for Christmas gifts from house to house, Dr. Bolita always had a candy cane and one nickel for each of us. This was the best gift to put into our bucket or sack.

Dr. Bolita was respected by us and our parents, but we never visited his house during the rest of the year. Dr. Bolita's stay at Embargo coincided with the war in Europe and there were whisperings among the adults that he was a German spy.

"What is there to spy on in Embargo?" I wondered out loud as we were having supper one day.

"*No hay nada aqui*" (there is nothing here), my father said.

"Maybe he is just hiding out. This is a good place to hide."

Doctor Bolita was an enigma to us all but he was purported to be suffering from tuberculosis. When he died some years later, his mattresses were burned and he left, just as he had arrived, with no one knowing much about the man with a "bolita" on his face.

During the time when Dr. Bolita lived among us, Father Smith, from his house on the hill in La Cueva had conducted siren drills at night and urged the residents of La Cueva and Cieneguilla, where his high powered P.A. speaker would be heard, to turn off their lights at night. In Embargo we could neither hear Father Smith speak to the people on his P.A. speaker nor could we hear the peeling of the church bells of San Cristobal del Rio.

Once, when I was at my Grandfather Lefevre's house in Cieneguilla, I had an opportunity to practice the "lights-out drill." But I wondered, *With the lights from the kerosene lamps hardly visible from outside the house how could the Germans possibly see us from high up in the air?*

A week after the lights-out drill at my grandparents', my Uncle Al and his friend Palomillo, unsuccessfully launched a makeshift airplane glider from my Grandpa's roof, resulting in Uncle Al, the pilot, dive-bombing onto the cellar door next to the wall and cutting off half his ear.

The Gatlin boys, Buddy and Jamie, were Mr. Lange's grandsons and our friends. They were a few years younger than my brother Vivian and me but they were active, energetic and mischievous enough to be fun. The fact that we were Buddy's and Jamie's friends was one reason, I'm sure, that we were always welcome at the Lange's store, more precisely, the Lange's porch. Because Buddy was the older of the two boys and because he had a seemingly endless supply of comic books, we acceded to his wishes. Invariably, Buddy wanted to play cowboys and Indians; with he and I, playing the cowboys and my brother Vivian and Jamie, the Indians.

In preparing for the battles, including the "building of the fort," I gave Buddy all the responsibility for getting us ready. Meanwhile I'd take some time watching for the enemy and read through a Gene Autrey, Lone Ranger or Green Hornet comic book while the *preparations* were being made. When the battle interrupted my comic book reading, I invented some way to get Buddy to take on the "Indians" while I got in as much reading as I could. Before too long he noticed what I was doing and cut off the supply of comics.

Buddy was a reckless adversary and a real danger for the Indians in our mock battles. Once, I was busy absorbing the contents of a Captain Marvel, when I heard him say, "Ivian, 'Ivian, catch this," he called out. My brother, thinking it was part of the game, caught a rag saturated with gasoline that Buddy had tossed at him. Buddy then quickly lit a match and threw it at him. The rag exploded and soon Vivian was on fire and I was trying to extinguish the flame with water from a bucket that Margie, the boys' mother, had handily placed nearby. That afternoon when I told my mother about the incident and seeing Vivian's singed eyebrows, she just said, "*ese muchito es un perverso*" (that kid is malicious).

The following day we returned to play with the Gatlins. Little was going to keep me away from those comic books and the journeys of fantasy they provoked in me. Buddy continued his extreme play and when my brother Vivian noticed that Margie was not around, took to punching Buddy out. Buddy was a brave trooper though. He took my brother on, even though he was a bit smaller, would say to him, "*quiere combate quiere combate?*" That sounded hilarious to us and often that broke up the fight.

"Where did you learn to speak that kind of Spanish?" I would ask Buddy. He'd then put up his fists, clenched inward and close to his chin.

"Put-em up, put-em up." I knew then, that he had been reading his comics too and all this time he had played and would continue to play one of the characters in his comics.

One day I noticed that Buddy had some pecans in his pocket. I asked him to give me one and he did. Then he turned to my brother.

"You want some nuts 'Ivian?" He started walking towards his grandmother Lange's house and waved us to come along. He climbed some outside stairs, went into the attic and yelled from within.

"Ivian, get ready," and peeking out the door pointed to the place where he wanted my brother to stand to receive the nuts. All of a sudden I saw a forty pound sack of pecans fly out the upstairs attic. It hit my brother right on the chest. He was knocked down, totally surprised. He got up, shook off the blow and ran up the attic stairs to punch out Buddy but by this time, Buddy had locked the door from inside the attic and Vivian and I had to satisfy ourselves with pockets full of pecans.

As we played together and often included MaCat and Andy in our play, Buddy learned to speak Spanish fast. He alternated between English and Spanish when talking with the gang, but one morning his mother said, as she took me aside.

"Gibo, what does, "*chingada, catherone*" mean?"

"I don't know. Why?"

"Buddy says that to me whenever I tell him to do something. Are you kids teaching him bad words in Spanish?"

I pretended surprise but because I was the oldest of the bunch, I promised that he would not learn any of the bad words from us. After that, and when I knew that Margie or Mrs. Lange weren't watching I tried to scold Buddy for the use of those words with his mother.

In front of the rest of the boys he narrowed his eyes, extended his head toward me and hunched down a bit, as if not wanting to be heard by those around us.

"Mira jodidito, te voy dar tus chingasos." The gang burst out in laughter and I knew that he was not really talking to me but was mimicking my brother Vivian's words when they clashed.

Our friendship with the Gatlin boys was as close as it was with MaCat and Andy. Buddy with his mischievous antics and Jamie taking it all in, together with the fact that they had access to their grandmother's store plus his comic book stash all made for a pretty comfortable summer. We would all snicker when at lunch or dinner time, Margie would yell out to Buddy and Jamie.

"Buddy Lester Gatlin, come here this minute. You too Jamie Bob."

We wondered why their mother always called out their full names. And I would hear my father's voice say.

"I guess that's how they are," as he would when I'd asked about something unusual that I had observed in one of our Anglo neighbors.

The Americanos all lived in Embargo except Mr. Jones, who lived closer to La Cueva. I never saw any of them mix with each other and the family members kept to themselves. I asked my father why he thought they were like that. It seemed strange to me since I knew that he did, in fact, mix with all of them.

"Some are Texans, others are Okies, and the others are just poor gringos," he'd say. As if careful not to be heard, he bend down to look me straight in the eye.

"*Y, no le digas a nadien de lo que yo y tu hablamos* (And don't say anything to anyone about our conversations)." Then he would wink his eye at me. I was beginning to understand why the Langes were so nice, sometimes even wonderful, and why the Hurds were so impulsive, aggressive and spoke differently. Finally, why Mr. Cooke, Mr. Mills and the old fishermen, Bud Parr and Slim McColmb were a bit more inviting when my brother and I would visit with them.

My mother had her version of the differences that I'd noticed.

"*Los gringos son muy escandalosos* (the gringos are very touchy), *no te les arrimes*" (avoid them)."

"*Umph, mira a quien le digo, al peste, numero uno*" (umph, look who I'm talking to, the number-one pest) she would tell me.

I think she was right, I spent more time at the Langes', Gatlins, Cooke's and Hurds than I spent at home.

Embargo was our world. The swallows, the flickers, the night hawks, the chipilotes (buzzards) and even the bats (which we called, flying mice) inhabited our sky. The river with it rocky beaches, the rivulets and the minnows with the red lines under their gills, the German Browns, the mutated fish in las Lagunitas, the genuflecting Dipper and the hellgrammites, as well as the swimming hole, all fit nicely into our universe. The Americanos, gringos or gabachos, whatever we called them, had also become part of this world. Who would have guessed that one day all the parts in this huge, comfortable puzzle would be unraveled and get scattered, never to be put together again.

The Resolaneros

La Cueva was built along a huge hill or grade. The houses along the road from Embargo north were either at cuesta arriba or cuesta abajo (uphill or down hill) and this is the way one described the location of a house or a business in La Cueva. It was either cuesta arriba or cuesta abajo. La Cueva had become the central place for the settlements in the area and which the natives called, "*la plaza*." To the southwest and extending for about three miles was "El Valle del Embargo." To the east and butted up against the huge mountains of *El cerro del almagre* was Cieneguilla (the meadows). To the northeast was Cabresto (*cabestro* for rope) and to the north was Llano, set on a high plateau between the huge mountains of the east and at the top of the cuesta arriba of La Cueva.

It was in La Cueva that the early settlers chose to build their church, San Cristobal del Rio. It was located in the center of an abandoned *plazuela*, now only ruins but in a central location to the satellite communities.

La Cueva had three or four businesses. There was the venerable sala (hall) belonging to Albino Rel, where we came to know the world of Tarzan and Gene Autrey through the movies brought in by an itinerant movie peddler. This hall was also used for dances on Saturday nights. There was a one-pump gas station belonging to old man Wallace. There was the post office, a bar and a grocery store called "The Mercantile Store," belonging to Jose Atilano Rel. The people called it simply, "*la tienda*" (the store). It was at this site or at least on the shady side of the store where the sages or wise men of La Cueva met.

The Rel store carried everything in it that the people there needed. There were canned goods, clothes, bundles of cloth, and of course, coca cola and ice cream. It also carried pocket knives, one of which I bought after saving up money for one whole year. La Tienda had the only telephone in town. Atilano would answer his and the community's telephone with a dignified, authoritative voice.

"*Hallo, dis is La Cueva one, Tilio, me 'peaking.*"

We snickered at his broken English but we knew that serious calls came through this telephone, otherwise why would people bother to use it. This store had a cellar-like entrance where Atilano Rel kept the dried sheep and cow hides that he received as barter from the small farms in the area. He also had big blocks of salt that were bought by those farmers that could afford this luxury for their cattle. The omnivorous boys also took the opportunity to break off a piece of the salt block with a rock and lick it as if it were hard candy.

On the shady side of the building, a long wooden bench had been placed, together with a couple of crude wooden chairs. It was in this unlikely place that the "wise men" of La Cueva, held council. It was called *la resolana* (the shade), a place reserved for old men, sleeping dogs and restless boys. It is here where Old Man Wallace, Abad Cisneros, Perfecto Martinez, Atilano Rel, and other guests engaged in verbal bouts. These were often sage discussions but most of the time they were simply verbal jousts among these old men. The sages shared their store of knowledge that they had accrued over three-fourth of a century, a knowledge which too often had been ignored by family members or dismissed as *having been heard before.*

The discussions these men held were on a variety of subjects and were often lively. These discussions resulted in challenges of elocution, of wit and knowledge, both worldly and biblical. The only young man that was in attendance at almost every meeting was a sixteen year old gadfly by the name of "Brownie" Valdez. Brownie was tolerated because he was a sort of messenger. He became the way in which the "words" of these men would be known to the rest of the community, for Brownie broadcast the essence of the discussions to whomever he came upon in La Cueva.

The gloves came off as soon as the main characters showed up, which was usually around ten o'clock, having given the septuagenarians time to have their breakfast and to walk to the center of town. Brownie's time was not predictable. He came and went as his fancy suited him. He only stayed if the deliberations promised the fireworks of controversy or gossip.

Long before encountering the deliberations of the wise old men of la resolana, I had wondered who or what first started a conversation. *How do conversations start?* I wondered. I had heard my mother and neighbors go straight into a conversation with the weather as the starter. Others started with someone complaining about their health (and it seemed that all the women did a lot of that) but I always wondered what the prompt, the cue or the starter of a conversation was. I learned the art of that science by listening to the wise men of la resolana.

The first time that I came upon these public conversations was a few weeks after I started working for Old Man Wallace in his one-gasoline-pump service station. I noticed that the old man would leave his place of business every morning. His wife, Mana Luz and I remained at the service station to take care of the occasional car that drove in to fill up with gasoline. One day, when the boss was out, his wife asked me to take a note to him, asking if she could extend credit to a man wanting to buy gasoline. As she handed me the note she said, "But don't bother him while he is talking, wait until you get a chance between their conversations."

When I arrived at the lively discourse, Henry saw me but he too knew that I had been given instructions to wait. I hadn't been there five minutes when I was captivated by the excitement of the discussion. The topic in question and the gravity of the men as they defended their respective positions just naturally held my attention. Despite the fact that I had arrived in the middle of the conversation, I soon gathered that the topic had to do with the ages of men, more specifically, men that had lived long ago.

"What do you think Perfecto?" someone asked.

"Well, I think that the reason that those men lived one hundred and fifty or one hundred and eighty years is because the people in those days didn't know how to tell time. Their calendars might have divided the year into four, maybe because they recorded each of the four seasons as years, hence, four years in one." said Perfecto Martinez.

"No, no!" retorted Abad Cisneros, '*El Viejo*

Testamento' (the Old Testament) clearly says that God, Jehovah gave those men that followed his word and obeyed his instructions many more years to live than he did others. Remember that most of these men were his priests or his 'true believers' and they were of special trust." At that moment of fervor in his voice, he seemed a prophet himself, with his beard and partly balding head.

Atilano Rel's position was somewhat vague.

"I believe like my grandfather David Rel, who told me once that man was born of woman and that he would die when his time came." Then everyone looked at Henry Wallace, as if to have him render a decision as to whose argument was the most convincing, or perhaps simply to bring the group back on task. They all quietly appeared to have discounted Atilano Rel's comments.

Old man Wallace, I soon surmised, was the mentor of the discussions, the leader of the group and too often, despite his irreverent views, the one to bring a consensus, a synthesis to their learned dialogues. Henry Wallace, now looked up, as if to ponder his answer.

"To my way of thinking, it was '*los tiempos*' (the times) when these men lived that caused them to get so old yet not be too old. What?" He asked rhetorically, "Enoch was one hundred and fifty years old when he died. Ezequiel was one-hundred and eighty and Methuselah almost three hundred years old. These men," he said, irreverently, "were the bulls of the tribes just like the bulls in the pastures of Maclovio Gallegos."

Abad Cisneros showed his displeasure by shaking his head and lowering his eyes to the ground.

"No Henry, now you've even surpassed your impudence of the past, these were holy men." The others smiled slightly, knowing that Abad was a fervent reader of the bible and that Henry had struck a sensitive nerve. They also knew that Old Wallace had not finished stating his position, besides this is the kind of point and counter point that these discussions were all about. I was enthralled with the discourse, but Henry Wallace continued.

"Look, after the deluge, there were very few men left to populate the world. God needed men from his tribes, David, Abraham, even Ezequiel, who wrestled with an Angel and other holy men who were in effect, the defenders of the one God." Abad now looked pleased. Henry continued, as a man convinced that his logic would win over his companions.

"The world was new then," he said. "The number of humans was low, and God needed to populate the world. These men were there to be the breeders of the women who would 'multiply' the human race. I believe like Abad, that these men did in fact live to be that old. I also believe that they were virile and let me tell you, I think that those women they bred were more than their wives. They were concubines, widows, even relatives of the women they were attached to," Henry Wallace expanded.

"There you go again," said Abad. "You're guessing at a lot of this. The Old Testament doesn't say all of that."

"Yes it does," asserted Henry Wallace and the other men of the group agreed that what he'd said was a real possibility.

The discussion ended, I hurriedly handed my boss the note sent by his wife and I ran back to my duties at the gas station.

A couple of days later I told my boss that I was sorry I'd left the station for as long as I did the other day.

"Mrs. Wallace told me not to bother you while you were talking."

"That's alright," he said. "What did you think of my friends?"

This was the opportunity I'd been looking for. I'd been captivated by the conversations that took on the level of high debate and since I had won the county schools' eighth grade speech debate that spring, I felt quite confident to answer his question.

"I have never seen grown men exchange ideas in this fashion. I think, that the development of your idea was not only logical but your focus was firm, even when people wanted to sway you from your argument." Henry looked at me, surprised that I had dared to analyze his comments. He smiled with a pride that I'd experienced when my coach at school had praised my own work that winter.

"Come on over any time you want," he seemed to invite. I didn't push it, but I said to myself, "*touché*."

My chance to attend this exciting gathering came a few days later when Mrs. Wallace said, "Henry wants you to visit with him at la tienda today."

"*Resolaneros*" she said with contempt. "Now, guess who'll have to do the work around here?" Shortly after Mr. Wallace left I stepped out, telling Mrs. Wallace that I would work an extra hour that day.

"Go, Henry says you're a smart boy."

When I got there, the discussions were already in full swing. The topic seemed to center on death and the here-after. Abad Cisneros was quoting from the bible to support his argument that although the Old Testament does not ascribe a heaven or hell that man can not just simply die and vanish. He stated, in his visage of an ancient patriarch himself, "Although the body will return to ashes from where it came, the soul will join the eternal in whose image we are made."

"Well," Perfecto Martinez added, "If you are talking about those among us that are perfect, that is, without sin, that's fine. But what about those of us who will be lucky to simply end up in Purgatory, for I don't know how long. What then?" Almost as if he truly wanted an answer to such speculation.

Henry Wallace then commented, as if playing the devil's advocate.

"Well, who is sure that there is a Purgatory? Just who are the candidates for such a place as we've imagined?" He then took on a role that I didn't know he could. Old Man Wallace was a reader and I knew that he was knowledgeable about a lot of topics but he started giving a lesson on a book that obviously he had read, and which he called, "El Infierno de Dante" (Dante's Inferno). He started by saying that Dante, *un italiano*, had written about eight levels of hell and who the candidates were in each of these levels. He lectured everyone there and I knew then why he had invited me. He wanted me to see him in his best hour. He continued:

"Dante's first level is that reserved for those unfortunate children who have not been baptized. And, although his book is not associated with the church," he said, "this level was taken into consideration by the church's teachings regarding the sacrament of baptism and the consequences of not obeying this doctrine."

Henry Wallace was exclamating and his voice was equal to the topic. He proceeded, rather dramatically, to say that the entry into hell's gate had a sign hung high for all to see. The sign announced, and Henry moved his hand, palm out and slowly swinging it from left to right as if reading the sign itself, "*Whoever enters will never return.*"

Henry Wallace then got into describing the entry into hell and the levels that he, through Dante, said were there and who the candidates were that were housed in each of these receding levels into the depth of hell in the eighth and final level.

"In the second level," Henry continued, "were those souls, that when alive, had been overcome by lust. They now resided in a perpetual storm symbolizing the power of lust to toss us about without the strength to resist it. The third level," Henry advanced, "was reserved for the gluttons. Their punishment was to lie in mud under rain and hail." Although Henry Wallace elaborated what Dante had included in each of the levels, I was looking for the key words as to who was condemned to each level and what was the punishment there. Wallace continued with the fourth level as being that level in hell where there lived those who coveted material things: It included the avaricious, the misers who hoarded possessions and the prodigal who squandered them. It was often hard to follow Henry Wallace's discourse of Dante's hell. Sometimes he did not explain what those words meant, but we all got the idea.

Henry Wallace had advanced well into the depth of hell in his story, but he kept coming up, just as had Dante, with the name of *purgatory*, describing a place midpoint between the levels of hell, when someone interrupted the sermon. It was Perfecto Martinez who had gotten up and interrupted loudly.

"No! No!" he yelled, "I cannot listen to all of this without getting sick to my soul. Have we forgotten who we are? Have we joined those who have destroyed our faith and made a mockery of our holy oath to Jesus Christ, who was whipped, humiliated, and finally suffered the shame and death in the road to Calvary? You, Mano Henry, *es facil para usted* (it's easy for you). You and your books and your views that are *laicos* (secular), forget. No! You ignore why we are all here in this country of *sufrimiento* (suffering). How soon we forget what faith, what sacred yearning, what sight on the cross coaxed us here, perhaps four hundred years ago. *Pues* (well), I haven't forgotten." And he did a strange salute that I had never seen anyone do. He beat his heart with closed fist then immediately opened his hand with fingers spread out and slapped his shoulder, twice. "That is penance," he said. Abad Cisneros lowered his eyes, he knew what Perfecto Martinez was talking about. Perfecto's visage remained hardened, his skin seemed to have darkened, his eyes were squinted and his forehead had beads of sweat.

Perfecto Martinez, I came to know, was a true zealot of the Hermandad, a 15th century religious confraternity that had been brought here by the ancient travelers to Embargo, La Cueva, Cieneguilla and El Llano and was now lost in the vagueness of time and the incidents of history. The fraternity was known, although covertly, as The Brotherhood of Light of The Nazarene, or *Los Penitentes.*

As if to add to the dramatic eruption of the religious manifestations of Perfecto Martinez, a lone figure walked down the street on his way somewhere in the tiny village of La Cueva. The man was a tall, lean individual whose head was bent down slightly and whose eyes looked straight ahead, as if his mind was lost in deep thought. "There," said Perfecto and he pointed to the man on the street. "There goes the last true believer, the only faithful in this town of cowards. There goes Tomas Avila, the last penitente."

Henry Wallace had abandoned his long discourse on Dante. Abad Cisneros remained with his head down, listening passively to the fervid reproaches of Perfecto Martinez. And I sat, like Ferravas the meddlesome individual in the old cuento (tale) who had been turned into a stone with eyes. I was excited at seeing such emotions in a grown man. I was perplexed and intrigued with his argument and certainly with his and the community's secret but most of all I wanted to hear more. The meeting of the resolaneros was over when I saw Perfecto clean a tear from his eye with a thumb, lower his head and walk away. About three weeks would pass before there would be another convocation of the *wise men of La Cueva.*

When Henry Wallace and I got back to his place of business we were both uneasy and neither one said anything about the outburst of Perfecto Martinez. I did not want to bring up the subject because I felt that Wallace had been upstaged, especially at his moment of glory. I knew however, that I could not let the thing go and I planned a subterfuge to get Henry Wallace to unravel the mystery regarding the proceedings of that day on the shady side of la tienda.

A couple of days after the incident at la tienda, I approached Henry Wallace one morning at work.

"I wonder if Perfecto Martinez has gotten over being so angry?"

Henry was leafing through some papers. He looked up.

"I knew you would ask me something like that, sooner or later. I saw you with your eyes wide open and eager for the argument to continue." He smiled and said, "Listen, let's talk about it this afternoon." He added, "You seemed surprised at what Perfecto was saying. Don't you know anything about the people here? You know that they're all Penitentes, don't you?"

"No," I said, although I'd heard a few rumors about "self whippings" from the boys in the area, but few knew any details. Today I would get an education on the history of an enigmatic people, my people.

The Secret Revealed

Henry Wallace and I had become good friends, or better yet, he had assumed a role of mentor towards me and I had welcomed this relationship. He said to me once, that he enjoyed my sense of curiosity. He said that I was like a blank slate, but eager to learn. He took me under his wing when I recited from a Lewis Carroll story, *Through The Looking Glass.* I'd said to him, early on my visits to the meetings of the wise men of La Cueva, "When I sit in on your meetings I feel like the Walrus in a book I once read." I began to recite (showing off).

"*The time has come, The Walrus said,*
To talk of many things, Of shoes and ships,
Of sealing wax, of cabbages and kings.

Surprisingly he retorted with:

"You are old, Father Williams, the young man said
'And your hair has become very white;
And yet you incessantly stand on your head—
Do you think, at your age, it is right?"

We both laughed, he had trumped me with another of Lewis Carroll's quotes in a conversation between Alice and the Caterpiller.

Henry Wallace was a back-country intellectual and he appreciated anyone that could at least, converse with him. With my little smidgen of knowledge acquired from Lewis Carroll I'd won him over and today I was going to hear what Perfecto Martinez was talking about and the Pandora's box that he seemed to have wanted to open for such a long time.

"As we were saying," Henry Wallace started his lecture that afternoon. "Perfecto Martinez had every right to berate us. Perfecto is a patient, sincere man but somehow carries with him, a guilt that is really neither his nor the community's or anyone else's. What Perfecto is talking about is a consequence of the history of change, of different times. You see," he said, "Perfecto's great-grandfather, grand- father and his father were among the leading members of '*La Hermandad*' (the brotherhood) or better said, '*Los Penitentes.*' They each had been the Elder or *hermano mayor.* They built the *Morada* (house of worship) in El Llano and presided in the activities of this society during the Lenten season and were central to the support of the families of El Llano during the long political neglect by Spain and later Mexico."

I think that Henry Wallace realized that I was lost in the information that he was giving me and so he stopped his lecture.

"Let me stop, I think that I am getting ahead of myself and confusing you in the process. Let me go back to what Perfecto said that day at la tienda, it might make more sense that way. You remember when Perfecto said, 'Have you forgotten who we are?' And I'll ask you, Did you know that all the people in these communities," and he counted off the names on his fingers: "La Cueva, El Llano, Cieneguilla, Cabresto and yes, even Embargo were, at one time, all of them, Penitentes? Yes," he continued. "Your grandfather Benito Lefevre, on your mother's side, your great uncle Ariel Herrera, on your father's side, all of them; Penitentes. You see, the history of this place goes back three hundred and fifty years. The Spanish king sent people to colonize these northern-most regions of New Spain, that is what this territory was called then. The King and later Mexico wanted people to live in this northern frontier and defend the land belonging to the crown. To my way of thinking, they wanted canon fodder and we were it. The King of Spain and his advisors made a good choice in the people they designated to 'protect' these lands. They chose the hardy Penitentes, whom they knew were up to the task of tilling a rugged land, defending against Indians and 'holding El torreon' (the defense tower) so to speak," he continued.

"The confraternity of religious people, called the Hermandad (brotherhood), was sanctioned within the catholic church. This group of colonists were granted large tracts of land that were held in common and given ecclesiastic permission to practice their form of religion. The Penitentes had a covenant with God, which was to follow the teachings of Jesus Christ and to emulate his sufferings through penance. This penance took the form of ritualized prayer, singing *Alabados* (medieval praise hymns) fasting, community support and self flagellation." Henry stopped to ask me if I knew what that meant.

"Whipping yourself?"

"Yes," he said and continued his lecture. "This covenant I mention is what Perfecto was talking about when he asked if we had forgotten the Oath that we had taken. The Penitentes and their families were, how shall I say? *muy sufridos* (hardy). They endured living in this place, with its climate and limited pastures and they seemed to negate pain. The children were taught not to show pain under any circumstances."

As Henry continued to talk, I thought of my own

experiences. I recalled that whenever I fell, cut myself or had some accident, my father would make fun of me. He'd say, "*Que no eres hombre* (aren't you a man)? Men don't cry." My mother would simply say to me or any of my brothers and sisters, "Don't cry. *no sean sinverguenza* (don't be without shame)."

Henry must have thought that I was wondering about the sufferings of the penitente families.

"You know why these people were so tough? Because," he continued, "They were stoics. One of these days," he said, "you will read about the ancient Spaniard of Greek descent by the name of Spinoza who speaks about the philosophy of stoicism. He talks about the virtues of being self-reliant, strong and not admitting to pain. These Penitentes came from Spain, where many citizens in the 14th and 15th century practiced this philosophy."

Henry was giving me a lesson that I know he relished and I was speech-less with wonder. I had no reason to think that what he was saying to me, was not the truth. *After all,* I thought, *If this man has read something as strange as the levels of hell in Dante's Inferno, he surely knows about this thing called stoicism;* After all, I had seen the endurance of my neighbors and members of my own family and the behaviors admonished by my parents.

In trying to absorb all that Henry Wallace had revealed to me, I thought back to an experience that I had about the time that I was six years old or thereabouts. We were living in the village of Culebra, named after the meandering, snake-like river by that name. My father had been working, temporarily helping to build a school house under what he called, *"El WPA."*

One morning in April, the weather was just breaking from its long cold winter spell when I heard strange sounds coming from the Morada a short distance away. I stepped outside our two-room house that my father had rented from Mana Dulcinea, a strong willed woman and no doubt, a true believer. The sounds that I heard came from a long column of men and women, walking toward a large wooden cross about one half mile from the Morada. At the head of the column were three men. One was playing a flute, the other was singing alabados from a book and the third one had a large rattle that he turned as they walked. The rattle held by the third leader of the column was so large that he had to turn it holding the handle with his two hands. The sound, I recall, was eerie and to this day I seem to hear it all: The shrill music coming from the home-made wooden flute played to a sort of death dirge with long monotonous notes and when joined in by the CRAA,CRAA,CRAA cadence of the rattle (matraca) and the medieval chants of the alabados, it all came back, flooding my memory. The sight, the sounds and the lowered heads of the men and women in the marching column, now became the metaphor for all that Henry Wallace had shared with me.

I had witnessed the symbolic march to the Stations of the Cross that Jesus had endured on his walk to his crucifixion and the basis for the covenant of the Penitentes. The Lenten activities and all of the rituals surrounding this cult were: sin, repentance, atonement and gracious acceptance of forgiveness.

To give credence to what Henry was saying to me and to show me that he too, sympathized with the society that he was describing he digressed from his lecture.

"You know that my mother is *mexicana* or *hispana*? My mother's maiden name is Esquibel," he said. "My grandfather was Toribio Esquibel. He too was a penitente but I guess that when he moved his family to Walsenburg he stopped practicing his religion. When my mother met my father, John Henry Wallace from Missouri, they chose to stay in Walsenburg where my Dad worked as a Fireman in the D&RGW railroad. Twenty five years ago I came to live in La Cueva and opened up this business. I was as curious about the penitentes as you seem to be," he said. "That is why today, I'm only too glad to share this with you. It surprises me, that your father has not shared this information with you. Your father is a smart man and I'm sure he is well read."

Henry Wallace then lowered his head as in deep thought, then he continued. "That is why so many of you kids, know nothing about your past. I mean, all that secrecy, all that worshiping God from within the four window-less walls of the morada, the oath of secrecy of its members, and the toll on them after the persecution by the American Catholic Church against the Brotherhood. These are among the reasons that the penitentes died off."

God, I thought, *this story is like the cuento de nunca acabar* (the never-ending story). It is such a long history of the people around me and I knew practically nothing about it."

"This evening," I thought, "I'm going to question my father about all of this." But Henry's voice brought me about and he continued.

"Yes, That is why the brotherhood ceased to exist and why Perfecto pointed to Tomas Avila, as 'the last of the faithful, the last penitente," said Henry Wallace.

"There are several reasons for the demise of the Brotherhood. Like I said, this was a secret society, but it was secret even from the families of the faithful. I suppose, that in order to give the religious practices the appropriate dignity and the serenity required by the stoics this kind of secrecy was necessary." Henry then said, as if talking to an audience of his fellow wisemen. "These practices were indelibly etched in the oral tradition, the religious memory of the original European Penitentes."

"Another reason, and perhaps the real reason why the penitente religion dead-ended was the tremendous pressure from the American Catholic Church. You see, in the early years of the American conquest of this territory, and I say 'conquest,' because my own grandfather was part of the Missouri Dragoons that marched from St. Joseph to Las Vegas in the *Conquest of the west.*" He recouped from his digression and continued. "Eventhough the Americans had promised that they would respect the religion of the conquered people, soon after their entry into Santa Fe there were huge disagreements with the leaders of the Catholic Church. It wasn't long before the Mexican bishops and the Archbishop were removed. They were replaced by French-American Catholics from Louisiana. And despite the fact that these new prelates were Catholic, a real difference was noted when it came to the religious practices of the Hermandad. The American puritanical mind soon labeled the penitentes as fanatics. The political and religious beliefs of the conquering Americans could not conceive of a people living under them as being so alien that they should be "christianized," as was one of the reasons for Manifest Destiny. The French American Archbishop pressured the remaining priests in the diocese and those having jurisdiction over the church in La Cueva to discourage, if not forbid, the penitente rites. The defense of the penitentes by Padre Martinez in La Villa caused the Archbishop to excommunicate him. This was the telling blow to the people that believed in the religious practices of the brotherhood."

Henry Wallace then took on a look of a lawyer defending a client, as I had seen in my father's court when I was younger. He said, "You have to give credit where credit is due. No one can refute the good that the penitentes brought to these communities. History will judge the passion of those defenders of the faith as being justified, just like Perfecto Martinez pronounced that day."

"First, there is the whole survival of those colonists that were left behind throughout these valleys: scattered, forgotten, isolated and without any kind of government." Henry Wallace now stood up, as if trying to convince me of his reasoning. "Spain withdrew the support to its colonists once it found that no riches were to be found here. Mexico too, after its independence from Spain, chose to consolidate its own power among its feuding caudillos (political chiefs) and frankly, I think that the territory was just too big for any distant power to govern. You know who kept the community together?" he asked. "It was the rule of order and religious morals and social direction that the Hermanos Mayores (the Elders) provided that kept the society together."

"They lived together and they faced their trials together. They called each other Hermanos (brothers) and Hermanas (sisters). Why do you think that they still call each other by 'Mano or 'Mana? They call me 'Mano Henry and I have never been a penitente. You see, the penitente elders, long time ago, when they first came to these valleys, elected to reject the common title of *Don,* which was used by the Spaniards to denote *De Origen Noble* (of noble origin) and chose instead hermano or 'Mano and 'Mana (brother and sister)."

How do I know all of this," he asked. "It is because I was both a participant, living among these people and an observer. The story of the penitente is a fascinating story. I think that although those days that Perfecto yearns for so much are gone forever, he has reason to feel proud of his family's history."

That night when I went home, feeling somewhat exhausted, but wise beyond belief, I approached my father and said. "Henry Wallace told me about the Penitentes today."

"Well, did you learn anything?" he asked.

"Yes," I said. "I think I learned more today than I have in all the years I've spent in school."

My father laughed. "You really think that?" He turned and did not pursue the conversation.

A few days later, after I asked him about his Uncle Ariel. He said, "Years ago, when I was a kid, younger than you, I was passing by the morada near the box canyon after sunset. I heard someone singing an alabado and a noise like slapping. I hid behind a crumbling wall of adobe and saw a man I recognized as my Uncle Ariel. He was the one singing the long sad alabado. I never knew who the other man was, but he was flailing himself with a short whip of many strands. The two men were slowly walking away and the slapping sounds coming from the whipping of the man's back and the singing soon faded. I quickly ran home, and never told anyone about my experience."

Later, I asked Henry who it was that had told him the history of the penitentes. He laughed and said, "No one and everyone. I got a bit of information from one person another bit from someone else and before too many years, I had made a picture, like a puzzle, that told me all I know."

The following summer I put this trick into practice when one day at one of the meetings of the wise men I approached Perfecto Martinez.

"Buenos dias le de Dios (God wishes you a good morning), Hermano Perfecto." My greeting was not uncommon among the people of the valley but my reference to him as Hermano (brother) not just the shortened 'Mano, got Perfecto's attention. He returned the greeting and he called me *Primo* (cousin).

"You are Prima Fina's son, aren't you?" he asked.

"Yes," I said and I knew that he was acknowledging the kinship through his mother, a Lefevre, and my mother's father, a Lefevre.

After the meeting of the wise men I approached Pefecto and I said, "'Mano Henry spoke to me about the brotherhood. He told me that the American Catholic Church had ordered the local priests to outlaw the brotherhood. Is that true?" Perfecto tried to control himself. His face seemed to darken but he waited a minute to compose himself, and then he answered.

"Sabes, primo, (you know, primo) that was not all that happened. Let me tell you about the vulgarity of the whole thing," he said. "The priests and the Archbishops themselves, lied and falsified the holy practices of the hermanos. They demonized us. *Nos hicieron diablos, y despues nos destruieron* (They first turned us into devils and then they destroyed us)." Perfecto spoke as if he had been of the generation that had suffered the original onslaught of the American Catholic prelates. "You know," he continued, "When we here in this valley get ready to hunt the deer of the forests, of the high mountains, we all first talk bad about our adversary. We speak of the deer as if he were a cunning, crafty, demonic creature to be hunted down and killed. That way," he continued, "we don't feel so guilty when we take the life of a beautiful animal that runs free in the forests and who harms no one. That is what 'they' did," he said. His metaphor of the doomed deer and the persecuted brotherhood, I thought, was pretty close to what I had heard Henry Wallace say.

Later that Summer, I approached Tomas Avila, the man Perfecto had called, "The last Penitente." Like my approach to Pefecto, I said, *"Buenas tardes, Hermano Tomas."* He was shocked that anyone would call him brother and not 'mano. He looked at me .

"I know who you are. You work for Mano Henry Wallace."

"Yes, But I have a very important question in my mind and nobody can answer it except you, Hermano Mayor (Elder)." No one had ever approached him in this manner, particularly calling him Elder. He was truly taken aback but true to his stoic upbringing he showed little emotion except for flushed cheeks, a fast flutter of eyelids and when I shook his hand, he had sweaty palms.

"Que es su pregunta, joven (what is your question, young man)?" he asked.

"Porque se abandonaron las moradas (why were the moradas abandoned)" I asked. I knew that because there were no longer any adherents to the faith that this might

be the answer. My intention, however, was simply to start a conversation, with this, "the last penitente."

Tomas Avila, a tall, lanky man, with dark skin and with a pigeon-toed walk took his time to answer.

"How much do you know about the brotherhood?"

I said that I knew little and only the things that I had heard from Henry Wallace.

"But isn't it true that one reason was that the priests no longer supported the brotherhood?"

"Yes, in part. Even then," he replied, "We still had a lot of brothers and sisters that continued to practice the faith." He then looked away, as if in deep thought.

"You know joven, it was the young ones that failed us. *Mas bien* (better said), we did not instruct the young men and women on the sanctity of our religion and they lost faith. When the older hermanos died off, there were no faithful among the youngsters to replace them."

I then, feigning serious thought, made the request that had prompted me to speak to Tomas Avila in the first place.

"I wonder if I could see the moradas that remain," I asked. Surprisingly, he readily agreed.

"*Por que no?*" (why not) he said. "I can show you what you want to see tomorrow." We agreed on a time, late in the afternoon of the following day.

Moradas, The Holy Vigils of Yesterday

The next afternoon, cotton clouds drifted slowly across the valley as if rain would soon follow. A light mountain breeze penetrated my light cotton shirt and the slight chill that I felt seemed to signal a foreboding. I met Tomas Avila at the tienda and he immediately took on the role of an eager host and tour guide.

"Let's start at the morada in La Cieneguilla. I know that Mano Ben Lefevre, your grandfather, was one of the faithful brothers at that morada."

We left the road from La Cueva to La Cieneguilla, about a mile from town and took a faint trail through the tall grass. La Cienegulla was mostly grassland with a few marshy spots here and there. The marsh looked more like bumps of short grass and when one stepped on these mounds, the ground gave way to soft cushions that gave one's footing a spongy, bouncing feel. The people of the

131

valley called this marsh, *estero* (estuary) but an estuary is a body of water that enters the land from an ocean at high tide and goes back out at low tide. Obviously, this was the best description that the early settlers had for a marsh and was perhaps, borrowed from the marshy areas of estuaries in far off coastal places in Mexico or Spain with which their forefathers must have been familiar.

Tomas and I followed the trail and shortly reached a stark looking building. The rectangular adobe morada had a dirt roof which we knew as an *azotea*. It had four window-less walls and a small wooden cross over the lintel of the door. Tomas authoritatively pulled out some keys from his pocket and opened an old lock. He felt compelled to tell me that the door had once had regular doorknobs with a regular lock.

When we entered the building it was difficult to see inside, even with the door wide open. When my eyes adjusted to the low light I saw that we were in a large bare room that took up about a third of the building. I noticed immediately, that the floor was packed earth and the smell of moist dirt permeated the room. The ceiling had been constructed with large pine beams to hold the four-inch thick earthen roof and young, thin aspen rails (called *latillas*), closely fitted to form a webbing to keep out the dirt. The walls inside had been white-washed with a local gray-white silica found in a pit in one of the hills east of the Cieneguilla morada. The room had wooden benches set around three of the picture-less walls. Tomas then led me to a second room that was also locked. After opening the door to the second room he walked directly to a candelabra with candle holders for twelve candles. It had been made in the shape of a even-sided triangle with one candle at the apex, four each on the two sides and three on the bottom cross member of this large wooden candle holder. Tomas struck a match with the tip of his thumb nail and lit six of the twelve candles. The room that had been almost totally dark was now lit enough for me to see the room's contents. The austerity of the room, like the one before, was softened only by the eight wooden benches inside. Unlike the benches on the room entering the morada, these ones were placed in two rows to allow for those in this room to face the wall opposite the entrance. At the corner of the room was a grass broom, made from the high grasses that grew along the fence lines of the neighborhood. Naively, I asked Tomas if the broom had been there a long time. He smiled and said that he makes one broom per year and uses it to sweep the floors and ceilings a couple of times each year.

"First, for holy week, in case someone wants to come in to pray and again in the fall just before winter when the morada is closed until next spring. Not too many people request to come in to pray anymore."

This room, unlike the outer room, had a couple of niches on opposing walls. These niches were about three feet high and two and a half feet wide. I guessed that these were used to hold crucifixes depicting the suffering Jesus on the cross. Tomas confirmed just such a purpose to which the niches were used. He then said, "We cannot keep the holy cross in here anymore, these holy icons are often stolen when thieves break in."

As we looked around inside this room, I wondered what type of worship my maternal grandfather had done here. *Had he beat his breast? Had he whipped himself in penance? Who were in his prayers and what were his sins?* For some reason I could not connect the place, the room the whole idea of the brotherhood with my grandfather. What little I remember of my grandfather was that I saw him as a serious, almost morose man. I never saw him smile, nor did I see him show overt love to anyone, including me, his first male grandchild. When he died I was only eight years old and he was forty-seven. My mother had spoken of her father in the same light that I knew him. My mother added that he had been a very superstitious man and that he thought that he had been *embrujado* (bewitched). My grandfather had developed a strange skin disease that caused the skin on his face and throat to turn white with brown blotches. A couple of other men in the valley had a similar skin condition, but concern by my grandfather, according to my mother, bordered on some kind of paranoia. I again wondered, *Had he prayed for deliverance from this leprosy, had he offered his bare back in penance for any real or imagined sins?*

I feigned wonder about my grandfather's history with this morada (dwelling of the faith) but I truly had little memory of him beyond a rare answer to questions I had made to him about his hunting skills. I remembered having seen my Grandfather as an old man yet I knew he was actually very young when he died. I chose to agree with Tomas Avilia's assessment that Mano Ben was indeed a faithful *hermano*.

We continued toward the back wall, which had an anteroom. It was small and was empty. Tomas said that this room had been used to store the cross carried by the faithful. It had been carried by some *penitente* during the enactment of the crucifixion during Lenten rituals. As the light from the candelabra penetrated the dark corners of this anteroom I noticed a glint coming from one of the corners. When Tomas started to walk out I picked up the tiny object and knew it was a piece of broken glass. I put it in my pocket and we walked out.

Outside, Tomas pointed to the site of the *cruz del calvario* (Calvary cross) a site about one quarter of a mile away. All that existed there now was a pile of rocks and traces of eroded adobe bricks.

As we walked away, headed toward the next morada, the one in Cabresto, we startled a flock of pigeons. The white, blue and brown birds flew in a panic and rose quickly against what was now a perfectly light-blue sky. The pigeons formed patterns of flight as they started to turn, first one direction then another. The birds had been gleaning the fallen grain and chaff from the recently-cut wheat field. They were now turning around behind us to land where we had surprised them.

Tomas suggested that we take a path across the fields instead of returning to the dirt road to Cabresto. "It's closer through here," he said.

It was late summer and grasshoppers were now full-grown. As the locust scattered before our feet I couldn't help but think of how nice fishing would be with one of these tasty morsels impaled ass-backwards in one of my hooks. We walked a couple of miles before we caught sight of the morada. We'd made the two miles quickly but I had gotten gramma grass seed and burrs stuck to my pant legs and socks. We had crossed several barb wire fences with pieces of wool from sheep crossing the lower strands of wire and we startled an occasional meadow lark.

Before we reached the second morada, I ventured an intrusive question to Tomas.

"Is it true that there was a lot of crying in the old *velorios* (wakes) and that sometimes the women that were crying were paid to cry?" Tomas did not miss a stride as he walked ahead of me, and hesitated only a moment to answer my question.

"Oh yes, they were the "*Magdalenas*," as if I knew what he was talking about.

"Who are the Magdalenas?"

He then stopped and said:

"Have you read, or have you been told about the woman who cried at the Holy Crucifixion of Christ? She was the woman who had anointed the feet of Jesus with precious oils at the Last Supper and was the first one to find the tomb of Jesus, the Christ, empty on Easter Sunday. She was Maria Magdalena (Mary Magdalene). Yes, she was a crier and the Magdalenas among us are complying with a holy act when they cry at the wake of a brother. It is to speed his soul on its way to heaven."

So the women, whom I had heard disparaged as lloronas (criers) were really emulating Mary Magdalene? I thought. I was getting more and more confused and more and more in awe of Tomas Avila, whom I had thought a poor laconic wretch with little to talk about. Tomas, I concluded, was not only a custodian of the old moradas but the custodian of the cultural memory of the people of this valley.

We arrived at the Morada del Cabresto. It looked very much like the one at Cieneguilla. However, instead of a wooden cross above the lintel of the door, like the morada in Cieneguilla, this one had a cross made out of river rocks embedded into the adobe when the plaster was soft. I was amused by the creativity of the different individuals that composed each of the moradas only two miles apart.

Like with the door in the previous morada, Tomas opened the lock at this one. As we entered this morada I began to see slight differences between the two places of worship. In the first room were niches on the north wall. In these niches, instead of holding any crucifix, both had murals of Christ on the cross.

What an ingenious way of having the icons of the faith depicted inside these niches instead of having statuary that could easily be stolen, I thought.

The benches around the three walls inside this room were much like those in the other morada but as we entered the second room, the one reserved for the penitente brothers only, I could see more care having been given to the benches there. These were benches with backs and fashioned at a slight angle to keep the brothers from having to slouch or to sit up straight. There was a similar candelabra as the one at Cieneguilla but Tomas chose to light up a kerosene lantern instead of the candles.

"I just wanted you to see the beauty of the candles lit before, but here I better conserve the candles. They are getting harder to get. My grandfather and father were both Elders in this morada," Tomas said. "And, even though you addressed me as an elder, I have never had the privilege of being one. This is my 'dwelling place'" he said.

"*Aqui moramos yo y mis antepasados*" (Here is where my ancestors and I dwell).

This is simply a manner of speech, I thought but the deeper meaning that Tomas tried to convey escaped me, except to deduce that *morar* means *to dwell* and *morada* must mean *dwelling place*.

Tomas led me to the anteroom of this morada and there I saw an adult size skeleton sitting on a bench-type seat on a two-wheeled cart. The cart had all the accoutrements needed for someone to hitch the cart to be pulled by a small animal. On the left hand of the skeleton was a bow and on the right hand the skeleton held an arrow.

"What do you think of this?" Tomas asked me. "*Le tienes miedo*? (are you afraid of it)? Before I could answer he ventured:

"*This is Doña Sebastiana, la muerte* (death). She is here to remind us of our frail lives and the end to which we must all come. This is the curse of our father Adam and mother Eve's original sin." He continued.

In my uneasiness, I could not help but think that the "old ones" personified death in order not to fear it. On one corner I could see another grass broom and I knew that Tomas would do his fall sweeping soon.

Tomas invited me to sit down in one of the benches in this inner sanctum. He sat in another. He surprised me when he asked, out of nowhere.

"I heard you played the part of Satan at the *drama de Los Pastores* (pastoral play) last spring."

"Yes," I said. "Mano Eugenio Ortega did a good job in training us to deliver a good performance."

"I heard too, that the Duran cousins, Beto and Linda Duran played the parts of Hilita and the Archangel Miguel."

"Yes," I answered.

"You must have a good memory then," he said. "I know that the script of the Devil or Satan was long and a lot had to be memorized."

"Yes," I said and thought, *What does this have to do with our visit to these ancient moradas?*

I began to wonder what this virtual hermit, this keeper of a promise to his ancestors had in mind. It wouldn't be too long that week that I would get, if not a complete, at least a partial answer.

When we walked out of the Cabresto Morada, heavy dark clouds threatened rain or perhaps even hail. The setting sun turned the clouds in the west crimson. To the east, less than a mile away, was the large mountain called Sierra Almagre. It had a huge glacial slide on the west side facing the valley. It is here, at the foot of the slide, that the Tiwa people, have their sacred cave from where they take the colored earth called *almagre* (ochre) for use in their ceremonies.

How fitting, I thought, *that the Christian Morada faced the Tiwa's ceremonial cavern.* And I wondered, *Which holy place is honoring the other?*

As we left the morada Tomas looked at the sky.

"It's getting late. What do you say if we don't visit the morada at Llano today? Maybe we can continue our visits tomorrow afternoon or the following day."

"Yes," I answered, almost too quickly. I had absorbed more information that day than I had done since Henry Wallace had related his version of the brotherhood to me. In today's experiences I had seen the real scenes of worship and I had listened to the voice of memory in the humble person of Tomas Avila. It would not be until Friday of that week that Tomas and I would meet at Jose Atilano Rel's tienda to continue our visit to the two remaining moradas of the valley.

That night I shared my experiences of the day with

my father. He was neither excited for me nor in any way upset. I pulled out the small sharp green glass from my pocket and handed it to him. I told him where I had found it. My father's eyes opened wide. He held it up, between his thumb and index finger and calmly asked me,

"Do you know what this is?" I simply shook by head to signal, "No."

"This little piece of glass was used by the penitente men to cut the surface of the skin on their backs in order to draw blood when whipping themselves. The bleeding also helped to keep from getting bumps or welts where the heavy leather straps met the skin."

On Friday morning, close to 10:00 o'clock I met Tomas at our appointed place. He had just come out of the store and was stuffing something into a large pocket of his coat.

"*Buenos dias le de Dios,*" I said. He repeated the same greeting to me and we started cuesta arriba, (uphill) toward El Llano. After walking about forty five minutes we reached that settlement's morada. It was much like the other two that we'd seen earlier that week. This morada was set on top of a small hill. During daylight you could see the building with its cross on the top of the adobe fringe silhouetted against a blue sky. To the west were the Cerro del Abra and Cerro Pelado, two prominent buttes jutting out of the llano or plain. This spot was the most scenic view of the mountains and the open gorge, which was the valley.

Tomas opened the door to the building. On the outside one could see that an effort had been made to clear the weeds from the front part of the morada but a couple of cottonwood trees had sprouted close to the east and north walls. Their branches were so close to the walls that I knew that if these trees were not uprooted they would threaten the structure itself.

We entered the morada and found it pretty much like we'd found the others: bare, austere and silent. In this morada however, I soon discovered crucifixes in each of the two niches and next to one of them, a leather-bound book. Tomas Avila did not seem surprised and calmly said that Perfecto Martinez's family often shared their private holy objects with the faithful. I assumed and later confirmed that Perfecto had placed these objects in the morada specifically for me to see. I commented that the Crucified Christ seemed so real and so sad.

"*Asi fue El sacrificio de nuestro padre santo* (This is the way of the cross and the sacrifice made by our Holy Father)."

I then turned to the leather-bound book and asked what sort of book it was. Tomas took the book, opened it and showed me the hand written *cantos* or *alabados* in it. Tomas, as if by cue from someone, started to sing. His song had a strange, yet somewhat familiar tone. My mind, in trying to find some association, took me to the Pastoral play of a year ago when even I had sung a similar dirge as the Devil, sang to the Archangel Miguel upon being defeated. But Tomas' alabado was distinctly different. Tomas' voice started each line of the song, with the first three lines on an even heel. His voice rose much higher on the third and fourth word and was sustained till the end of each line:

Le dieron MU-ER-TE, a-a-al   SENO-OR-OR
Los clavos le RE-E-EMA-CHA-A-ARON...

(They've given death to our Lord)
(The nails they've truly riveted...)

Tomas' alabado went on for a while longer and while I understood the words, the tune was strange. It was a quivering of the voice as it was sung acappella. This, together with the high rise of the voice in each stanza made this a death dirge, if anything.

Much later as an adult, I recognized this characteristic quivering of the voice as Middle Eastern music. I thought back to that time and said to myself, *It's no small wonder that the penitentes had used this form of musicality since less than one hundred years before the brotherhood came into being in Spain, the Moslem Moors had held sway over Iberia for eight-hundred years.*

I could not help but comment that the alabado was very sad, that it told the story of the crucifixion quite realistically and that he, Tomas, had mastered the alabado well. Tomas' reply was simply, "*Sea por El amor del Señor* (Be it so, by the love of our Lord)."

The morning of that visit to El Llano's house of worship passed as if in an instant. I entered the second room in this morada and saw in one of the corners, a staff and standard with the Crucified Christ depicted to almost life-size.

"This standard was carried by the faithful at the head of the column on the walk towards Calvary."

Since I was able to see and hear so much more than I had seen or heard in the other moradas, I suspected that Perfecto had made it a point to have Tomas Avila, whom he admired, show me as much as possible. All this was in the interest of showing me what it was like to be a penitente. Tomas' questions about my ability to memorize, his singing and even his props, I surmised, were all intended to reward my curiosity with the responsibility of carrying on the cultural memory. I asked myself in the silence of that morada, *Do you, really want to know?* I should have guessed that it was not yet over.

We left what I thought was the most beautiful site of all the moradas that I had seen. The great expanse of the llano with its surrounding buttes, huge mountains and this lonely hill top chapel silhouetted against an azure sky made this the perfect setting. I couldn't help but feel the love that Perfecto and his family and fellow faithful still had for this relic of the past.

We made our way toward the morada at Embargo, our last place to visit. Tomas suggested we walk the fringe of the summit of the high hills north of Embargo. In this way we could descent into the valley by the box canyon at the end of the valley. I was surprised that Tomas had chosen this arduous trail but I was young and he was a stoic. Tomas never asked me what my impressions were as we visited the holy places. Instead, almost as soon as we started toward the last morada, some three and one half miles away he started another story.

"Do you remember the question you asked me about the Magdalenas?" I didn't know what part of that exchange he was referring to, but I answered.

"Yes I do."

"Well," Tomas then said, "The only tragedy for us (meaning the brotherhood) which was almost as bad as our loss of faith was the great plague that fell upon us when I was just a child." He kept talking and made sure that I was listening.

"When I was a kid, no more than eight years old, a great plague overtook our people in this *poblado* (habitation).

"No one knew what was happening. People started dying. People of all ages: old people seemed to die first, then younger and younger ones became victims to the scourge. At first, each of the moradas cared for the people in their *vecindad* (neighborhood). They cared for the sick, ministered to their needs and prayed day and night that this death pass us by. The Magdalenas cried, the brothers sang, prayed and sacrificed themselves as we buried our dead, and then, they too began to die. The Elders of the four moradas got their people together and jointly built coffins, buried people and tried to survive this visitation from the old testament. Nothing seemed to help," he said. "When whole families died off, the brotherhood closed up the houses, burned bedding, turned out the animals from their pens and cried to God for deliverance."

I noticed that Tomas' voice was breaking as he told me this story of so long ago. It was as if Tomas Avila, himself had been in the middle of this terrible tragedy. He related the story as we walked. He spoke of cases where people had been buried alive and some who, when being prepared for burial had suddenly come back to life. I saw Tomas wipe the tears from his eyes and I was overtaken with emotion.

Tomas' tale of apocalypse was as vivid as if it had happened yesterday. I was surprised at the strength of Tomas' memory and especially, the emotional bond attached to this memory. He told of how, as the epidemic began to subside, the people of the valley and the llano and the hill side all prayed together and asked not for deliverance anymore but for God to do his will. They lay their dead to rest, some in unmarked graves and others with the simple initials, D.E.P. (*Descanse En Paz*) Rest In Peace.

"The crying of the remaining Magdalenas was more subdued now," Tomas said. "Those people that remained, returned to work and thanked God for having been spared. At a time when there were no doctors and no clinics and no civic authorities, all we had was each other." He said, "But with the will of God we returned from Hell."

The three-mile walk to the morada at Embargo seemed but a short distance. We descended the sparse juniper hills and entered the valley, a very different country from the llanos. As we approached a minor canyon adjacent to the Box we saw a dilapidated building ensconced between huge volcanic boulders. The building was in ruins. Its vigas were fallen and some of them were rotting on the ground. The front wall, facing east, still had its door frame standing but it had no door. The west wall was completely gone and the others were severely eroded. I wondered why Tomas Avila had brought me here, to these ruins. I didn't wonder long, for the voice of Tomas brought my mind back into focus.

"I imagine you are wondering why I brought you here, to this place of abandonment. You are a good student," he said. "You have all the qualities of a good Hermano. You are smart and you are oblivious to suffering. But before I tell you why we're here, let's eat something."

Tomas went into the pocket of his coat and took out a can of sardines and a small box of crackers. He pointed to a couple of large rocks near-by. We sat and he opened the flat can with his knife. He handed me some crackers and he placed one sardine in each one of them with the point of his knife. He made the same snack for himself and we ate. I hadn't noticed how hungry I was but I mimicked the way he ate, slowly and quietly. After our brief lunch the world seemed brighter, even though dark clouds were slowly approaching from the west. After eating we got up from our rock seats.

He signaled with his arm, inviting me to follow him. We walked several yards to someone's well. Tomas took a bucket with a thin rope attached to it and dropped it into the shallow well. He retrieved the bucket full of water and invited me to cup my hands. He poured enough water into my cupped hands for me to get a full drink of that clear, cold water. He repeated the pouring of water again and I had my second drink. He then invited me to pour water into his cupped hands while he drank. So was our meal outside the ruins of this ancient place of worship.

Tomas Avila stood away from the derelict building and seemed to survey the setting, the ruined walls and even the erstwhile path to the site of the Calvary. He walked toward a large volcanic rock a few yards from the old morada and I followed him. When we got there he pointed to an etching on the black rock, D.E.P., it read.

"Who is buried here?" I asked.

"It is more like what is symbolically buried here," He corrected me. He then started his story of the last morada; the last moral battle of the Hermandad itself.

"Lonicio Duran," he said, "was the last Elder of La Morada del Embargo. This morada, according to my father, had the most faithful of any of the other moradas. Lonicio was a true 'Hermano' and one that would defend the faith to the death. One day, after the brotherhood had become the target of the demons out of the church as well as those in the church itself, Lonicio went to his brothers, the Elders of each of the Moradas: El Llano, Cabresto, Cieneguilla and even those of the neighboring communities, El Cerrito and Culebra. He went to them, according to my father, to propose a strategy to defend the faith against those enemies *que acababan con ellos* (that threatened to finish them off)." Tomas said. "There was much discussion because each morada considered itself independent of the others and the long history of each, together with the different 'sentiments' of the adherents in each one, made a common goal a problem. The confusion, doubt, suspicions and mistrust within the community of moradas made Lonicio's task almost impossible. The detractors of the faith had done a good job in planting the seeds of discord and had begun to successfully be able to divide and conquer." Tomas paused as if carefully measuring his words.

"Lonicio then went to the principal defender of the Hermandad, El Padre Antonio, in La Villa. Lonicio stated his case; that if the Hermanos Mayores did not take the initiative in this conflict that each morada would fall, one by one.

The priest agreed with Lonicio and he sent a personal representative to each of the Elders in those moradas that I have mentioned," said Tomas Avila. "The priest's message was simple: 'Plan to meet with me at the Morada de La Atalaya, in Valdez'. He had also sent this message to the Elders at Los Cristobals, the three moradas at Arroyo del Hongo, the two in Arroyo del Monte and the two in Valdez. On the appointed date, all these Elders traveled to Valdez and the Morada de La Atalaya. The convocation was a matter of days, not just one. My grandfather attended and he related the story to my father. It was a beautiful event and it was a heart-wrenching event," said Tomas Avila, and he looked down to control his emotions.

"The meeting took three days and in the end, a terrible decision had been reached by all those in attendance. The pressure on the priests in each of the communities was so great from their superiors, that it was decided to disengage from an open battle and instead retreat to each of the moradas and hold the sacred rites in secret. Of all the Elders attending, only Lonicio disagreed but he was out-voted and ordered to comply with the new strategy. Lonicio was heartbroken. All the Elders returned to their communities and to their moradas. Lonicio however, returned a broken man. He knew that this was the beginning of the end and his reaction was one of personal blame. He returned home and fell into a deep sadness. He was not seen by anyone for a long time and one day he took seriously ill and died."

"Lonicio's 'Hermanos' were devastated. They buried him with all the honors of a holy Hermano. He was buried in the *Campo Santo* (Holy Ground) behind the Church of San Cristobal del Rio. The Morada at Embargo had suffered a terrible loss: the families were now confused and leaderless and the future course of the brotherhood in Embargo, was unknown. As if this were not enough, people started to equate Lonicio's death with his public disagreement with the other moradas and the sin of disobedience. This claim was advanced by some of the priests, now against the brotherhood. The worst was yet to come however," said Tomas Avila.

"Less than two weeks after Lonicio's death, the rains came to Embargo. Huge black clouds came out of the western sky and seemed to settle just over the Guadalupes and the Cerro Pelado, immediately west of the site of the morada. It rained, and it rained." Said Tomas. "It rained for thirty three days and nights right on this site." With a wide sweep of his arms of the whole area near the morada del Embargo, Tomas continued. "My father said that it appeared that the rain cloud was not moving and that it seemed as if it would just rain at this place."

"First, the *asotea* (the mud roof) began to leak, the inside of the place began to flood and suddenly, see those big boulders?" He broke into his own conversation. I nodded that I did.

"The whole mountain seemed to slide down, bringing these rocks, gravel and a lot of water down into the valley, right through that arroyo. The rocks blocked the arroyo and water came gushing right into the morada. The walls buckled and then they gave way. In short," he said, "The morada was pulled down and destroyed. The people were shocked and terrified. *It must be a visitation or punishment for Lonicio's sin of disobedience;* many of them thought. Someone, later came and etched D.E.P (rest in peace) on that boulder there," he said.

Tomas had painted a vivid picture of the last days of La Morada del Embargo and the fate of the champion of the faith, Lonicio Duran. He had also connected the desertion and total isolation of the site with the events following the convocation of the Hermandad.

"From that day forward, my father said," related Tomas Avila, "No one wanted anything to do with this morada. No one had the spirit to renew the faith, no one had the fervor to rebuild the morada."

"Now you know, what I know," Tomas said, and his words sounded much like those of Henry Wallace after his lecture to me.

"Joven" (young man) Tomas Avila said. "I believe in your sincerity, I believe in your faith and I believe that you will keep these events in your mind as long as you live. If these were different times, I think, that perhaps you would have become one of our Hermanos and maybe someday, an Elder, but for me this opportunity to share this sacred memory with someone like you, I consider a blessing." He then invoked a religious wish in *"Bendito Sea Dios* (blessed be God)."

He continued, "Don't forget these sacred stories, nor forget the sacred images of the dwelling places of Jesus and our people. Share these things with your children and with those serious enough to honor and respect the passing of this great faith of our brothers in Christ."

"*Que te vendiga Dios, Hermano,*" he said. I was choked up with emotion with his words of faith in my ability to be a keeper of the memory and to address me as an Hermano. Tomas shook my hand, turned and walked away over the hill, back toward his home near his morada.

I often wonder if Tomas Avila, Perfecto Matinez and perhaps others, had duped me into becoming the vessel of memory of a religious practice, now long gone. I laugh at myself for thinking that I had manipulated them into revealing their secrets when all the while, I had been selected over a period of time to "hear" this journey of my forebears. Whatever it was that brought me in contact with Henry Wallace, the Resolaneros and Tomas Avila, was for me a fortuitous view of a life unknown outside the valleys of northern New Mexico. I wondered too, if perhaps I was entrusted with enough information, that in another time, I might have become the "Last Penitente."

El Cambio

During the summer, before the start of my senior year in high school, I experienced what I thought was a lifetime of learning. I was welcomed into the adult world as sanctioned by Henry Wallace and the "wise men of la resolana." I was led through the backdoor of memory into the holy brotherhood of the penitentes and I witnessed changes in myself, in Embargo and in the people around me. I also experienced two life-changing experiences that would not soon leave me.

Close to the end of the summer, you could smell the melancholy days of autumn approaching the high valley. One morning, when rain clouds came in low, and splattered the sky with sheep-images, the wise men of la resolana were well into the warm-up stages of their discourse. I came by their haunt near the store and sat down to listen to the debates and was acknowledged by the men of the group. Perfecto touched the tip of his hat as he looked at me, Abad Cisneros nodded his head in my direction and Henry Wallace simply smiled at his protege. I had apparently been adopted by the wise men. They had all heard about my tramping across the countryside on my pilgrimage, visiting the moradas. They must have heard from Tomas Avila about our conversations during my impressionable visit earlier that summer, and without a doubt, Henry Wallace must have spoken to them about me. I pretended not to notice their new respect for me and I sat down to listen.

"The obvious thing about this world," Abad Cisneros said, "is that, there is a time for everything." Then he started to quote from Ecclesiastics: *"There is a time to sow, and a time to reap, A time to laugh and a time to weep, A time to live and a time to die."*

While Abad was now a member of the Seventh-Day Adventist Church, he and his family had been penitentes and his sympathies were still with these people. He was as comfortable with Perfecto Martinez's Catholic penitente past as he was with Henry Wallace's heretic views.

After Abad was finished with his discourse, Perfecto Martinez stood up and took the stance of a trial lawyer, as I had remembered Amarante Martinez had done in my father's court, so many years before. Perfecto said, "The most obvious thing about life is CHANGE." He emphasized the word, *El Cambio* (change) and immediately started making his case.

"Yes, change is everywhere." He addressed his fellow wise men with a sweep of his arm. "We are all changing. We are all getting old, some of us are missing teeth, all of us are missing hair from our head. Even the mountain is losing its head. Look!" he said, pointing to Columbine Mountain to the east. It was quickly becoming a bare slide. "That's what change does."

The mining company that for years had been tunneling through that mountain was now surface mining and denuding it, by scraping the entire mountain.

"What changes do you think that change will bring?" Perfecto asked rhetorically. "I'll tell you what change it will bring. First, it will poison the rivers, it will kill the fish, it will sicken our animals, it will foul the air, it will kill our grand children, it will kill the birds."

"Oh, by the way," he added, this time to drive his point home, "Have you noticed that the birds are already gone? It's only August and I don't see the swallows anymore, do you?"

I was taken by surprise with that last question because I realized that in my changing late-teen world, my work at Henry's, my focus on things that had little to do with my former life as a river waif, I hadn't noticed.

That evening, when I went home, I asked Vivian two important questions that would reveal whether or not Perfecto's prophecies were possible.

"Are the swallows still flying over the river in the evenings?"

Vivian gave me a strange look and asked, "How would you know? All you do is chum around with those old men at La Cueva."

I knew my brother was impudent but I insisted, "Have you seen the swallows?"

He turned serious and said, "No, I don't know what is happening, they're all gone. Why has it taken you so long to ask me that question?" he admonished. "Besides," he said, looking away, "The fish are also gone, well, they're not gone, they're just so few and the ones you catch are freaks."

"What?"

"More and more," he said with disgust in his voice, "I'm catching fish with no dorsal fin, with crooked mouths or some with eyes out of kilter. What's happening?"

Shocked I could not answer. My first thought was, *These guys, are truly wise men*, and my second thought was, *It has to be the mine*.

That evening, I approached my father with these questions. He had worked at the mine for about five years now, and he tried to dismiss the implication that the mine operation was the culprit.

"Let's wait and see," he said.

The next change that seriously impacted my life was

when Deluvina, my girlfriend of a year, suddenly told me that her family was moving away and she had to go with them. I knew Deluvina through her older sister, Lizabet and we dated throughout the previous summer and the school year. Her family lived in a big tin-roofed, adobe house by the edge of the forest. Her father was an itinerant miner who worked in places like Red Cliff and Minturn. Her mother was a tough, hardworking lady.

Deluvina was a petite, beautiful girl with a round face and cherry red lips. She had light green eyes that were so green that they looked as if she had just cried. At a time when most of the girls in high school did not use any lipstick, Deluvina, two years younger than I, used a cherry red lipstick that made her look older than she was. She was funny and had a laugh, I once told her, "like the rippling waters of the high mountain streams."

I thought back to that time of innocence when we walked down the box canyon and sat down on the grassy bank of the river to watch the dipper bird, to laugh and to talk. I remembered the time when I walked to the river's edge, cupped my hands in the water and returned to splash it on her face. She recoiled and yelled "You-stupid!"

"You know that the kids in school say that you're a smart guy, but I think you're a silly boy," she taunted me with half-closed eyes as she laughed.

As a silly boy would do, I went back to the edge of the river, splashed my own face with water then chased her, caught her and kissed her still-wet face.

But now Deluvina was going away. I saw her the day of her family's departure. Her two older brothers were waiting for her in their car when she came to say good-bye. She had tears in her eyes and I thought my heart would break. She told me not to worry, that they would be coming back soon and that she would write me. She gave me a soft kiss and as she joined her brothers in the car, I knew that she would never return.

Deluvina and I wrote to each other every day for a couple of months. The start of my senior year was consumed with writing to her and awaiting her replies. My obsession for her was such that I sent her a poem I'd copied from a book which Henry Wallace had lent me. It was a love-lost poem by Thomas Moore written in England in the mid-19th century.

> In The midhour of night
> when stars Are weeping
> I fly to the lone vale we knew
> when love was young in your eyes.......

She wrote back and said, "Gibo, I showed your poem to my English teacher and she commented that my friend must be a romantic egg head." She said she liked that, but she did not tell me how she felt about my eternal love for her.

For the remainder of the first semester and into the second I tried to lose myself in the affairs of school and involvement in my changing family. By this time in my life I had three more siblings; there was my sister Flo, who was quickly becoming a woman, my brother Vivian a handsome kid who had outgrown me by three inches and now played in a junior varsity basketball team, and my little sister Jo, now a seventh grade cheerleader. We now had, as my father said "Three more mouths to feed." The oldest of the second team was Van, a quiet, sad eyed and frail kid. I felt a special love for him, because of his frailty and because he looked to me, his oldest brother, as his hero. From very early on, we discovered that Van had an uncanny mind. I would relate stories to him from El Cid Campeador, the Spanish epic hero, and later he could recall them in detail. I shared some of my sacred excerpts from *Alice in Wonderland* and he readily retold them to me, adding details that I had added on later. Van recalled dates, times and details of events. His memory was so vivid that the joke within the family was that he remembered when each sow in the valley had given birth to her piglets.

There was Eva, a green eyed, red-headed tomboy

who had an aggressive nature, much like my sister Flo, but this one was dominant. By the age of eight, she was dominating my timid brother Van.

Finally, there was the baby, Cleve. He was dark haired, and so quiet and unobtrusive that we called him, "The Shadow," after a radio show by that name. Vivian, now an aggressive teenager, would say to little Cleve, "Who, can tell what evil lurks in the minds of men?" and he would answer "The Shadow do." Cleve would just look at him with big dark eyes and grin shyly. We all loved Cleve.

My sister Flo and I starred in a school play, she was my leading lady. I was also getting ready to deliver the valedictory address during graduation exercises.

My correspondence with Deluvina continued. In our letters we reminded each other that we would always be in love with one another. She wrote me about her new adventures; about making friends and about how different her new school was from La Cueva High School. I told her how much I missed her and that I would wait for her forever.

As time went on, her letters started taking a little longer to arrive. When they did they were about some of her new friends and about going to the kind of places, which did not exist in La Cueva. She mentioned a friend who she said reminded her of me. His name was Bobby.

In a jealous mood I wrote back and told her not to be fooled by this "Bobby." Her next letter assured me that he was just a friend and that he made her laugh.

"Besides being a friendly guy, I call him Booby."

By December, her letters stopped coming. Mine were not returned but were never answered.

I began to apply to trade schools and universities in an effort to forget my loneliness. My plan was to escape my love-sick pain by leaving the valley. It seemed nothing else would help. My companions were the then-popular songs of *Vaya Con Dios My Darling* by Les Paul and Mary Ford and *My Heart Cries for You*.

I'd resigned myself to forget Deluvina.

Belica

Change comes despite our efforts to keep things the same. That was the point that Perfecto Martinez had tried to make on that day last summer when he dropped the bombshell about the loss of place and, in my mind, the loss of someone you love.

March rolled around and graduation was only a couple of months away. The elementary school basketball teams from across the county came to the La Cueva High School gym to hold their annual tournaments. I had often helped at the scorers' table and I was assigned to do just that during the three days' duration of this tournament.

The teams from the different schools started coming in the morning of the first day. The continuous flow of strangers as well as locals, parents, fans and teams in their respective uniforms and in their variety of colors, seemed endless.

The first teams for that evening's games had come

out and were shooting hoops and otherwise warming up for their slated contest. Ten minutes before the buzzer, I noticed a young girl walk in with her parents. The parents went in one direction and she came to the side where the scorers' table was located. My eyes followed her as she made her way toward the benches of the teams from Arroyo del Hongo. They were scheduled to play next.

She was a petite beautiful girl, with short curly black hair. She wore new Levi jeans. I had never seen any girl carry herself with such self-confident aloofness. I noticed as she passed by my table that she had a small upper lip and dark serious eyes, a small, slightly turned-up nose and high cheek bones. I wondered how old she was, she looked about seventeen or eighteen. I also wondered how any woman could be so beautiful.

My eyes followed her as she climbed the wooden bleachers and sat with the Arroyo del Hongo fans, making small conversation with a couple of girls. It wasn't five minutes before my friend and classmate, Roman, came and whispered,

"Did you see what came in?"

"Yes, but she's mine, I saw her first."

"We'll see," he laughed.

I had not dated anyone since Deluvina had left me. I liked this girl and I was going to do my best to find out who she was and what I had to do to meet her. The game started and the teams were on the floor, but between my duty as timekeeper and my obsession with the beauty from Arroyo, I was as nervous as a young freshman. As the game progressed I began to think of ways to meet her or to have her notice me. I had a plan; I would showcase the scorers' table that night.

I began to take longer on the buzzer, I feigned problems with the scoreboard, which I quickly appeared to fix and I gave the team from Arroyo del Hongo all the advantage I could when it came to turning in the ball, time outs, etc. Once when a loose ball flew into the section where the Arroyo del Hongo fans were seated, I pressed the buzzer and asked the referees to come to the table for consultation. I suggested that they look into that section where the ball had fallen and inquire if there were any injuries. I saw her turn slightly toward me in that feigned commotion and my eyes met hers. I smiled but she pretended that she hadn't even seen me.

During half time I got off my table and walked over to where she was with her friends. I asked patronizingly.

"Are you ladies ok? We don't want our guests to get injured by a stupid ball."

One of the girls was more than happy to answer my questions.

"Oh yes," she said, "our pride was hurt." She and the

other girls giggled.

The beauty did not respond but simply looked straight ahead.

"You haven't said if your pride was hurt." She ignored my direct question and pretended to speak with the girl who first answered. My friend Roman showed up all of a sudden, but before he could make some stupid remark I said, "Ladies, this guy's name is Roman, he is a senior and a ladies' man, watch out for him."

The talkative girl said, "I'm not scared of seniors."

More giggling.

"What is the name of that girl?" I asked one of the girls close to the first row and pointed to the dark haired beauty.

"Oh, her name is Belica Artiaga."

I didn't want to embarrass myself by remaining there and not getting any response from Belica Artiaga. Before I left, I addressed the group and said,

"I hope your team wins."

Roman sheepishly followed me and suggested that I had tried to embarrass him. I told him that the girl who said that she was not afraid of seniors was giving him the eye. He smiled and went back to his seat. As I made my way back to my post I thought to myself, *I know a guy from Arroyo del Hongo, by the name of Saul Artiaga. I wonder if they're related?*

It was almost time to resume the second half of the game, with Arroyo del Hongo ahead by ten points. I hurriedly took a small piece of paper and wrote on it, "Do you know Saul Artiaga?" I signaled to the young girl who'd given me Belica's name, gave her the note and asked her to give it to Belica Artiaga. Belica read it but gave no sign of acknowledgement. I raised up my open palms to the young messenger and she nodded and whispered, "Yes, he's her brother."

"Halleluya!" I said to myself. "I now have something in common with Belica Artiaga."

As the game resumed and the excitement shifted to the teams on the floor, I thought back to a summer about three years ago when I had met a young Saul Artiaga at my Cuate Leve's house. He was related to Cuate's mother somehow and he came to spend a week at Embargo where the Cookes lived. My brother Vivian and I made friends with Saul immediately. He was about thirteen years old, one year older than my brother and about two years younger than me. We invited him fishing but his luck at fishing was the worst that I'd ever seen. We teased him that his problem was that he was left-handed and would always have trouble casting his fishing line. He took our teasing in stride, even though he was a whole head taller than any of us. He met my sister Flo and our cousin Lisa. Both tried to flirt with him and they teased him about his name.

Flo would ask, "If your name is Saul why is it not pronounced 'Sol,' like Paul?" Saul never reacted to their taunts.

After we had become good friends, I did what I often did with friends, challenged him to wrestle. I did this because I had a trick that was almost one hundred percent effective, otherwise I would have never risked defeat. My trick was to position myself in a slight crouch with my arms offered for the opponent to grab. They almost always grabbed one of my arms, usually at the wrist. I quickly grabbed their wrist, twisted my own arm away from their grip and holding their arms now, move quickly to the left placing my leg behind theirs. A slight push and they went down. Saul fell prey to this trick and I tossed him on top of a bunch of cactus. I discovered however, that he was stronger than any other boy that I had wrestled down before, I could not keep him down. I quickly let him go but I had gauged his strength, and he was strong.

Now I had an ace up my sleeve when it came to getting to know Belica Artiaga.

After the game was over and the crowd began to exit, Belica passed in front of my table. I called out, "Belica!" She looked at me for an instant.

"Tell your brother Saul that Gibo Herrera says Hi."

She continued as if she hadn't even heard me.

That night I dreamed about Belica. Next morning, I thought, *Funny, I've never dreamed about Deluvina, this must mean something.* On this new day I felt an excitement that I hadn't felt in a long time and I vowed that today I would have a talk with this silent, proud, beautiful girl.

The day's games went on fastidiously slow, or so it seemed to me. It wasn't until that night that I would see her again since I was sure she had to go to school during the day. Promptly, at about fifteen minutes before game time, I saw her and her friends come through the door. She was even more beautiful than the night before. She surprised me when she approached the table, smiling ever so slightly, and finally speaking to me.

"So you know my brother, let's see how well you know him."

Just then a big guy came through the door and made his way towards us.

"Hey, Gibo!" he yelled from afar. I offered to shake his hand, but instead he moved into the scorer's bench and grabbed me at my shoulders. He whispered, "You still want to wrestle?" We both laughed and I knew that, with this big guy now at about one hundred and sixty pounds, that suggestion was out of the question.

Meanwhile, Belica and her friends had walked away to their former seats on the bleachers. She had called my bluff and I now saw her smiling and much more animated than she had been the night before. Saul and I made small talk. He told me that he was now playing football for the La Villa Tigers, as he showed off his orange and black jacket. I thought to myself, *Even if he is only a sophomore, he has the body and, I know first-hand, the strength to play high school football.* Saul and a couple of his friends soon moved to the opposite side of the gym. The game soon got underway, with Arroyo del Hongo playing for the championship or second place in the tournament.

My antics of the night before were much more subdued. I looked to where she was from time to time. One of those times I saw her look at me. I was now the one being challenged and I vowed that during the half time break I would go over to where she was, despite the fact that her brother, my friend, was in the gym. The game quickly progressed to half time with the Arroyo del Hongo team a mere two points ahead of their opponents, a feisty team from La Piedra, a school some forty miles away at the far end of the county. By the time the buzzer sounded, I noticed that Belica and her friends were no longer sitting in their usual place. Surmising that they had gone either to powder their noses or to the concession stand, I walked towards the bleachers anyway.

Still seated there was the younger girl, whom I'd used as my messenger the night before. Saul and his friends were walking out of the gym and I was glad about that. I preferred to talk to his sister than to him at this critical time. I sat down next to the young blond, green-eyed girl and asked her name. She said her name was Yewela. *That's a strange name,* I thought, but recalled Henry Wallace's recitation, "*What's in a name? A rose, by any other name would smell as sweet.*" However, my interest was in Belica Artiaga so I began to question Yewela about her. She proudly said that they were first cousins, that Belica had seven brothers and that she was the only girl. Her cousin was a freshman at La Villa High School and as far as Yewela knew, she did not have a boyfriend.

Soon Belica and the group of six girls headed back to the bleachers. The talkative one whispered something to Belica as they approached. They both looked at me sitting with Yewela and laughed. I quickly got up and sat down next to Belica.

"You thought I was lying about knowing Saul."

"I knew you weren't lying" I had already talked to him about you last night."

"I'm Gibo," I offered her my hand.

She did not take it but said, "Well, I guess you know a lot about me already, you've been asking a lot of questions."

I was surprised at the seriousness of her comment, but I saved the moment.

"I'll tell you what, you let me talk to you and I'll just ask you the questions that I want to know about you. Deal?" She inclined her head slightly and smiled, saying, "Deal."

We spoke during the entire half-time break. I asked her if I could see her sometime. She told me that on Saturday next, she would be at a dance at Arroyo del Hongo at a place called La Sala (hall) de Mano Victor.

"Don't come to my house," she admonished, "my parents would not understand."

"My friend Roman wants to meet your friend, the talkative one, what's her name?"

"Oh, her name is Rosa. She'll be at the dance too, he can meet her there."

We promised to meet at the dance within a week and I returned to my job at the scorer's table. The Arroyo del Hongo team won the game and were crowned tournament champions. After the ceremonies I visited with Saul briefly and said goodbye to Belica. I was ecstatic thinking, *I'm falling in love with this girl. What's wrong with me?*

All week I thought about her. I saw her smiling, I imagined her dancing with me, looking into my eyes and laughing her mischievous laughter. I couldn't wait to see Belica Artiaga again. Saturday rolled around and Roman and I got his father's car, a 1952 DeSoto, prepped for the trip over the mountains to Arroyo del Hongo. We gassed up the car at my friend Henry Wallace's station, bought a pack of gum and headed south.

The hall was full of people when we arrived. There were a few cars parked along the dirt road leading to the dance hall, telling us that those attending would not only be the people from the village of Arroyo. Roman and I nervously made our way to the Sala de Mano Victor, knowing full well that village rivalries often erupted into fights between young men from the different villages. We first looked through a window to get a feel for what to expect when we went in. People were sitting on benches around three of the walls, couples were standing in some of the corners, and on a makeshift wooden stage was the band. I could not see Belica nor her friends but I took her words as a promise that she would be there.

Roman and I made our way into the dance hall. The entrance was so crowded that we had to ask to be let in. Then I saw her. She stood with her friend Rosa next to two older women. She was beautiful. She had on a tight navy-blue skirt and a white silk blouse with long sleeves with ruffled cuffs. I was mesmerized, but I knew that I could not stare. Her friend Rosa was dressed in a modest yellow dress but she wore high heel shoes. I immediately moved to where they stood. Belica blushed, but Rosa just gave us a big smile. Belica, rather self consciously, turned to one of the ladies and said "Mother, this is Gibo, a friend of Saul's and this is his friend," and she asked me, "what's his name?"

"I'm Gibo Herrera I said, and my friend is Roman Rangel."

"I'm pleased to meet you."

Her mother was as serious as Belica had been when I first saw her at the tournaments. She did not extend her hand in greeting, but simply said, "Mucho gusto."

We moved to the girls' side, me with Belica, Roman with Rosa. The dance hall was packed, the dance floor was full. The band was an odd outfit, composed of a fiddler, a guitarist, a drummer and a saxophone player. The music was spirited, but definitely geared to an older crowd. I noticed that in fact, the majority of those there that night were older folks. At least to us, they seemed older.

Rosa pulled on Roman and they were among the first to be out on the dance floor. The band was playing a waltz and the fiddle sounded like something from another time. The people didn't care. They were enjoying themselves. I asked Belica out to dance. With no objection from her mother, we walked into the middle of the floor. Belica's hands were sweating and she was uneasy but she smelled as sweetly as she looked beautiful. I could tell that she didn't have too much practice at dancing, or at least at dancing in public. We danced and she spoke very little. I talked about the night that I had first seen her and how I was impressed with her seriousness. I commented that I thought Roman and Rosa made a nice couple and I asked about her family.

As the night rolled on, the tunes got livelier. They went from waltzes to polkas to *corridas;* a mix that made for the fun that everyone was having. It was getting hot inside the hall and Belica's face was turning a bit flushed. I asked if she wanted to go outside for some fresh air, but she said that her mother would not allow it. I then told her that Roman and I would be right back and we went out into the cool night air.

We noticed some of the men from the dance hall were smoking. Some were chatting and taking occasional swigs from their bottles. I had made a special provision in case Belica and her friend would have joined us in the car. I had bought four Coca-Cola bottles at Henry Wallace's station. We took them in and I gave a coke to Belica. I offered the other to her mother, but she declined. I had already popped the bottle caps and placed the caps on the open bottle tops which impressed Belica. The drinks quenched our thirst and cooled us enough to return to the floor when the musicians returned from a break.

It was a scene from a fairy tale: The musicians and their old tunes from another time, the old adobe-walled dance hall, the total abandon of the happy dancers and Belica dancing in my arms. I knew without a doubt that I had met the girl of my dreams and that this time my love was going to last forever. I was euphoric.

"I'm going to tell you something that maybe it's too early to say, but I think that I'm falling in love with you."

Belica inclined her head slightly, as if someone might hear me but she squeezed my hand. I knew that this was it. We didn't pursue the subject again, only because I had extracted a promise from her that she would see me again the next day. We had agreed to meet at the school grounds, "where the kids often meet," she told me.

The night seemed to end no sooner than it had begun. Belica's mother stood up at 11:30 p.m. and Belica said that it was time for her to go. The four of us walked out the door, her mother a few paces ahead of us. I asked Belica if they wanted a ride home but she said they lived very close by and wouldn't need one. In a brief moment, when her mother had disappeared into the crowd I brushed my lips against her cheeks and the side of her mouth. She didn't pull away but she did not reciprocate my kiss. She smelled so good; I carried the scent of her body, her clothes and her breath with me home that night.

I convinced Roman that we had to return to see the

girls the following day. He said that due to the screeching of the fiddle and the aura of the place, he had a name for this experience. He called it, *El baile de los gatos* (the dance of the cats). I thought it demeaning but went along with his perception because I needed him to drive us back to Arroyo the next day.

My own experience had been that of magic. My love was on fire. I did not confide to my friend my deepening feelings for Belica, nor my serious intentions to pursue a relationship with her.

Just before noon, the next day we again took the DeSoto down to Arroyo del Hongo. The vistas along the highway had never seemed so beautiful. The tall Douglas Fir with its golden bark rose up to meet the clouds and the piñon trees asserted their eternal place on the face of the hill sides.

We drove into the school yard where several girls were seated on the school swings. I immediately saw Belica, Rosa and little Yewela.

Yewela ran towards us and teased loudly,

"My tia Lita wouldn't let you take Belica home from the dance last night, huh?"

Belica, called out,

"Yewela, come here!" as if reprimanding an errant child. We approached the girls and Belica introduced us. I remember having seen some of them at the tournaments.

They all smiled at the "guys from La Cueva."

Our meeting that day was really the introduction into each other's lives. I walked with Belica towards the small river that bordered the school grounds and Roman immediately invited Rosa for a ride in his DeSoto. I wanted to have Belica to myself and we waved to them as Roman spun out of the schoolyard and into the dirt road leading to the Rio Grande.

Belica and I walked under the hovering branches of the yet leafless cottonwoods that lined the south side of the river. It was mid-March. Because Arroyo del Hongo was set in a true valley, quite a bit lower than the mountain valley of Embargo the weather here was warmer. Belica and I walked hand in hand and we talked. I was surprised to find out that she was a regular chatterbox, not the silent type I had seen at the tournaments. She was a happy, beautiful girl, who was particularly animated when she talked about her family. Her spontaneity kept me transfixed.

Belica Artiaga, told me she was a middle child, and the only daughter. She was obviously the center of attention at home and the only one that "got away" with getting what she wanted from the brothers and father, but not her mother. Belica had seven brothers. Three of them were in the armed services and the rest were still at home including my friend, Saul. She rattled off their names and said something special about each of them. The oldest was Mel, named after their grandfather, Melquides Rel. He was stationed in England. Danny, whom the family called Chato (but she didn't know why) was stationed in Japan and had just graduated from La Villa High School a year ago. The third one, was Beto, but they call him "Liters" at school.

"You know Saul," she said.

"Yes," I started, "I met him at Cuate Leve's about three years ago."

"I know, I know," she said. "He talked so much about you and your brother that, quite frankly, I was surprised when I figured out who that pesky guy at the scorers table was that night of the games."

"Was I really pesky?" I asked feigning hurt.

She laughed her spontaneous laughter.

"Hmm, Nah, I thought you were kind of cute."

"But how could you think that, you didn't even look my way."

"I couldn't be as obvious as you. My parents were sitting right across from your table. Besides, how could anybody miss you. Has anyone told you that you are a big show-off?"

Then she recanted. "But a cute, show-off." She laughed and continued her family history.

We spent several hours by the noisy river that

afternoon. Clouds came up and it turned a bit chilly. It seemed as if I'd always known her, as if we had been waiting for each other to appear and now we were simply getting together. For me she was the midday sun. I had never seen the world so bright and my heart felt like it was hanging from one of those cotton clouds above the little river at Arroyo del Hongo.

I noticed a small store as we came into Arroyo, about half a mile from where we were. I invited her to a coke and she readily agreed. We walked to Fito's market and I bought her a coke and some frito chips and got myself a coke and some Planters peanuts. We walked back to the school yard and sat on a teeter-totter. Quite adroitly she mounted her side of the see-saw, moved as far back as she could in order to maximize her weight and pulled me up into the air. She laughed, having taken me by surprise. I had to immediately adjust my own seating to balance the teeter-totter. "Saul told me that when he first met you, you had wrestled him down on top of a cactus. Is that true?"

"That was about three years ago," I said, "and he was a lot smaller then. Besides, I'm a wrestler."

"Nah," she said, and we both laughed.

A couple of times that afternoon I tried to kiss her but she pulled away. One of those times she said to me,

"Do you want people to see us? I don't want my

mother to know that I'm kissing some boy in public."

She was setting the rules and I could not help but admire her convictions. My guess was that her mother had inculcated in her some traditional values. I began to see that her upbringing was what I preferred in girls. I then said,

"But you're not with just any boy, you are with Gibo Herrera, from Embargo."

"Oh, yes, that's what you call the place where my mother's cousin, Meme, lives," she said, serious again, ignoring my attempt at levity.

As I look back now, that day was a journey through a dream. My love for this beautiful, talkative yet somewhat naive girl, seemed boundless. I liked everything about her, and I did not mind her admonitions. I promised myself that I would do whatever it took to know her better. I asked her if I could come to see her the following week and she said, "No," She could only come out on weekends, but that if I wanted to, she would see me on the weekend that followed. I took this as both a promise and, to my dismay, a prison sentence.

Close to five-o'clock that afternoon, Roman and Rosa returned from their car ride. Belica said that it was time for her to go. Before we got out of the forest of cottonwoods I took her hand, pulled her toward me and kissed her long and hard. She seemed surprised by the kiss and she lowered her head, embarrassed.

I softly told her, "I love you, Belica Artiaga."

She just smiled broadly and said, "I'll see you next Saturday." She refused a ride home and, before I knew it, Roman and I were on our way north to La Cueva.

On Tuesday of the following week I wrote her a letter addressed to General Delivery, Arroyo del Hongo. Since I had no mailing address for her, I took a chance. I told her that I had thoroughly enjoyed being with her, both at the dance and at the river. I took the liberty to ask her, formally, if she would be my girlfriend and said that I would be true to her for as long as she wanted me. That Friday I received a reply. She simply answered, "YES!" I took this to be an answer to, as the Platters would sing, *My Prayer*.

Saturday rolled around and early on I made plans to go see her. Since Roman could not go I found my own transportation and I borrowed my father's old Chevrolet pick-up. Because we had not talked about where we'd meet, I went straight to her house. I was met by three of her younger brothers.

The oldest of the three approached the pick up.

"Your name is Gibo, eh?"

"Yeah," what's yours?"

"Oh," "I'm Nilo, he's Charlie Roy and the little one is Roque, but we call him, Que. I know who you're looking for. You're looking for my sister Belica. She's in the shower," he said. "You're going to have to wait."

The youngest one tried to open the passenger door and Charlie Roy got on the bed of the pick up. Only Nilo stood outside talking to me. Just then Saul came out of the house and invited me up to the porch where we sat down on a car seat from some pick-up truck and we talked. All three boys were now inside the cab and Nilo pretended to drive.

Belica came out of the kitchen several minutes later.

"Gibo, you be careful with my sister, she's a tomboy, you know," Saul said.

Belica, looking gorgeous in an ash-gray cashmere sweater and black gabardine slacks, suddenly pivoted and gave her brother a hard straight punch that must have hurt.

"See what I mean?" Saul said.

She blushed with a bit of anger.

"How could you be a friend to this big horse?" Saul just laughed.

"Hey, you guys take care," he said.

I yelled out of the pick up window.

"We're going to La Villa, in case your parents ask."

We rode around the plaza at La Villa, drove up to her school, then drove up the canyon and talked about lots of things. When I figured that it was a bit past noon, I said,

"Let's eat. Do you like hamburgers, pizza or something new?"

"Lets try something new."

I drove to a restaurant that I had visited earlier that winter with Henry Wallace's son John. He was slowly taking over Henry's business and we'd been in La Villa on a business trip.

"Do you like fish or a steak or what"? I asked my gorgeous girlfriend.

"Is the fish like the one in the river?" she asked.

"What they have here, I think, is Halibut, a fish from the ocean, want to try it? I'll have the same thing that you do," I said.

When our plates came, the fish covered with little green capers and other condiments, she asked, "Are you sure this is a fish, I don't see a head, nor fins."

Before I could answer, she gently slapped my arm and said, "I'm joking. I know what fish fillets look like. We lived in California when I was a little girl. My father used to work in the shipyards in Alameda. I've always loved Fish and Chips since then."

As we ate our butter-brushed grilled halibut, she said to me, "See this small scar that I have on the side of my chin? I got that when I fell off the stairs in the house we rented in Alameda."

"I believe you lived in California," I said. "You have

the most beautiful scar that I've ever seen. I'm going to kiss it after we get out of here."

She looked at me reproachfully. "That's not why I told you about it."

I realized then and there how authentic she was, how naïve and so beautiful, and that she didn't even know it or didn't care.

I said to her as we drove home that day. "I can't bear to think that you might have stayed in California and that I would have never met you."

"I don't think like that," she said. "I think that what will be will be."

Our days together were, for me, a heaven that I didn't know could exist. I realized too that she was still a young sophomore and that I, despite my having grown up in an isolated mountain village with little outside experiences, was older and perhaps wiser. I was happy with any relationship that I could have with this girl and simply wanted to stay with her as much as I could and as long as I could.

Spring came, I graduated from High School. I was the Valedictorian for my class and I was honored by my English teachers for my role as the principal actor in most of the school's plays. Yet all of these end-of-year school activities were unimportant to me because I was in love and nothing else mattered. One terrible thing kept looming in my future; I had to leave that Fall. I had not told Belica that I would be going away to a trade school in August. Before I met her my father had enrolled me in a trade school to learn telegraphy so that I could work in the railroads. This was my principal preoccupation as summer approached.

We dated that entire summer. Scheduled to leave in mid-August, I finally got the courage in mid-July to tell her that I would be leaving for school in Colorado, that I would be studying railroad telegraphy.

She said, "Jeff Rel, from down the canyon, is going to a similar school. Maybe you guys can be buddies when you're there."

I was surprised at her apparent lack of concern for me leaving. I then said, "The place is about one hundred and seventy miles away, and I promise you that I'll come to see you as often as I can."

She then said, "My brother Mel has a girlfriend by the name of Mimi, she promised to wait for him while he is in the service. If you want me, I can wait for you too."

Leaving Paradise

The time to leave arrived too soon. My father and I had taken a trip up to "The Pittsburgh of The West," as Pueblo, Colorado was called and where the telegraphy school was located. We had made arrangements for renting an apartment. I'd be leaving in a week. Belica and I went out one of those late summer nights when the wind is a little crisper and the signs of autumn are slowly appearing. This particular night, we were double dating with a couple from La Cueva. The girl had attended school in La Villa a year ago and Belica knew who she was. We'd driven up a mountain road where the vista of the valley of Arroyo del Hongo could be seen in its hallowed-out setting and the few lights gave the place an enchanted look. The guy and his date got out of the car and Belica and I stayed behind in the back seat. I wanted her so badly, I felt so terrible about having to leave that I leaned over and said that I was going to miss her terribly and asked her if she would keep true.

Uncharacteristically, she grabbed me by the neck, and kissed me with a sort of desperation and said "Yes, I love you!" For some unknown reason I pulled back and said, "It's not that bad." She pulled away. The magic of the moment was broken. It would be a long time before she would tell me that she loved me again.

Telegraphy school was a totally different experience. I was away from home and going to school among strangers. I met Jeff Rel, and surprisingly, Fito Vasqez from La Cueva, who had enrolled in class the last minute. The two guys were staying at the YMCA and since I was living alone in an apartment, I invited them to live with me and share expenses. It wasn't long before we were room-mates and telegraphy school classmates.

Morse code, which is the medium for telegraphing messages through an electric current, was the content of the class. Rather than learning from written letters on a page, you learned through sounds in an apparatus called a telegraph key and sounder. At first it was a challenge to make out letters that were represented by clicks and dashes. Then you gradually started to recognize the combined clicks, pauses, and briefly delayed releases of clicks to make a dash. Attempting to relate some experience that I might have had to this totally aural learning, I remembered the tap, tap, tap of the woodpecker on the tree. I remember counting one, one-two and one-two-three taps of the woodpecker's beak. I converted the same frequencies of the on/off electric current to these wooden sounds in my memory. One quick click (*) was an (e), Two clicks (* *) was an (i), three clicks (* * *) was an (s). When there was a slight pause between clicks, then different letters were formed: (* * *) was a (r) and the reverse, (* * *) was a (c). I was hearing letters made everywhere. Finger tapping, short horn blasts, drumming, etc. cued the mind to form letters, then words and on the telegraph sounder, sentences.

I committed myself to learning telegraphy, wholeheartedly. The harder I studied the skill, the less I would think of Belica. I made fast progress, Jeff made moderate progress and Fito just couldn't seem to decipher the sound combinations. When I had been given a task before, my goal was to finish it with something good happening at the end. I was on a rat's treadmill in order to, hopefully, get back to the comfort of home and to a life with my girl. I didn't know what was at the end of this experience but I knew I couldn't go home and I couldn't make any decisions until I finished what I'd set out to do.

Days rolled into weeks, weeks into months. I saw Belica once a month, when Fito, the only one with a car, chose to go home. We would visit on Saturdays because we'd have to get back to school by Sunday night. Belica and I wrote at least once a week and I never failed to tell her how much I missed her and how I would give anything in the world to be with her. Her letters were long stories about her family and her friends at school. She told me that she missed me. Occasionally she would ask outright, "When am I going to see you?" In my desperation I worked harder at my task to keep from going into depression.

Mid-December rolled around. We had been in school about three and one-half months when the head teacher, Mr. Cosner, called me into his office. He was a retired railroad dispatcher and not only taught us how to master the skill of telegraphy, but often lectured us on job conditions on the railroad and on the personal and competency requirements for prospective telegraph operators. Mr. Cosner was a tall, slightly hunched man with big hands and magical fingers which made the telegraph key sing. He rose from his chair when I entered his office.

"Do you want to work for the Santa Fe?"

I was surprised by his directness.

"Yes, I'd like to work for the Santa Fe someday."

"Well, young man," he said, "if you'd like that, that someday is today. The Santa Fe Railroad's Western Division has an opening for an apprentice. I have reviewed your competency tests. I see that you are up to forty words per minute on the key and you seem to have a good hold on The Book of Rules." He wrote something on a paper and handed it to me. "Go see Dispatcher J.D. Horns at the Colfax Depot and tell him you're the new candidate for the apprenticeship in Maxwell. Congratulations. Tell Horns I said Hi"

With that brief meeting, I had successfully completed, in three and one half months, what was normally a six-months course.

That same day I met the Colfax Street Depot Dispatcher. He gave me a simple test for color blindness and authorized a doctor's visit for me to take a medical examination. I was on my way to becoming an apprentice telegraph operator. This would happen in a town I'd never heard of, for a job I had only a small inkling about, dealing with trains on which I'd never ridden. It felt so strange. Things were evolving faster than I'd ever experienced before.

"After your medical exam tomorrow," the dispatcher said, "I want you to make plans to report to the station agent in Maxwell on Monday, December 15th."

All of a sudden, I realized that my work there at the school was done. That night Fito made plans to quit school and return to La Cueva and Jeff said that he was going to stay in school a bit longer and see if he could get assigned to the next spot available.

That night I called my parents with the news. I located Maxwell on the map and planned to take the bus there to check it out, as was suggested by one of my teachers when I returned to the school that afternoon. I asked Fito, since he was going to go home, would he take some things of mine to my house in Embargo. He was only too glad to do so.

"Thank God, I never really liked this school," he said, "I'll never learn that crazy telegraphy."

Suddenly, rather than being excited for my new prospects, I wished so much that I was going home with Fito.

But the whole world would never forgive me if they thought that I was a quitter, I thought.

Perhaps my brother was right. Perhaps I was a penitente, a stoic, after all.

I had about a week and a half before I had to report to Maxwell. It was close to Christmas and I wanted so much to see Belica during the holidays. Already I had plans to buy her some Christmas presents and I kept thinking of how to spend my free days with her. During my last couple of days, going to see the doctor for an employment exam and other personal matters, I received an unexpected letter on the mail. It had been addressed to me in La Cueva but someone forwarded it to me at this address. The letter was from Deluvina. It was almost two years since I had last seen her and, about that long since she had stopped writing. I opened the letter nervously. Her letter included a small 3X5 picture inscribed on the back.

Dear Gibo,

This letter will probably come as quite a surprise to you, but I felt a real need to write it. I'm sorry we stopped communicating, I missed your letters. I have been thinking a lot about things and the truth is that I have been very lonely.

You see, Gibo, and I hope that you understand, I know you will. It's hard for me to tell you this but when I first came here, I met a guy. His name is Bobby Valdez. At first we were just friends. We ran around with the same crowd. We started dating at some point and we started getting serious about each other. Last month Bobby joined the Army and before he left he asked me to marry him when he returns in two years. He asked me to accept an engagement ring and I did. Gibo, I don't know what to do. I miss him so much.

My mother wants to go to La Cueva and I have volunteered to drive her there. My Uncle Abie is very sick and my mother wants to see him. I've taken out some time from work and we plan to be there by the 15ᵗʰ of December. I want to see you while I am there. I need someone to talk to. I've always considered you a cool guy. You are smart and

I know you can help me resolve my problems.

Will you see me when I get there?

Your Always Friend,

DeLu.

At first I was appalled at her audacity and then I felt sorry for her. I thought, *Isn't it ironic that she, who has caused me so much pain when she dumped me, now wants me to ease hers?* I read the letter again and realized that by December 15th I would be in Maxwell. I thought that this was the best excuse in the world not to have to see Deluvina. I felt a twinge of guilt about getting a letter from someone I thought was my girl not so long ago, and about my new-found love in Belica.

I looked at Deluvina's photograph. She looked prettier than I remembered her. She had tinted her hair a light blonde color, her face seemed more mature but she still wore her cherry red lipstick. On the back was written,

To Gibo, My Forever Friend.

DeLu.

I made up my mind right then to write her, even though my letter would probably not reach her before she got to La Cueva.

Dear Deluvina,

Your letter was a pleasant surprise and I'm sorry that you are as lonely as you say you are. Believe me, I know the feeling.

Congratulations on your engagement to 'Booby,' Wasn't that what you used to call him? No, I'm sorry for being so mean but I think that all this loneliness will disappear when your husband-to-be shows up. Besides, someone told me recently, 'Don't worry about the future, because, what will be, will be.'

I like your picture. You are turning into a full-grown woman and you are as pretty as always. As far as meeting you in La Cueva, I will not be there when you visit, you see I've just taken a job as a railroad telegrapher and I will be reporting to work on December 15th.

A lot of things have happened since you left to Junction and someday maybe I can tell you my story. Where is Lizbet these days? Please give my regards to your brothers, Willie and Mono.

A Friend, From the Past
Gibo Herrera.

Up until the time that I met Belica I had made irrevocable plans to enroll in telegraphy school and leave home, to a future that I had no idea about. In my rush to escape the sadness caused by Deluvina's departure from my life I had not counted on meeting and falling in love with someone living, as it were, in my own back yard.

Yet, here I was, getting ready to go away from my home and from Belica. I was committed to pursue this future as much as I wished I would have the power or the will to change it. Even after the end of my high school experience I somehow entertained the remote idea of staying where my heart was; at home and close to Belica.

My life had always been directed by love of family and Embargo, by my respect for others and my adherence to unspoken rules, like keeping your word and, others, which were passed on by those with whom I had spent my life up until now.

I seemed committed however, to follow these and a new set of rules, The Book of Rules, that would guide me through my employment and personal future. These promised to take me somewhere far, in spite of my misgivings.

I was going into another world that would present me with situations that would soon test my sense of right and wrong and to a journey into this new world of experiences. My past, growing up in a naive sort of innocence, my future away from my love and my home and my new commitment had become for me, *a reluctant journey.*

Into The Real World

All the while that I attended telegraphy school I had thought of myself as simply being away from Embargo and from Belica for just a while. The one-hundred sixty miles from home was close enough to make it possible for me to see Belica and my family often. Now, I was being assigned to a job a lot farther and I had this uneasy feeling. I was beginning to believe that I might leave and never return. The thought was unreal but it persisted. Already many of the people that I knew from La Cueva and Embargo had left, many to cities or towns relatively close, others, like my friend Roman had enlisted in the army and was on his way to Germany. I thought of Belica's brothers and I thought of Mimi's promise to Belica's oldest brother Mel, that she would wait for him. I was suspicious of these kinds of promises. The now, DeLu, had made a believer out of me on the inconstancies of relationships. I thought of another classmate of mine, Robert Romero, who had dated Mariam for most of the years they were in high school. After graduation, Mariam left to the big city to attend a business college. After three months there, she met a "fly boy" at the airforce club, fell in love and eloped with him. Robert was destroyed. In his case he took to drinking himself senseless every night.

I left Pueblo, never looking back. I went home, broke the news about my new job to Belica. Surprisingly, she was excited for me. We got involved in the excitement of Christmas coming soon and made plans for the absence that awaited us. She continued to be the happy girl that I had met just months before and whom I had learned to love. In my thoughts were the moments we'd shared, our walks through the cherry trees in the spring twilight, where the blossoms fell on her hair and where the silver-plated moon tracked our walk under the branches of the trees.

Belica, did not seem as perturbed as I was for my leaving. She just said to me, "take better care of yourself, you've lost weight since you left." She would then laugh and say, "I'll make you a baloney sandwich at my house, if you'd like."

If I weren't such a coward, I would think to myself, *I would just stay home, work for Henry and John Wallace and see Belica everyday.* But that was not an option for me. The die was cast and I had to complete what I had started. I told Belica that my trip to Maxwell would be brief and that I would probably be back for Christmas.

I was right. I met the Station Agent at Maxwell, made arrangements to rent a room in an old hotel, the only lodging in town, and after introducing myself to some of the men in the rail work crew I returned to Embargo in my father's Chevy.

After the Christmas holiday, I had my father drive me back to Maxwell. I had no car and I decided that I would buy a used car as soon as I got my first paycheck. The Santa Fe Railroad, for whom I would work, had a contract with the Brotherhood of Telegraphers Union, to provide for moving expenses for its members. To my amazement I was included in it. My three-hundred dollar allowance gave me the money to put down for one month's rent at the Quinlan Hotel, one which had seen its better days, and a down payment for a car in near-by Raton. I was now working in earnest and couldn't wait to drive to Arroyo to see Belica.

The world of work in the railroad was a brand new experience. The nomenclature was alien, the work tasks were new and the assignments by departments made this, a closed system. It seemed a world of work on to itself. My experience with my father's work at the mine at La Cueva, was the only thing that gave me an idea on how to relate. I knew I was in for a lengthy time of learning.

The duties included the loading of milk cans, destined for the creamery in Trinidad and mail for distribution, starting in Raton. Unloading of mail and merchandise for the stores took place off trains going south. I learned quickly that the west bound trains had odd numbers for identification while east bound trains had even numbers. East bound trains were given preference when meeting those heading west. This meant that west bound trains took the siding, allowing those in the opposite direction to pass. The principal task of a station agent and the telegraphers was to monitor and help direct the safe flow of trains. Train orders were the principal means of communication between the dispatchers, some five hundred miles away and the conductors and engineers of the trains. There were passenger trains of a first and second class, with these, taking precedence over all other trains. There were the freight trains, work trains and local trains, called "hogs" used for car switching in yards or spurs. These trains served the mines or lumber yards in the area.

There was a hierarchy not only in humans and their ant-like tasks but also between inanimate trains of different classes. I began to see what I had seen on my father's job, the need by workers to "bind" themselves to their work on the demands made by the organization. In La Cueva, that organization was the mining company, here it was to the railroad. I would soon learn the term used for these men. They were called "company men."

"Your first month," Agent Charlie Mitchum said, "is to listen, pay attention to what's going on and learn all you can on how to run a railroad." He continued, "your skills as a telegrapher are secondary. That, you learn on your own time."

It was a wild ride but I learned brand new stuff quickly. I watched Old Charlie Mitchum, as he expertly jumped from one task to another with precision.

"Will I ever be that good?" I naively asked Charlie one day after seeing him receive a train on his block (three mile boundary for an approaching train), deliver its train orders and dispatch it with all necessary tasks safely completed.

"You'd better," he answered simply.

The entire affair reminded me of the bull fights that I had read about: First, the train, like the bull, announces his presence. In the case of the train, it trips a bell signal when he is three miles out. Secondly, the Operator, in this case the agent, announces the train's approach with a quick telegraph message to the dispatcher, OS, MX, or *train approach, Maxwell.* The dispatcher would signal back immediately: CY 4 or *make four copies of a train order.* The operator or agent would then hurriedly insert three double sided carbon papers with onion-skin paper into a typewriter. He would then telegraph the dispatcher; GA, MX, or *go ahead, Maxwell.* Meanwhile the train is coming at you. The dispatcher is now telegraphing the orders and the operator is typing on his typewriter: *Order No. 124 to C & E. Number 1511* (order number 124 addressed to Conductor and Engineer on Train number 1511). The receiving operator is completely focused on that message coming in on the telegraph key and he's typing away. The dispatcher continues: *No. 1511 meet No. 22 at Springer at 9:45 a.m. .*

The agent, in his black half sleeves, immediately begins his confirmation to the Dispatcher by repeating each number, letter and period that he has received. Meanwhile, the train is still coming, perhaps at fifty miles per hour, and he is getting closer. It's been a full minute and a half since the transaction between dispatcher and operator started. Upon receiving the correctly verified train order, the dispatcher gives the time received and signs off: 8:55 a.m. HBG (his initials). The operator or agent jumps up, rips the multi-copied train orders off the typewriter and folds and inserts them on a "Y" shaped set of sticks. The telegrapher quickly runs up a metal ladder and hangs the three sticks each holding one train order: One copy is high, for the engineer, the second set at a middle level, this one for the brakeman and the lowest one is set for the conductor riding in the caboose.

An instant after the agent has set his sticks, the train roars through. The engineer sticks his arm out the window of the locomotive at the precise level of the stick and snaps off the string holding the first copy of the train order. The second and third strings are, in turn, grabbed off their sticks by the bent arms of the brakeman and the conductor. The engineer sounds two quick bursts of his whistle to acknowledge receipt of the train orders and the adrenaline generated in those intense five minutes, begins to come down. The final communication goes back to the dispatcher as *OS, MX 9:00 a.m.* The bull has been slain, the bull fighter, with precise, quick stokes and focused attention has fought and won, yet another bull fight.

I internalized the emotion involved in the task and tried to mimic Charlie's rapid-fire moves, and knew that these were the real skills that you needed to master in order to qualify to be a good telegraph operator in the Atchison, Topeka and Santa Fe Railroad. I admired Charlie's skills and soon started to think that I would soon learn to "fight the wild bull too." I also learned what those black-half sleeves were for. They were used simply to keep the operator from getting all that carbon from the double-carbon paper on his arms and shirt sleeves. Charlie watched me respond to the motions necessary to execute this time-compressed task. He assigned me the task in reverse order of the actual procedure.

First he asked me to fold the train order copies as they were completed and place them in a running knot in the hoop and then hang them on the pole. This he allowed only when the train was not yet in sight. He then asked me to copy the train orders on a piece of paper, as he was receiving them himself. This task was the hardest, because the orders were coming directly from the telegraphed message on the telegraph sounder (receiver). We repeated the tasks again and again. I was given the responsibility to "throw" the semaphore signal board when no orders were forthcoming and to remain outside to do a running inspection of the trains as they hurled by. Soon the tasks became logical steps and I began to master them.

During all this first month of work as an apprentice telegrapher I only visited home once. I saw Belica and she seemed to be faring well in my absence. She talked about school, her classes and her friends. She looked for a paper and pencil in my car's glove compartment and she wrote some glyphs on it. I asked what they were. She said, "I know code, just like you do, this is short hand that I'm taking with Mrs. Jara."

"Do you know what I'm saying here?"

"No"

She smiled and said, "That means *I love you*." I tried not to get too emotional when I was with her and when

I returned to work I thought of her daily, but I did not brood, as I'd done before.

I got a letter from Belica about three weeks after I'd seen her. She asked me not to go see her on the week-end when we had agreed to see each other. She said in her letter that a new student, an exchange student from Mexico had enrolled in school and that she and a couple of male friends were going to escort him to a school dance on that weekend. She said, in her naivete, that she didn't know why he had chosen her over all the "gringitas" that were after him. She also hinted that she had been with him to the movies before this formal date. I thought back to a time when I was getting similar letters from Deluvina. I also remember once, this last summer when I had found a letter sticking out her back pocket, from some guy I didn't know. But, I resigned myself to believe, "What will be, will be," as she had once told me.

Girls from Maxwell had been coming to the station with one excuse or another to see the *new apprentice*, but in my self-imposed fidelity, had feigned indifference and most of them went away.   All, except one, who asked me questions about certain train schedules, even when passenger trains no longer stopped at the Maxwell station. On one of these frequent visits she pretended to be listening. As I was talking I caught her looking straight into my eyes. When I caught her looking, she laughed and said, "I guess you caught me gawking. But hey, you are, a good looking guy and I've asked myself, "Does," she hesitated and looked around my arm to where a name plate on my desk read: *Gibo Herrera, Apprentice.*

"Yes. Does Gibo have a girlfriend? Has he found a girlfriend here in Maxwell? Well, do you?" she asked. She took me by surprise.

I said, "Yes to the first question and No to the second one." She offered me her hand and said, my name is Patricia.

"I can't do anything about your first problem but I can do something about the second one."

"Are you asking me for a date?"

She looked away.

"What do you think?"

I was cornered.

"If you can get permission from your parents this weekend, let's go to a movie in Raton."

She replied immediately.

"You're on! Do you know where I live?" She drew a map with directions to her house on the train schedule and asked me to pick her up at 4:00 p.m. on Friday night. I'd been a bit peeved at Belica for her change of plans to my anticipated visit this weekend and to her increasing involvement with this new kid. *Now,* I thought, *It's payback time.*

I picked up Patricia on the agreed-upon time and we drove to Raton. When we arrived she said she hadn't yet eaten. I invited her to a café near the railroad depot there. We each had a full meal and before leaving she said, "I've drank so much pop that I'm going to burst if I don't pee."

That was a bit more information than I needed, I thought, but I had discovered in the short conversations that we'd had that she was different. She talked different and thought differently from any girl that I'd been with before. She was an avid conversationalist. She seemed to know a lot about a lot of places and things and she was funny. When we got into the Drive-in, she grabbed my hand and insisted that we go to the concession stand together. I noticed a couple of the guys there looked at her at least a couple of times. One of them said, "Hi Pat, where've you been, ain't seen you in a while."

"Oh, Tod, this is a friend from Maxwell, his name is Gibo." As we walked out she said to this Tod, "Hey Tod, check you out later."

We continued our conversation in the car and she cuddled up to me as if we'd been boyfriend, girlfriend a long time. She wasn't interested in the movie it seemed to me, and she put her hands under my shirt ten minutes into the movie.

"You know that I never kiss on my first date," I said

in an attempt at being funny.

"This is not our first date," she said. "Our first date happened at the Maxwell depot, remember?" She was insistent and when I kissed her I felt disgusted with myself for betraying Belica, angry at her betrayal of me, sad and confused. I feigned illness after about an hour at the Drive-in. I asked her if we could go home to Maxwell. She seemed surprised.

"Don't you like me? Don't you want to be with me?"

"Of course I do," I said. "You're funny, you're smart, you're pretty, who wouldn't want to be with you Patricia? It's just that remorse is getting the best of me. You know that I'm engaged to my girlfriend back home?" I lied. I felt like a real heel. She thought for a minute.

"I've been looking at you since you got to Maxwell, I've asked about you and tonight I've kissed you and felt your body. I like you a lot, and wouldn't mind making it with you."

"Whoa, I'm a twenty-year old engaged man, I can't screw up."

"You want the honest truth? As matter of fact, you're a twenty-year old engaged man and I'm a seventeen-year old married woman."

"What?"

"Yes, I've been married for a year now. My husband is in the airforce, he is ten years older than me and I know that he has been cheating on me forever. Forgive me for telling you," she continued, "I think that your little fiancée is probably going out on you too."

"How would you know that?"

"Well, you don't look as happy to me, as you should be. Besides, I know that you haven't gone home to see her in a month, I even know where home is, and you could get there from here in a couple of hours."

Patricia had disarmed me. She was too cool, too perceptive and too in tune with the real world. Mine was a world of denial, blind obedience, and now turmoil.

"Give me some time, I'm not sure of anything right now."

I had to get her home. I had to think. Belica's declaration to me on her letter had hurt more that I had wanted to admit and now ironically, a young married girl was opening my eyes to reality. I was in a box. I had thought that I'd gone out to a movie, popcorn and holding hands and instead I'd come face to face with my own stupidity. I could not break off with Belica simply because she'd gone to a dance with a guy, even if it hurt me, but I most certainly wouldn't try to find any kind of relationship with a married woman.

We traveled for a long while in silence. Then, overwhelmed by rage and confusion I said to Patricia, "Listen, I think that you are a wonderful girl but I know that you are married, and I don't want any trouble." I then turned the car around and drove back to the city.

"I'm in a very vulnerable mood tonight, you are a genius and after all, you're a woman. I need a friend tonight but if you promise that you won't hurry things with me, we'll get drunk together and cry on each others' shoulders. Deal?" I asked her. I remembered Belica saying "deal" to me long ago, or so it seemed. Patricia put her head down for an instant, and repeated, "deal."

I stopped at a liquor store back in the city. I bought a half-pint of Jim Beam and two cokes and asked for two paper cups. We drove up to Look Out Butte on the east side of the city where we could see the city lights like a hundred fire flies in the late evening sky. The night was clear and the stars were winking their summer dreams. We drank and talked. She cried and told me how lonely she was and that her forwardness was just a sham to hide her sadness. I broke down too, with the help of the liquid spirits, and told her about Belica and my agony of being away while she dated some "asshole."

That night, on that lonely mesa we kissed, we were lovers and we promised each other that tonight would be the only time that we would ever be together. We drove home early next morning and I had discovered a friend with a deep hurt and regrets greater than mine but I knew that ours could never be. Our destinies had crossed paths just briefly and a future together was out of the question. We kissed at the gate outside her parents' house.

"I'm sorry Gibo. I don't want to ruin your life like I've ruined mine, life is cruel. I just met you yesterday and today I have to let you go," she said.

After that night I never saw Patricia again. Some said she went away to join her husband in Nevada. Others said that she had simply gone away.

A Visitor

In time I reconciled with the idea of Belica going to dances with guys and when I saw her a couple of weeks later, she seemed undisturbed about anything. When I asked about how her date had been with that Mexican kid, she dispelled it with, "Oh, we danced only twice. He danced all night with a lot of different girls and I danced with my cousin Tony most of the night. Those 'gringitas' just wouldn't turn him loose and I didn't really care." Our relationship was back on track but my absence could not bring any permanence to this relationship. I just had to hope that someday we could make real plans about our future.

I again returned to Maxwell and one day I asked Charlie Mitchum if he knew the Jaramillo family up the hill and if he knew the daughters. He looked at me straight in the eye and said, "You mean the married one, the one that's been here pestering you? Well," he continued, "Jaime, the Daddy, is a good man. He works at the sugar mill on the north end of town. The oldest daughter, she can't be more that eighteen years old, got involved with an older guy from Springer and poof, they're soon married. The Daddy was very unhappy but then the husband went into the air force and left her with her parents. You are a good boy Gibo, and I don't want you to get yourself fooled and taken advantage of. Going around with a married woman is a serious matter and who knows, there's been cases of fellows being shot by jealous husbands. You don't want that, besides," he continued, "It's bad for you, its bad for her, it's bad for Jaime, her father and it's bad for the depot."

I was sorry I'd brought up the subject and when I said that I hadn't been aware of the fact that she was married until that night, he said, "The talk around town is that someone saw you drive her home in the wee hours of the morning." I remembered an admonition made by the head teacher in Pueblo and he made it more than once: "Boys, don't drink in the town that you're at." This advice didn't seem too far from what I had done. "*Don't date a married woman in the town that you're at*," it seemed to say.

After a couple of months in Maxwell, I got a surprise visitor. He arrived at the Trailways Bus depot in the middle of town. It was my brother Vivian. He announced, in a carefree manner:

"I've come to see that you don't get into any trouble."

"Hey," I asked, "who's the older brother here?"

He laughed and said, "Dad says I'm getting into too much trouble in La Cueva and maybe I'll straighten out here." Vivian continued with what Dad had said, "…that the Springer Boys' Reform School is just about twenty miles away and that if I mess up here, that is where he'll send me. You believe he means it?" he asked.

Vivian made himself at home. I'd rented a small adobe house near the tracks and could accommodate him easily. He enrolled in school a couple of days after arriving and before long he seemed to take over. He was an aggressive, tall, good-looking sixteen-year old. He had a surplus of self-confidence and he was a charmer. It wasn't very long before the girls from the high school started coming over to the house. I wasn't too keen in him bringing girls home because, mine was a bachelor's quarters, bereft of furnishings and not always tidy. The surprise came, however, when he announced to me that he had met a girl by the name of Louise and, he added, "whose sister you've been dating. What's up old fox? Louise seems to know all about you, Belica and your affair with her sister. It sounds pretty real to her, I don't think she's lying. Level with me older brother."

I told Vivian all about the mistake that I had made

that one night when I'd taken Patricia out not knowing she was married. He listened and said,

"I know all about it, but Louise is not married and I intend to get close to her." Their romance was intense and it was real. She was only fifteen and the relationship worried me because we were both living among strangers and I knew Vivian could do something impulsive and get us both into a lot of trouble. Nothing happened for a while. Vivian became a member of the Maxwell Bears basketball team and was an excellent player. He intimidated his rivals on the court, he helped the team win all of their games and when tournament time came and Maxwell was seated number two in the division, trouble started. The coaches from opposing schools, especially the bigger rival to the north, who had never been beaten by the Bears at a tournament, objected to Vivian being in the team. They called it, "a case of ineligibility." They stated to the tournament officials that Vivian did not live with his parents and therefore they couldn't allow him to play in that region. We talked to the Maxwell school administrators, but they had been out-maneuvered and Vivian was out.

Vivian continued to live with me even when I had misgivings about him, since he was rather aggressive for the kids here. We went out regularly, especially to the drive-In movies. Some of Louise's friends would join us but we never spoke of Patricia. One girl that came around quite a bit was Thea. Eventhough I had never asked her out, she said she did not want to date me, "because," she told me one evening when Vivian had walked away into the darkness with Louise, "You like married women. Does the name, Pat ring a bell?" she asked. "At least that is what Louise has told me."

"That never happened," I said, like a coward. I didn't want Patricia's husband's family to hear this scuttlebutt and come after me. Thea kept a subtle pressure and would get great pleasure out of turning an expression, "See you later alligator," into, "see you later Alley Gator." I asked Vivian to tell Louise not to invite Thea out with us anymore. So essentially, Patricia was, in fact, the only girl that I ever dated while in Maxwell.

At the end of a six month period as apprentice telegrapher, I anticipated being given an assignment elsewhere and it came before very long. But not before Vivian did what he did best however; get into trouble.

Vivian and some of his friends had remained after school shooting basketballs. He and one of the boys got into an altercation. Vivian, it appeared, punched the kid a couple of times and his friends reported Vivian to the Town Marshall. The first inkling I got, was when Vivian and his friend, Jake rushed into the house, saying nothing to me. I was outside wiping down my car when I heard a siren, faintly at first and then it became louder. It was the local law enforcement approaching the house in an old, green 1949 International Harvester pick up. When the Marshall stopped by my car he was livid. The man could hardly speak.

"Where is your brother?" I knew that if I revealed where Vivian was this man who was in such an excited state, would undoubtedly rush into the house and grab him. I stayed pretty calm. I asked the obvious, "Are you Marshall Butchel?"

"Yes," he answered.

And before he could insist on the whereabouts of my brother, I said, wiping my hands, "I'm Gibo Herrera. I work at the Depot with Charlie Mitchum. What seems to be the problem, officer?" I feigned great concern. "Your brother has just beat up on one of the kids in town and I've come to arrest him." "Whoa," I said. "I'm sure that we can get all this resolved if you share with me the information I need in order for you to do your duty, starting with any warrant that you might have to arrest my brother."

"I don't need a warrant" he blurred out, trying to intimidate me. I remained calm and retorted.

"Now Marshall, I'm my brother's guardian, while he is here in Maxwell and you and I both know that a warrant is the first thing that you must show in order to effect an arrest."

The man turned red with frustration, but he hesitated long enough for me to add:

"I'm sorry for this whole thing, but it's an issue of due process for both of us. Won't you agree? My father was a Justice of the Peace back in the county where we come from and I know a little bit about the law," I bluffed.

"I'll work with you on this believe me, but either you talk to me as this kid's guardian or a lawyer in Raton will be asking you the questions I want answered."

The Marshall knew that, at the very least, I could talk up a good game. He cleared his throat, he was now considerably calmer. I beat him to the draw again.

"Whose family does this kid who allegedly got beat up belong to? I know most of the families in Maxwell and if it isn't more than boys whacking each other around I'm willing to fez up to the kid's parents."

"It was my kid," he said.

"Oh well Marshall, I'm truly sorry, but this puts a whole 'nother light on the subject. Don't you agree? At this time I'm going to have to insist that there be a medical report on this, so called assault, or that I get a chance, with the parent's permission, to see the alleged victim. Otherwise any rash action on your part might be interpreted as a conflict of interest."

Just then Jake, who had been listening to our

conversation from inside the house came out and said, "Marshall Butchel, Butch was not hurt, he threw some good blows himself. Vivian just fended them off and just got in a good one along side Butch's head."

At that very moment, three boys came running toward us. One of them was Butch, the alleged victim. Jake moved to my side and whispered, "That's Butch Butchel" and he pointed to a tall, lanky kid with a crew cut. Butch and his friends had ventured here, perhaps thinking that the Marshall was going to arrest my brother and take him away in shackles, instead they discovered a stalemate. The Marshall was not a very big man and did not present the stereotyped imposing figure that sends fear through a man. He had already stepped out of his pick up. He was by now, a bit red-faced, but addressed the boys that had just arrived.

"Just what in the dad-burn tarnation is this all about? I was told that you had been beaten to a pulp," he said to his son. "You don't even have a scratch." The son said nothing except lower his head. He knew that he had, somehow, embarrassed his father. Then he said, "Ever since 'Avian came to Maxwell everybody thinks he's so tough, he's always trying to embarrass me because he thinks he's a better player than me…"

"Stop!" the Marshall yelled. "Is this what this is about? Some, macho, bullshit jealousy? Get in the truck," he ordered his son. "You boys," he told the others, "go home."

The Marshall then idled up to me and whispered, "A damn pissing contest, that's all it was, Mr. Gibo." He then said to me, loud enough for anyone in the house to hear, "I'm sorry for the misunderstanding, but if you don't mind a bit of advise, please keep an eye on that brother of yours, next time it could be real trouble."

He drove away and that night Vivian and I made plans for his return home. At first he made a hundred promises that he would behave. He said that he didn't want to leave Louise. While I felt truly sad about his last concern, I leveled with him and told him that it didn't really matter, that my apprenticeship here was over and that it would not be more than a week or two before I got reassigned. Vivian was on the Trailways Bus the following day.

Tears Of An Old Man

During the time that I spent in Maxwell I met a lot of the people that inhabited this small farming community. There were several different ethnic groups in the community, unlike Embargo or La Cueva with only one or two ethnic groups. Many of the people in Maxwell were from another part of the country, others from other countries. Many of Maxwell's citizens were of Italian descent: The Quinns and Pasaventos and others. Hispanics with Anglo names were such families as the Olmsteads and the Mitchells. There was old man Lazaro, an eastern European who raised chickens, sold their eggs and brewed a wonderful wine that he made from chokecherries, grapes or any fruit that he could find. My brother and I liked to buy his fresh eggs. We Knew that we would get a sample of that home-made wine every time we went there.   Other Hispanics included those whose grandfathers had run large flocks of sheep in the plains in the early history of the region.

There was a collection of single men too, who might have came with the railroad and stayed. I often asked about these loners and was led to believe that in some cases these men were fugitives from justice or simply recluses with no place to call home, except Maxwell.

My favorite person in this mix of people living in Maxwell was a store owner by the name of Solomon Hatta. He said he was from Yemen in the Arabian peninsula and he had come to Maxwell thirty five years before, at a time of great activity in the coal trade up in Dawson, lumbering in Cimmaron and gold mining in Vermejo. Solomon was among many of Middle-Eastern people that settled as merchants among the scattered Hispanic villages.

During my lunch breaks early on my arrival at Maxwell I often walked over to a store surrounded by tall large leafed cottonwoods located a few yards from the train depot. This was the "Hatta Store."

Solomon Hatta was an astute merchant and a personable individual. From the first day I stepped into his place we became friends. He said when we first met, "Welcome, welcome, my good friend, how can I serve you today?"

"I just want a coke and a cupcake, I'm going to have a small lunch today," I said.

"You work at the depot, don't you?" He asked. "I've

seen you empty the burned-out coal from the stove every morning and I see the smoke come out of the chimney right after that. You are study to be Operator, Yah?"

"Yes," I said. "I just started to work about a week ago."

"Don't be in a hurry my friend, stay, stay, have a chair." And he pointed to a chair next to boxes of bulk candy, peanuts and dried red chiles. I offered to pay for the coke that I had taken from a small ice box and a cupcake that I found near a clutter of assorted snacks.

"No, no, keep your money. Today I treat for you because you become my neighbor. We also eat together. Wait a minute for me I bring us something. You like cheese and crackers?" he yelled from back of a cold case.

"Yes," I yelled back.

"I know a fine person, when I see him, and you are that person to me."

"Well," I said, now sitting in the chair that he had designated, "My name is Gibo Herrera."

"Ah, what a nice name you have Herrera," he said and seemed to savor the sound of my last name.

"My language is very similar to your language. Lots of words in Arab language are same as Spanish." And he proceeded to give me the source of many of the words in Spanish that were similar in sound and meaning to Arabic. He rattled off a half dozen words: *almohada* (pillow) *albud* (dry measure) *El alba* (dawn) etc., he said that the Spanish word Ojala, (I hope it is so) is really a prayer to God, literally meaning *"Be it the will of Allah."*

Salomon Hatta was talking all this time from a table by the cold case. He then walked out to where I was sitting. He had a tray with cheese, crackers, figs and a tea kettle. "I know you young people like coke, but one day, I serve you tea, you'll like tea better." He placed the tray before me and invited me to partake. I was surprised at his generosity. In less than ten minutes Solomon had offered me his food, had not charged me for my coke and cupcake and had given me a lesson on the history of language.

"Why?" I asked.

"People forgot that peace and friendship is firmed up when you eat together. Today you and I, Herrera, are become friends."

Salomon Hatta, the humble store keeper and I, had because of his actions, become friends.

I tried to visit Solomon at lunch time or sometimes after work. I got to know a lot about him and how he'd come to this country and how he ended up in Maxwell. I got some idea of what the culture of his people was like and as our visits came and went, he also learned a lot about me.

One day around ten-fifteen in the morning, right after the Greenwich Time check had come over the wire, Charlie sent me there to buy some household items for him. I found Salomon kneeling on a small rug and then prostrating himself as he repeated a prayer, then repeated the ritual again. I did not ask him about his prayers but he offered me the information himself. He said, "I pray to Allah twice a day. You see Herrera, Allah for my people, is the fountain-head of all off our lives, what we do, what we think, how we behave." He spoke as if he was a tour director, much like Tomas Avila had been.

"In the morning, the criers at the towers of the mosque call the faithful to prayer. Everybody, no matter what they are doing, take out their prayer mats, as you would say, and offer their prayers to Allah."

After that, I tried not to go there during this time of prayer even though he never locked the door of his store during those times. Solomon Hatta spoke frequently about his life before coming to the United States. He told me about his mother and father as well as his brothers. He offered me lessons on living a better life along the way and he said that he wasn't sure that his self-exile from his country had truly been a good idea.

As we continued to be good friends, Solomon Hatta, heard about my life. He learned, among other things, about my love for Belica. He suddenly became animated after my story of homesickness, my own doubts about being away from my family and my girlfriend and my commitment to some future that I could not yet define.

Solomon Hatta began to talk more and more about a young love that he'd had back in his village in Yemen. He told me that he was about my age when he came to the U.S. but that he had been friends with this girl for two years before that time.

"I still think of her, Gibo," He was now using my first name.

"For me, I think, she gets more beautiful every year I think about her. She was the daughter of a distant cousin of mine, her name was Sarah. The family was opposed to us ever being together. My father had already made arrangements with a man from another village for me to marry his daughter. My father had said to my mother that the girl from the next village would bring more, what you call, dowry?" He said. "But I love Sarah, so much that I spend long hours at night, outside our house, thinking how I could take her away, far. But I couldn't do it. How funny, I think now," Solomon continued, "I used to meet Sarah on the hills far from the village where her father and my father used to graze our goats. It was forbidden for boy and girl to be close to each other before marriage, but Sarah love me and I love her, I swear by my love for Allah."

As he was telling me his story, a customer came and Solomon had to stop the conversation and I had to return to work. Before he went off to tend to his customer he whispered, "Tomorrow, Saturday, I want you to come have lunch with me. I have to tell you a lot more. Come around one o'clock."

I had not planned to go home that weekend and I had little to do on Saturday so I made plans to visit Solomon Hatta and have lunch with him. I knew that he always had fruit in his house so I went across the tracks to Solomon's competitor, Old Man Friske, and bought some oranges and dried pears. I took the fruit to Solomon's house which was simply a couple of rooms in the rear of the store. He was in good spirits and was finishing his cooking when I got there. He placed a "Will Return" sign on the window informing his customers that he would return within the hour.

Solomon's cooking turned out to be some of the best food that I had ever eaten. He had skewered pieces of lamb and had cooked them in the oven. He had steamed a long rice that he saturated with a yellow liquid he called "saffron." He had made a salad from tomatoes and cucumbers and had sprinkled it with goat cheese and he had made some small, sweet cakes that also seemed to be made out of rice. Before the meal he repeated some words in his language and then poured us a dark, hot tea from a tea kettle, not into cups but rather into small clear glasses. He was a good host and we ate. He said, "I had a thought to invite Charlie, your boss, but then I said, how Gibo and I talk about those things that are personal with strangers here?" We ate a wonderful meal and afterward we moved to a couple of cloth chairs in a space he used as a living room.

Solomon made small talk, then asked me, "Gibo, your girl, she come from a good family?"

"Yes. She is an only girl in a family of eight boys. Both parents are well respected in the community and one of her brothers is a friend that I had met when we were boys."

"How long you know your girlfriend, Gibo?" I told him that I'd known her for almost two years now.

"I can tell you love this young woman, like I loved my Sarah."

He then looked away and continued the conversation that we had started the day before.

"The older I get, the sharper my memory becomes of my life before I came to this country. Lately I been having dreams of my mother. She sits on the floor in her kitchen cooking the bread, and she calls to me. I never dream of my father, but I feel his presence in the other room. I often think about Sarah and wonder what happen to her. You know why I come to this country

Gibo?" Before I could venture a guess, he said, "I have no choice. My father was making plans for me and I also hear the most terrible news in my life. One day I took the goats up to the hills, where Sarah and I grazed them on the thorny bush that grow there, but no Sarah. I ask her little brother where she was but he put down his head and did not answer to me. Next day she did not come and the day that followed. Sarah did not come to the hills. I went to her house and pretend I was asking if she was sick or something. Her aunt went outside and told me, angry, 'You better go Sahal,' my name back home. 'Sarah not here anymore. She go away to the next town. Her father, my brother in law, he take to offer her in marriage to a merchant son. Better you go. You embarrass her and you embarrass our family if you stay to ask."

"Gibo, the rocks tumble from the mountains, the sun cry and I go crazy. Why I be punished like this? I ask." I noticed that as Solomon spoke on, that his speech was altered; that he seemed to have forgotten his English and he sounded to me as if he was trying to speak as he had spoken on that day of his betrayal. "I ran way that night," he said. "I sneak away, took the family donkey and rode south until I got into the low desert. I just keep going until I reached the ocean three days later. I don't know how I got water or food but I made it to a city, a port on the ocean." Solomon now seemed to be talking to himself. He continued, "At first I beg for food then I went to the mosque and prayed to Allah for help and he gave it to me in a strange way. In one month after I left my village, because I could never stand to be where Sarah had been taken away, I got a job cleaning the decks of ships in the port. I worked for an Egyptian captain first and then when an English ship came to port I offered to work for free if he would take me to Egypt. I got the job working on this English and in six months, after stopping and taking cargo in other ports, we got to Egypt. One year later I made my way to this country."

"I never tell anyone this story before, my friend Gibo. Now I want to go back even if I have to work so hard in somebody's ship. I feel trapped here now. I know I'm getting an old man and I think more and more of my village. You know Gibo, don't wait forever to marry your girl. Life goes too fast. It happens like that," he said, snapping his fingers. "To be young is to be a god and your virgin bride is a badge of honor to you and to your family. Don't wait too much time, Gibo."

And as he looked away, I saw tears flood his eyes. Solomon Hatta, my good friend, was pouring his heart out to me.

He assumed we were kindred souls and the tears in this old man's eyes, sealed our kinship.

Time To Go Again

Two weeks after my brother returned home I received a Work Assignment Order by telegraph. It simply read, "G. Herrera, Report to Division Headquarters in Las Vegas for Book of Rules Exam on May 5th. Please acknowledge. Signed C.J. Barnes." I immediately acknowledged receipt of the work order and made plans to leave Maxwell. This order was in effect, the end of my apprenticcship period and if I passed the book of rules exam I would be promoted to Operator/Telegrapher. Charlie Mitchum thanked me for being a, "good apprentice." He congratulated me for having made the grade. I knew that his evaluation of my work was instrumental in the completion of my apprenticeship period. I thanked him and told him that I'd see him around. I said good-bye to my friends including Solomon Hatta who bowed slightly and said something in Arabic and then he said to me, "Allah be with you my good friend, I enjoy our long talks together."

I left Maxwell a couple of days later in the early

morning when the sun had just broke the horizon in the eastern plains. I took one last look at the railroad depot and the familiar houses of people that I had gotten to know on my brief sojourn in this community. I felt a sad, forlorn feeling just as I had felt when I left Embargo for school in Pueblo. It was just about ninety miles to Las Vegas but the trip was one of reminiscence. I thought of my friends: the Mitchells, with Molly playing "Charmaine" on a record. I could almost hear the yells and cheers of a Bears basketball game and see my brother Vivian shooting from the corner on the court. I could see the track inspector Arbicrombe, an old Norwegian, who stopped at the depot on his way south. He rode in an open track-car, summer and winter and would call me "Herıy" and called Charlie "Chowrly." I remembered our trips to the Drive-in up in Raton and I thought of my night with Patricia.

When I arrived at Las Vegas, I made my way to the Depot located by a big Hotel called the Castaneda and where the railroad people, I later learned, held their parties and dances. I introduced myself to the staff and I was offered a cup of coffee. I was led into a room and handed a multi-page exam, and in the presence of a retired station agent, I took the dreaded test on "The Book of Rules." It took me about two and a-half hours to finish the test. Having done so, the dispatcher gave me something he called a "warrant" and told me to present this at the Castaneda, that it would pay for my lunch. He reminded me to return after lunch and find out how I had done.

The meal was excellent. I ate a hot beef sandwich with mashed potatoes, gravy and a coke. The place was extraordinary. Tables were set with white tablecloths, the chairs had padded seats and red cloth napkins adorned the table setting. I was relaxed after the test, but in the back of my mind was an exciting thought.

I hope I fail, then nobody can blame me for going home.

But this fleeting wish was not to be. I returned to the dispatcher's office. He got up when I entered his office and kidding me said, "Are you sure you didn't cheat on this test?" He laughed then offered me his hand and said, "Mr. Herrera, you did very well. Congratulations! You answered 297 questions correctly out of 300 on the test. In other words, you scored a 99% on the Book of Rules. I guess," he continued, "those long lonely nights in Maxwell, with nothing to do, gave you plenty of time to study." He smiled, turned around and said, "Take a week off, but on Monday, next, I want you to report to Hohnes in Colorado, take a couple of days to 'break in' at that station and protect that assignment until further notice. Welcome on board!"

Charlie Mitchum had once said that the job of a starting telegrapher was that of a substitute operator. "You'll be placed on the 'Extra Board,' where, for the first year or so, you will replace other telegraph operators when these men take vacation time, are ill or are unable to protect their assignments." *Protect* was a term used to mean "to cover a job or to make yourself responsible for it." I knew from the start that I would not hold a permanent position, but rather, to always be on call to take over for a fellow telegrapher at such a time as the dispatcher ordered me to do so.

"Don't worry," Charlie had said, "you'll have more work than you need, you'll see a lot of country and you'll have free passage on most of the passenger trains in the system."

These were some of my thoughts initially as I drove home. I had been given a week's vacation and I intended to see Belica as much as I could.

As I contemplated a continued absence from home and from my girlfriend I had begun to formulate a strategy of mental and emotional survival during these future absences. I saw myself starting on an odyssey and I could not continue the heightened emotion brought on by my love for Belica. I also had to take into consideration that events, like her dating that exchange student would probably happen again and I could not punish myself when this happened. I knew that she was a young high school girl and she must be able to grow and mature without the restrictions imposed by a protracted relationship. But I resolved, in these conversations with myself, to live for the moment and to enjoy the times that I would be with the girl with whom I had so deeply fallen in love, so long ago, its seemed.

I left Las Vegas at the edge of the plains and entered the mountain valleys of Porvenir, Chapello and Mora. I passed the ancient villages of Guadalupe and Holman and began the steep ascend on the highway into and over the huge mountains that had historically kept these villages isolated for centuries just as it had done to Embargo and La Cueva. I crossed the road to La Piedra and other isolated villages: San Juan de la Llegua, Vadito, El Llano and others, hidden in the mountains. Life here had not changed much in the last one hundred years. I topped the first mountain range and entered another formerly impassable sierra. I was in the heart of the Sangre de Cristo Mountains.

An hour later, I descended into the valley, or better said, the alluvial stretches of La Villa. I knew that I would be passing by Belica's school and I got a crazy idea. *Why not call her, leave a message or just drive up to the school and ask to see her?* My old-fashioned respect for others had always kept me from making rash decisions, but today I was called by the *sirens' song* and I stopped at her school. I wondered as I walked up to the offices whether I would be thrown out, if my actions would get her into trouble or that she would chastise me for embarrassing her. *No matter,* I reasoned, as I entered the office.

At the desk was a young office assistant. *A high school senior no doubt,* I thought.

"I'm Gibo Herrera," I said. "Is it possible for me to leave a message for one of your students?"

"Yes, yes, so you're the Gibo I've heard Belica talk so much about?" "Wait," she then gestured a stop with her hand and smiling, "I think I can get her for you."

Hey, I said to myself, *This is cool.*

I had lucked out. In a couple of minutes Belica appeared. Her face was reddish and moist with perspiration and she had on a black and orange head band to hold back her hair. She was dressed in gym shorts and sneakers. She had burst through the door, surprised and a bit embarrassed.

"What are you doing here?" she whispered, and offered me her hands. The office assistant beamed with joy at seeing two lovers awkwardly coming together in a public place. Belica was stunning. Her petite body looked alluringly gorgeous in those gym shorts. Her legs were strong and beautifully contoured and her smile all but melted my soul. I was on fire. I quickly suggested that she let me take her home later that day. She thought a second.

"Wait for me at the parking lot. Let me shower and I'll leave with you right away."

It was still some time before the last class, I guessed but I was more than willing to wait. She returned to her physical education class and I went out to my car to wait. Before I left, the student office assistant put out her hand and introduced herself.

"I'm Margie Fernandez, Saul has mentioned your name to me." I thanked her for having called Belica. The student was still smiling when I left the office.

I met Belica at the parking lot twenty minutes later and she let me sneak a quick kiss as we met again. She was now dressed in a grey pleaded skirt and a light pink blouse with a light pink neck scarf. She had a faint smell of a rose perfume.

"What do you have on? You smell so good."

"It's just jergens lotion," she stated nonchalantly. We got into town and went straight to a hamburger place called "The Pig Stand." Teenagers particularly, frequented this hangout. It was a small place, with a juke box and it made the best tasting hamburgers in town. We sat close together in a booth and once in awhile when no one was looking I'd sneak in a small kiss. I punched in a couple of songs by the platters, "It's Twilight Time," and "My

Prayer," and told her that no matter where I was, that these songs reminded me of her. We lingered, talking and laughing until some teenagers started to come in. She quickly rose and said, "Take me home, I want to get there the same time the bus does." We left, with the cook looking from under the counter hood and smiling at two teenagers, well at least one of them, in love, without a doubt.

I dropped Belica off at her house just as the school bus passed her neighbor's. The three little brothers had come out of the house. Charlie, the shy one, followed his sister into the house, Nilo came up to the car.

"You know, I think I can drive this car. You want to show me one day?"

"Sure." "We'll take a spin one of these days."

Roque came up to me.

"Did you bring us something?"

"Yes, matter of fact I did," thinking of something that I might have for him. I put my hand into my pocket and pulled out three quarters.

"Roque, you take your brothers out for a coke at Fito's Market. What do you think of that?" He jumped up and looked at his quarters.

"Thanks Gibo, I'm going to show this to my mother."

I visited with Belica that night and every night before

my dreaded return to work. Belica told me that on the early part of the summer she and her cousins were going to visit her aunts and cousins in California and they were going to travel by train. I told her that I had no idea where I'd be working this summer and I explained to her that I was now on "The Extra Board" and that I had no notion where I would be from one day to the next. I didn't realized then, how true my comments would be.

On one of those wonderful nights with my girl, we chose to walk toward the old school house. We sat on the swings for a while and talked. It was twilight and we could see a path leading away from the school grounds, which seemed to go no where. I asked her about it and she said, "Let's walk it and find out." We crossed the barbed wire fence which she adroitly handled and we made our way up a hill and into a meadow. We walked around the meadow and up into a grove of beautiful cedar trees aligning a ditch. The ditch was one of the major acequias (community ditches) that watered the farmlands on the south side of Arroyo del Hongo. The ditch was carrying quite a bit of water and its ripples and rushing water sounded every bit like a small river. We decided not to cross and instead sat on the banks facing the village. We talked until the graying sky to the west started darkening. The silhouetted mountains were quickly disappearing. Belica scrambled up, shook the dust off her seat and said, "If we don't hurry we won't be able to see the trail, let's go." I followed her down the path that was also disappearing in the dying light. As we walked farther down the trail I realized that we had missed a turn or simply gotten lost. We were in the meadow now and I thought nothing of having lost our way. I noticed suddenly, that the meadow had the feel of those soggy, spongy patches of grass in La Cieneguilla, where I had walked with Tomas Avila some time ago.

"Hey, be careful I think we've hit a marsh."

"Ya, There's one here." We kept walking and suddenly she said excitedly, "Gibo, this place is sinking," and she grabbed by arm. I too, felt the sensation of a wobbly unstable earth under me. I knew that these patches or tuffs of trapped water would not give nor that we would fall through. I think Belica knew that too.

"Let me carry you across." She gleefully agreed and jumped on my back. I got a big kick over this and started to walk with her laughing and shrieking. I hadn't carried her more that forty or fifty feet when I slipped on the wet grass, we both fell and immediately got all wet. We laughed as we lay side by side.

"What a poor horse," she said. "Can't even carry a girl on its back." I grabbed her wet body and kissed her there. We laughed and kissed and made fun of the "poor" horse. When we got up we were both almost completely

248

wet. We made our way back easily enough by seeing the lights in the houses near the school. I left her on her porch and knew she had some explaining to do and I went home in my wet clothes.

The magical moments of that week soon passed. I kissed her good-bye on my final night there and told her that I'd drop her a line from Hohnes, Colorado where ever that was. She said she'd miss me and told me to hurry back. I made plans to drive up to the Colorado border and find Hohnes by the use of a map and start my new career as a newly promoted telegraph operator.

My long trip to Hohnes was uneventful. I had traveled part of that route many times on my way to school in Pueblo. On the first leg of my trip I passed the old village of La Culebra. It lay at the foothills of the Latir Mountain, an eleven thousand foot peak with seven natural lakes, all at different elevations from each other. There were waterfalls, with moss covered rocks on the watercourse and large ferns touching the cascades of water as if teasing them. The town of Culebra (snake) derived its name from the river that flowed from this mountain. It formed a giant snake as it meandered into the alluvial fan and through the town. I crossed the border into Colorado at a nondescript place totally inhabited by blue chamiso (sage brush). The only landmark was a wooden sign now needing a paint job. "Welcome to

Colorful Colorado."

The twenty miles north to the village of San Luis was similarly inhabited by chamiso to the point of monotony. This Hispanic village prides itself in being the "Oldest Town in Colorado." It's one main street is essentially the road north. It betrays the fact that the village and its environs have not changed much since its founding, two hundred years ago. To the east of San Luis loom huge mountains, so high that snow caps can be seen on some peaks all of July and into August. A skinny female dog with withered teats chooses to cross the road as I approach and continues oblivious to any traffic on either direction. It probably knows that the lay-back, timeless tempo of the town and its people makes hurry or caution irrelevant.

Fort Garland, a former American army fort, looks abandoned and simply appears to exist as an outside museum. This site is the start of the road east and across the Rockies. The road quickly meanders up into the mountains crossing the Denver and Rio Grande Railroad tracks just east of town and the road quickly begins to climb. The mountains are formidable. I quickly climbed into and over La Veta pass, and just before I reached the summit, I could see a saddle shaped depression on the ridge of the mountain. I had read that it was through these saddles that the French trappers and other earlier travelers had been able to cross these mountains on their way to the isolated Hispanic villages and rivers with their prized beaver. Once having crossed the pass I went through the town of La Veta. I could see the imposing Spanish Peaks to the south. Today they were a hazy blue and looked as mysterious and enigmatic as portrayed in the book by Zane Grey in <u>Raiders Of The Spanish Peaks.</u>

Next, the town of Walsenburg. It was once a shipping off point for the coal from that region but for me it was a place of mystery that my great grandfather had emigrated to in an effort to start a new life for himself and his family. It appears, with some secrets not revealing the whole story, that he had left his newly born son (my paternal grandfather) with In-laws back in Embargo and had fled to Walsenburg with his wife. I never found out the truth of this exodus, but I know that at least it resulted in my last name being that of my paternal grandmother, Maria Herrera.

After Walsenburg I turned south on my way to Trinidad, where I planned to stay the night and drive the twenty remaining miles east to Hohnes the following morning. I passed the ghost town of Aguilar and approached Trinidad from the north and into brick-layered streets. The radio was playing "In Days of Wine and Roses," which did not do much to assuage my melancholy. I stopped at the railroad depot and asked the operator about a good place to spend the night. I told him that I was reporting to Hohnes in the morning. He welcomed me and said that he had often heard me on the wire and that I would find Hohnes peaceful. He recommended the Columbia Hotel.

"That's the place that most 'trainmen' stay," he said.

I spent the night at the Columbia and told the desk clerk that I might be coming back the next day and perhaps the next two weeks, having learned from the Trinidad operator that Hohnes had no accommodations. That night I slept soundly and early next day, after breakfast at a little Italian restaurant next door, I headed east to Hohnes.

The twenty odd miles to my first real assignment was quick. I left the last appearance of mountain terrain and entered the grassy plains and had I continued east, would have taken me into the heart of the prairies.

Hohnes was a lone railroad station that was situated, as if in the midst of a huge meadow. There was one small store that was also the site of the post office. I went into the station, introduced myself and was welcomed warmly by the station agent. He asked if I had a place to stay. I assured him that I would stay in Trinidad. He echoed the information that I received in Trinidad, that most of the trainmen stayed at the Columbia Hotel. The station agent said he was going back east to see family and was taking a two-week vacation. He said he was happy that I was available to fill in for him. He added that the shortage of operators on the extra board made it difficult for tenured agents or operators, who had been waiting for over a year, to take their vacations. I knew then, what Charlie Mitchum meant when he had assured me that "There would be plenty of work."

I got acquainted with the station and its idiosyncrasies as I would discover during my experiences in different stations. The set-up at Hohnes was rather standard and I did my two days of "breaking-in" before I took over this lone, isolated railroad depot on the edge of the prairie. At the end of my instructions on the first day, the agent surprised me with an announcement that a minor railroad crossed the Santa Fe Railroad at a point about ten miles east. He said it was the Colorado Southern Railroad, coming from Boise City Oklahoma and ending in Walsenburg, a destination usually associated with coal.

"My only concern is that if we have trains coming from the west that you might have to take "train orders" instructing the eastbound S.F. trains that a C.S. freight train would be crossing over our tracks. The C.S. does not always tell us when they have trains coming."

He said that the Colorado Southern railroad had a tower near the crossing that would instruct their trains of our schedules. He had placed some doubt on my mind and so this fact was the only thing that bothered me. But as I took over my duties and as the days turned to weeks, I had only one occasion to issue a "wait" train order to a freight train of our own in an instance of a crossing by a Colorado Southern train.

The work at Hohnes was singular. Other than the usual dusting of this non-passenger train depot, I had time to read. My experiences with Henry Wallace, had left me infected with the reading bug. My interest was varied and either because I had a genuine interest in a subject or simply because I used reading as an escape from whatever was obsessing me, I read every chance I got. While in Hohnes I not only read about the Santa Fe trail and the impact it had on commerce between the United States and the Hispanic/Mexican province of New Mexico, which included the present state of Colorado but the history of that immediate area as well.

What made a real impression on me was the history of the so called, "Ludlow Massacre." It was a story of an event in the history of the coal industry in Trinidad and Ludlow. It was, I concluded, a shameful and inhumane act of repression of the miners in the early 1900's, whose only sin was to attempt to organize a miners' union. The outcome of a strike by miners was the massive firing of men, the expulsion of families from their company-owned homes and the murder of men, women and children by the monopolistic mining company and its hired thugs. This whole episode in the history of this region, was surely a black eye on the early settlement history of this now peaceful area.

Every day, after working in Hohnes I drove back to the Hotel Columbia in Trinidad. I ate my dinner at the same Italian restaurant and went to my room and read. Approaching the town was always a pleasant sensation when driving over the brick-paved streets. I imagined that I was riding over some cobble-stone streets in Europe, of which I'd only read about. And with the radio playing I would transport my thoughts far away from Trinidad. One evening, the radio kept playing the Nat King Cole song, "The Lazy, Hazy Days of Summer," and like Mr. Jinx in the L'il Abner comic strip, I invariably returned to the melancholy induced by the cloud raining and lightning crashing over my head.

The two weeks at Hohnes were over before very long. Three days before the end of my assignment I received wired instructions to report to the Rowe depot, near Pecos, New Mexico with no time off to go home. On my last day there I checked out of the hotel which had seen its better days, but was clean and accommodating for me and my fellow railroaders. Not unlike all those hotels that I would later frequent, it had a Gideon Bible in a bedside desk.

On this last day in Trinidad I decided to leave after work. I traveled south on my way to Raton, where I planned to stay the night. I went south and over the Raton Pass, a narrow passage for both the highway and the railroad. This place in history, I recalled, had been witness to railroad giants competing (to the point of armed conflict) for the right to lay a railroad south across the mountains into Santa Fe and beyond. The Santa Fe Railroad and the Denver, Rio Grande and Western, both wanted control of this pass. A central figure in this conflict was an astute land grabber, by the name of Jim Wooten. He laid claim to the pass as it existed in those early days of the American takeover of the region, and when it came time to choose between the two parties trying to woo him, he chose the A.T.& S.F. Ry Co., "The Santa Fe," for short. I imagined all this historical turmoil as I drove down grade to Raton.

While I was in Hohnes, my father had written me and said that a family from La Cueva was living in Raton and because they were members of the same church as my parents, he asked that if I had the opportunity, to stop and visit with Mana Cleotildes. He also mentioned that the woman, two of her daughters and son Teddy had come to see the father interned at the Miners' Hospital. What my father had failed to tell me was that this

family was going through a crisis. The husband of Mana
Cleotildes had really been an outpatient at the hospital
and had readily found himself a younger woman there.
I knew Teddy well and I made it a point to look him
up that evening. It wasn't difficult to locate the family
and they were as happy to see me as I was to see them.
They were a decent, kind family who insisted I stay the
night. The mother, soon after I arrived, started telling me
the sad story of a family torn apart. It wasn't long before
the mother started crying, bemoaning the treason of the
husband and the ruin of her family. The two younger
daughters seemed extremely saddened by their mother's
disillusionment but Teddy soon broke what would have
become a wake by suggesting he and I drive downtown
to a movie.

Teddy and I drove to town from the little suburb of
El Salado (saltburg) where most of the city's poor lived.
He suggested we pick up a couple of girls that he had met
and even though I objected, we ended up picking up two
girls whose names were Rhonda and Freida. Teddy had
obviously chosen the girl he was going to pair off with and
I was left to deal with Freida, a girl with a terrible cold.
We drove around a while. My old haunts reminded me
of my previous visits there. I suggested we see a movie
and ended up at the Drive-in theater where my brother
and I had so often frequented. I did not see anyone that

I knew from my former visits. Tonight's movie was "Love Is A Many Splendored Thing." The theme hardly fit my situation tonight, but Teddy was soon ignoring the movie and concentrating on Rhonda, both on the back seat. I evaded the romantic scenes by inviting Freida to the concession stand where there were tables and chairs and where we could eat and talk. I spent the night at Teddy's and early the next day, I drove south on my way to the Rowe Train Depot.

Following The Rails South

In the semi dark of the morning I soon reached familiar ground. In the early dawn I could see the silhouetted mountains of La Tinaja. I passed an old abandoned railroad station named Shoenfeld and I thought of Arbicrombe, the old Norwegian who patrolled the track in an open rail cart, suffering the cold of the winter and the heat of the summer. I passed Maxwell as the sun was rising and I crossed myself in thanks for my successful experience and the wonderful people there who had made it possible. I passed another closed station named French Corners and went right through Springer, another place that my brother and I had often frequented. From here I simply counted off those places that I had seen time and again in train orders as meeting places for trains on their way to eastern cities and west to California. I reached Las Vegas, the Division Headquarters, with its roundhouse used for turning trains around for their return. Then there was the majestic Castaneda Hotel and roads leading east into the plains and west into the mountains.

I reached Rowe just before noon. It was a station on the top of the mountain. I had begun to climb immediately at Las Vegas, going from the flatlands on the fringes of the plains and on to the top of the mountain that divided the direction of the rivers on the eastern watershed and those flowing west on the western side of the mountain. The legendary Pecos River flowed south by south east from these mountains.

My arrival at Rowe, was expected by the station agent, whose name was, Lem Robinson. The man acknowledged my arrival with a nod and a comment about knowing Charlie Mitchum, my mentor at Maxwell. With his head down he told me that the young man, sitting at a desk and smiling broadly at me, would help me during my two-day break-in period. I wondered how anyone could be so bereft of common courtesies. *Perhaps it was the years of being an operator in lonely places like Watrous, where he had been working prior to his Rowe assignment,* I thought. The obvious thing about Rowe and the one thing that concerned me was that this station was an "Inter-locker." It was a train depot that had multiple tracks used for switching engines used in assisting long trains on the steep climb from the west and through Glorieta pass. The multiple tracks were controlled by switches that were operated from within the station. The problem for a novice like me was in learning to switch trains on or off designated tracks in a sequence. Unless the sequence required was followed, an operator could disable the switches and create delays and confusion on the part of the conductors and engineers of the trains waiting on the main track.

The agent quickly moved to instruct me on the use of the interlocking levers and the signals that were triggered upon a successful interlock. He said that Hernan Gallegos, whom he introduced to me perfunctorily, would help me when we used the interlocks. Hernan was immediately up off his chair. He shook my hand and laughingly winked his eye.

"I'm Hernan or 'Nan,' as everybody calls me. I can help you with the interlocks, but the telegraphing, I'll leave it all to you."

I was relieved by Hernan's self-confidence and offer to help. After a few minutes of my arrival, he and I were driving into the town to have lunch. In the town of Pecos, we went into a restaurant/drive-in called, "The Panther's Lair." Here, Hernan was immediately approached by all those there, mostly teenagers. He seemed to command a respect and admiration, almost to the point of celebrity. Before I had a chance to ask him about his fan club, a beautiful, tall brunette walked in and immediately walked toward Hernan. He stood up immediately and with a beaming, almost idiotic look, he hugged the girl and kissed her. She immediately sat down with Hernan and said,

"Hi baby, I've missed you all morning."

"I've missed you even more, my pumpkin." Then, turning to me he said,

"Gibo, this is my girlfriend, Mimsey. Baby, this is Gibo Herrera, the new operator at the depot."

"Glad to meet you Gibo," she said. By then a young waiter came and asked us if we wanted to eat. Each of us ordered hamburgers, with Hernan suggesting I try the mushroom burgers.

"They're something else," he said. "These mushrooms are picked by hippies in the fall and sold to the drive-in for use in their hamburgers. Sometimes a few leaves of pot are thrown in with the mushrooms."

He was laughing an infectious laugh and all those watching us, laughed with him, even those that didn't know what he'd said.

"No, don't believe this guy, Gibo, he is always joking," said his girlfriend. We ate and made small talk. Mimsey wanted to know if I had a girlfriend.

"Cause if you don't," she said, "I have a friend who would love to meet you." I told her that I was practically engaged to this girl back home and so the conversation drifted to other topics. Hernan continued to joke and laugh and soon there were more people trying to cluster around him. Mimsey didn't seem to mind, obviously she was used to this scene. We left the diner with Hernan and Mimsey hand in hand and they kissed profusely, each whispering to the other that they would see each other after work. Hernan and I got into my car and he asked me If I had gotten a room. When I said that I hadn't, he drove to the Deer Lodge and said, "This, Gibo, my man, is the only game in town." I went in, asked for a room and despite not seeing any part of the motel, rented for one week. We headed back to the depot.

"Hey, 'Nan, what's with all the popularity? Looks like you're some kind of a star."

"Well, Gibo, I'm the lead singer in a band called the Railroad Conductors and these people think that I'm maybe as good as Elvis." Then he cracked up laughing. "Na," he then said. "Remember how, when we were growing up, how we nailed a bucket to a backboard and shot any kind of ball through the bucket and pretended we were playing basketball? Well, I did that, then I played on outside courts and then the gym, I have always loved basketball, then I must have got good at it."

"You mean you're a good basketball player and these people admire you for it?"

"I guess so," he said, as we arrived at the depot.

Two very fortuitous coincidences happened for me on

my coming to Rowe. One was that Hernan Gallegos, a part-time clerk was working at that depot and had learned the most intricate workings of the Interlock system and two, he was a man with a plan. He was scheduled to enroll in the University, or College in Santa Fe that fall. I felt that 'Nan and I had hit it off the moment that we had met. As we worked together, he took over anytime we needed to usher trains into the intricate system of tracks and I was in charge of taking train orders over the wire and delivering them to the board where the trainmen would grab and take them.

We had some long conversations about a variety of topics. I told him about Belica and he told me about Mimsey. He said, at one time, "I love this girl Gibo, I've been encouraged by Clem to go to telegraphy school and learn to be an Operator but I'm not stupid, I don't want to lose my girl so I'm not leaving Pecos."

By this time I had also learned that Hernan Gallegos, a five-foot eleven inch student at Pecos H.S. had taken his basketball team to the state tournaments where the team, *The Pecos Panthers*, had won first place in their division for two years running. I learned that he was high-point man and Captain of the team. Now I knew why all the adulation. I learned too, as I mingled among 'Nan's friends at lunch, that just as I had thought that he was my new "best friend," others, also thought, that he was their best friend. I figured that with his charm, constant laughter and command of basketball, 'Nan Gallegos, was everybody's best friend.

One day when we were working at the depot, a car drove up with two people in it. One was 'Nan's girlfriend, whose full name was Mimsey Redding. When I first saw her I'd taken her to be a Hispanic girl. The other person in the car was Mrs. Elsa Torres Redding, her mother. I was introduced to the mother and 'Nan and Mimsey started to kiss in front of the mother. I thought back to my relation with Belica, and knew that she would have never allowed for these public demonstrations. The mother was an Hispanic woman married to a Mr. Redding, obviously, an Anglo American. I thought later, as I traveled beyond the confines of my mountain village, that the Santa Fe Trail had not only brought trade goods to New Mexico but strangers' interactions, marriages, racial mix and as a result, the new citizens of this region. I remembered the Mitchells and the Olmsteads in Maxwell, the Rimberts, the Legers and the Cassidys in Las Vegas and in my own family the Lefevres. These names now belonged to Hispanics, obviously from a racial mix, if not intermarriage.

The second good happenstance for me in meeting up with 'Nan Gallegos; the gregarious athlete, railroad clerk and all-around good guy, was that somehow he inspired me. He said that he'd received a full athletic scholarship to attend St. Michael's College in Santa Fe and that on Monday, one of our days off, that he would be traveling to the college. He invited me to join him, and I did.

We traveled to Santa Fe and when we arrived at the college we were welcomed by the Dean, a Christian Brother, who formed part of the faculty and administration of St. Michael's. Hernan was recognized on sight. He was welcomed profusely by those we met, obviously, 'Nan had star recognition. I was warmly welcomed, principally because I was with him. The Dean picked up the phone and announced to us that 'Nan's future coach wanted some words with him and that later he was to return to the business office to sign some papers. The Dean then offered to have me toured through the campus. "Perhaps we can interest you to join us at St. Michael's," he said. I was given a tour by a young Christian Brother, who was rather reserved, but who showed off all the important features of the college while down playing those weaker aspects of the small all-male Catholic college.

He spoke of their academic program, their commitment to learning, the Christian Brothers' teaching tradition of excellence and their library. He pointed out the large Spanish language library and even the college's humble but, as I perceived, serene chapel. He did not talk too much about the on-campus housing. He did admit that the college was a former army hospital and the living quarters were the humble barracks of the army personnel working at the hospital. When Hernan returned a couple of hours later I thanked the Dean and my tour guide and said that I was impressed with the college. Actually, this was the only college that I had ever visited. And it was here, that I began to formulate my possible future upon leaving the railroad. Hernan and I returned to Pecos and he was anxious to return to see the love of his life, Mimsey Torres Redding.

The following week, I drove home, about one hundred and forty five miles away, with my intentions of getting together with my love, Belica Artiaga. *Mimsey is a beautiful girl,* I thought, *but does not hold a candle to the woman that I have chosen to love, every bit as much as 'Nan has chosen his Mimsey."*

I arrived at Belica's home about eight o'clock on Saturday night and found her doing her chores in the kitchen. I was welcomed at the porch but, unlike Mimsey and Hernan, no kisses were exchanged. Her father, who had become accustomed to seeing me around, now shook my hand and asked me to join him in the living room while Belica got ready to come with me. Her father was a serious man, but he was talkative. He told me that he had to work away from home a lot and that he didn't recommend that for any man with a family. He said he wished that more jobs were available closer to home. He talked to me about the time that Belica and his sons were still small, when he had worked in the shipyards in California.

"Having your family with you is the best time of any man's life but you do what you have to do," he said. Then, he surprised me with, "I guess you know that, with your work in the railroad and all that. Belica tells me that you are a telegrapher with the railroad."

At this point in our conversation, Belica came into the living room, looking like I had always seen her on my mind's eye, beautiful and lovingly attractive. She had on a long flowing skirt and a light full arms sweater. She told her parents she would be back by eleven that night

"Because, Gibo and I may go dancing down at Sirilio's."

"You kids take care," said her father. Her mother had already disappeared into the dining room.

"Hey, Babe, I'm not ready to go dancing, I'm not dressed for it."

"Don't worry, it's just a neighborhood dance and my brother Sonny will be playing tonight."

I knew then that I had been out of touch. First, I didn't know that her teenage brother Sonny even played any musical instrument, and second, I'd never been to a dance at Sirilio's, a small dance hall next to a bar by that name.

"Ok, but isn't it a bit early for a dance?"

"Take me to La Villa and buy me a coke, that way we'll make time before we get back to the dance." She said.

We did that and returned when the dance was in full swing. As we entered the dance hall everyone seemed to look at us. Belica hung on to my arm and two minutes after we entered the hall, she had pulled me back onto the dance floor. Her brother Sonny played sax and he sounded pretty good to me. The band was made up of all teenagers and they were doing pretty well. I loved to dance with Belica because she seemed so happy when we danced. She held my hand tight and pulled slightly on my waist when we went out on the floor. At about an hour or so into the dance, I told her I wanted to rest a bit and as we sat and watched the crowd of kids dance, one of the high school boys, whom I knew, headed our way and asked Belica if she wanted to dance. She looked at me and at that moment I stood up and pulled her gently towards the dance floor, leaving the would-be dancer standing, looking embarrassed.

"That wasn't very nice," she said to me, looking as if she was pouting.

"Let him bring his own lunch, Or is he like those people that go to a picnic and all they bring is the ants?"

I was trying to be gentle but I was seething with anger. I never told her how I felt, but I think she could see it on my face.

"He's just Randy. He my brother Sonny's age."

"Not when I'm around," I simply said and no one else tried to invite her to dance that night. Belica was a good dancer, well she was a lot better dancer than she had been when we danced that first time. I knew she loved to dance and I had no doubt that she was getting plenty of practice. I asked sometime during the dance that night,

"So, who do you dance with when you come to the dances by yourself, or do you come here with someone?" She looked surprised at my question and quickly said,

"Oh, I dance mostly with my cousin Teddy, you know him, he is my Uncle Mel's son. I also dance with some of the guys from school," she continued. "You're not jealous, are you?" she asked. I didn't answer her question and we were rather silent as I drove her home.

"Oh, she said, I forgot to tell you that my two little cousins and I are going to California to visit for a couple of weeks."

"When are you going there?"

"We're leaving next Wednesday. We're taking the train at Lamy. My Uncle George, Yewela's father, is taking us there. Remember Yewela?"

"Yah," but by this time, I was beginning to feel the

panic of the unknown when it came to her.

"Belica, I'm a damn fool. I'm sorry I've acted so childish but you have to know that I love you and sometimes I feel that I'm going crazy, not being with you." I then told her about Hernan and his girlfriend, Mimsey.

"I wish I could always be with you, like Hernan and his girl, but you know that I can't."

She reached out to me and kissed me hard and said, "You're silly, I know you love me, and we will be together one of these days soon."

We were together Sunday and again on Monday until about five o'clock that last day. I was happy to be with her but I was counting the days when she would return. We walked down the big river, later we took in a movie and we played music and ate hamburgers at The Pig Stand. Sometimes we would return to her house and sit and talk on a back porch which wasn't used much but was next to their living room. She had a radio in the living room and she would often break out in a dance by herself. She'd often say when I wanted to join her.

"I don't want my mother to find us dancing, but I'll dance for you."

I loved this girl, and to watch her dance did a number on me. I wanted to hold her but I knew that her mother was very conservative and would not approve of us dancing there at their home. When she danced by herself I'd often dance too, mimicking her dance steps but dancing a good five or six feet away.

"I feel that I'm dancing with you," she would say "but we can't dance together here."

Before I left that Monday evening I told her that I would be moving on to another station, that my assignment at Rowe would be over at the end of the following week. I asked her if she knew what train they were taking. She said that it was called, El Capitan.

"First class train," I said. "I'll be looking as El Cap passes by our station on Wednesday, knowing that it will be taking my baby away on a long trip."

She laughed, "I'm excited about the trip," she said "but I know that I will miss you too."

We parted and I returned to Pecos that evening, thinking of Belica and thinking to myself, *Every song that has been written has been about my love for Belica.*

Wednesday came and by the end of that week I had received my instructions to report to Bernalillo, near Albuquerque on the following Monday.

East and West,
The Directions For A Train

My itinerant work assignments, from Hohnes and Rowe to Bernalillo and to the twenty-two others that would follow were essentially duplicates of each other. The work stations differed only slightly and even the men working these stations were of a singular mind set. It was only in consciously seeking out the "other persons" inside those railroad workers which I met, that I could glean that these men actually had other lives.

At Bernalillo, I worked with three men who had chosen to be there, within the rigors of the seniority system. Their respective roles were determined by their commitment to company rules, to company whims and to the ever-present demands of routine. These, were company men. They and I, as their temporary relief worker, filled a specific niche in a large company's operation in the running of trains: passengers, freights, maintenance, service and the occasional, covert carriers. Two directions determined the flow of traffic on these trains, east bound or west bound. My own destiny started me heading west and as any road that ends, must simply turn, only to return on the opposite direction. So flowed the clanking iron wheels of my train.

Beyond the station at Bernalillo and the work-flow of that place I encountered very little that "filled me." Perhaps because the town was so close to a large urban center or perhaps because changes were coming so fast that people did not relate as I had expected. During the time that I was there, approximately a month, I saw faces that in my memory I simply see as blank. One aspect of this old Hispanic community, associated for so long with the Tewa Indian Pueblos of that region, were some unusual religious practices. Unlike the Penitente Brotherhood, from my hometown of Embargo and La Cueva, Bernalillo had a religious fraternity called "Los Matachines." This group of lay and religious adherents performed religious dances in masks that were reminiscent of Indo-Mexican pagan religions. The masks on these dancers were those of animal fetishes with headdresses that exhibited tassels and facets on masks with inlaid mirrors. I found out, soon after I first witnessed these dance rituals, that many of the town's noted citizens were prominent members of the Matachines. These two in-group features of the Bernalillo experience was all that I can remember: faceless citizens and pagan dancers.

Later that summer I was assigned to a train depot some thirty miles east (train east) called Domingo. It was located some five miles from the Kerisan Indian Pueblo, Santo Domingo and three miles from Peña Blanca, another old Hispanic village ; who, like so many others were former satellites to an Indian village or pueblo. My assignment to the Domingo station was for two weeks only and essentially to protect the operator's job, while he was out on sick leave. The man's name was Frank Lucero, originally from Trinidad, but for the last twenty-five years had been spent serving at the whims of the job, wherever it took him.

I met Frank soon after leaving Bernalillo. The first impression I got of him was that he was sickly and second, that he was a company man. Frank was kind and humble and an able person at his job but one who had sacrificed his family, now all grown up and accustomed to living without him. He told me that he was thankful that I could be there while he went back to Trinidad for much-needed medical attention. Frank seemed to worry about everything. He went over tasks with me that were required at the station but, which I felt he had personalized and focused on unnecessarily:

"On Mondays and Fridays, you drive to the Rosario

Gypsum Mill, pick up the company's bills of lading for cargo. Get these bills ready for the conductors of the trains that pick up the box cars with wall board located at the spur that goes there," he said in a worried tone.

"I'll take care of it Frank," I said, "If you remember something else, just write it down and I'll take care of it." I felt that this man was overdue at the doctor's office and he was overdue in *feeling the love* of his family again if he was to survive another summer in these lonely, desert and juniper days.

During my short stay at this isolated railroad depot, I had a chance to visit a unique place at this little village called Peña Blanca (white rock). It was the Catholic Church there. The story I heard about this unique church was that a former priest there, a Father Chavez, who was also an artist of sorts, had painted two giant murals on the inside walls of the church, depicting the stations of the cross. The interesting feature about these murals, was that the biblical personages in the paintings: the Christ, the Roman soldiers, the crowds of people along the road to Calvary, were depicted with the faces of the citizens of Peña Blanca. I'd heard that this had initially been controversial, after all no one wanted to be the Roman soldier with the whip, nor the Pharisee who placed the crown of thorns on the Christ, nor even a witness to this biblical shame and the question that this prompted: "Who really crucified Christ?" It appears that Fray Chavez, had answered that question.

I left Domingo on one of Frank's days off and I never got a chance to see him again. I went west to another temporary assignment and I'm not sure whether Frank survived his illnesses of the body and the heart. I knew however, that if Frank Lucero was well enough that he would return to his post at the expense of his own life and the need for his family. He would, I knew, because Frank, was a company man.

From Domingo I went to Abajo Yards, the network of Interlocks on the south Albuquerque tracks. It was thanks to my friend Hernan Gallegos, who had taught me the essentials of Interlocks that I survived the Interlocking tracks of Abajo Yards. I was there until a permanent replacement would take over the job vacated by a fellow La Villa County citizen, Robert Acoque. Robert had been recruited into the Korean conflict. I remained there a short three weeks because this position was one of those coveted jobs on the railroad and soon a suitor showed up to claim the prize.

Summer was soon history, Belica returned from California and again got back to school. I moved farther "west" and was assigned to Socorro at a stifling 97 degrees in late summer. From there I worked at Rincon (the corner), located about thirty miles east of Las Cruces.

This place was the epitome of the living desert: with coyotes, quail, owls and wild bands of dogs filling the moon-lit nights with their noisy yelps, hoots and chatter. I worked this corner of the world during the midnight to morning shift, otherwise known as "grave yard" shift. Rincon was at the junction of the railroad to El Paso and west to the Coast Lines Division of the A.T.& S.F. Railway Company.

Fall came and winter threatened, but in this southern climate winter was mild, unlike the deep freeze of Embargo and the mountains of the north.

The Las Cruces depot was my final assignment of the year and unwittingly, my last assignment before a total change of direction and railroad territory. While in Las Cruces I performed the usual telegraph operator's routine. I ushered and reported the train traffic coming through on either direction. We sent and received Western Union telegrams, processed freight assignments and even sold passenger traffic tickets. We also handled the heavy job of loading and unloading mail for the town and the University Station. Just before Christmas there was a lot of mail including all types of packages, and the work was not easy. I remained there until the twenty-third of December with three days scheduled as free days. I had planned to return to the north and be with my family and girlfriend for Christmas.

On the night of the twenty-second, I noticed a tall man come in and proceed into the office, which was off limits to the general public. I was told that he was the station agent at Mesquite, the next depot on the road to El Paso. The man did not acknowledge me but I caught him a time or two looking my way. He took the liberty to get on the company telephone and several times, obviously not having completed his call, returned to call on that phone. Just before ten o'clock that night he left smiling and said good-bye to the other operators there. Twenty minutes after he left I got a telegram from my dispatcher ordering me to protect the Mesquite depot for the following three days. This opportunistic agent had found out that I was free during the following three days and he chose to take his own vacation then. That was the end of my own plans. I returned to Las Cruces three days later only to find another work order, this time to an assignment, that for me, was a world away.

Go East Young Man

On a cold night in January I found myself disembarking on a long brick platform a little after midnight in Stafford, Kansas. The order to go there read:

"G. Herrera, Please report to the Stafford Kansas depot and protect the position of Operator, swing shift, starting January 7th and remain until further notice."

/s/ E. J. Barnes

The train had dropped me off on the far end of the platform and I could see a bright light illuminating the depot some yards away. It was mid winter and the night was cold but not over-powering. I saw an operator working feverishly helping a trainman pull a huge rectangular wooden box from the mail car located toward the front of the train. Before I reached the depot I determined that it was "remains," or an outer box for a coffin. *Someone was coming home*, I thought. The operator turned my way and unperturbed by the task of helping unload "remains," as bodies were called, turned to where I was approaching, and almost apologetically said, "Hello there, you're the new operator. Go into the depot and warm up. I'll see you in a couple of minutes." He then started to pull a platform wagon, with the remains on it and wheeled it into the baggage room. Jacob Abernathy, the swing shift operator introduced himself and welcomed me to Stafford as if I had been some long awaited celebrity.

"I'll be finished here in a few minutes, the new guy is a bit late, but once he gets here I'll drive you to the hotel."

Jacob was a friendly guy and quickly set me at ease. He said that he had called for some relief time some months ago, and "thanks to you," he said, "I'll finally get a chance to go home and visit my ailing mother."

Jacob drove me to the Stafford Hotel. He knocked on a window and an old man with his hair disheveled, emerged from a back room. Jacob said, "I'll see you tomorrow, around noon, I want to show you as much as you need to know to take over my job. The café at the end of the street is the best one for breakfast, see you tomorrow."

I entered the lobby of the Hotel, the old man sleepily handed me a key and said, "You're upstairs, room 250, you can register in the morning." The musty smell of hotels in general, greeted my nostrils but I knew that if the rooms were clean that this smell would probably go away in due time. When I walked into my room, close to 1:30 a.m., I was too tired to care how it looked. I opened up the steam heat valve completely and before long I was drifting into the warm grasp of sleep.

The Stafford depot was located on the main line of the Santa Fe, extending from Chicago to Los Angeles. All the traffic that I had experienced in the stations in the New Mexico Division also came through Stafford. Trains like El Capitan, Number 21 going west became Number 22 going east; the Grand Canyon, Number 123 going west became 124 going east. The rules of traffic were the same: east bound trains took precedence over trains going west, meaning that west bound trains took the siding while the eastbound trains remained on the main line. The El Cap' was a first class train and it always had precedence over second class trains like The Grand Canyon, which I had ridden into Stafford from Las Vegas New Mexico. Stafford, like all A.T.S.F. stations relied on semaphore "boards" or huge metal arms with a light in the center of a long metal post to signal an approaching train. The boards were manually operated from inside the operator's office and were tripped down from its 180 degree position to give the train a green light to indicate "No Train Orders." The boards remained on a horizontal position and the light on "red" to indicate, "Pick up Train

Order." Or do not proceed farther than the station, if you don't pick up a train order.

I met Jacob around eleven o'clock on the following day and he asked me if I'd had my breakfast.

"Only the best pancakes, ever," I said and we went directly into the idiosyncratic demands of the Stafford Depot. I remained with Jacob until two o'clock and I saw him sign in, and take over from the day-time operator. Jacob was a joy to watch. He made every task seem fun. When the wire seemed to be frantically calling for SF, SF, the Stafford call sign, he would deliberately, but without any kind of panic, sit down on his chair and calmly answer, "I, SF." Immediately the message would follow. It often went, "SF, cy 4," meaning Stafford, make four copies of a train order." Jacob quietly inserted four onionskin paper sheets layered by carbon paper and started to take the message:

"To: C&E, No. 123 period.
Meet train number 22 at Kinsely.
At 4:56 p.m. No 123 take no 2 siding
At Kinsely period.
/s/ J.B.Cooper."

Jacob quickly repeated the train order verbatim on the wire and when given the GA, "go ahead" instructions by the dispatcher, he methodically took out the typed orders, folded three separate papers and hung them on pre-tied strings on a hoop. He then walked out to the platform and climbing up the steel ladder, he hung a copy of each train order at a level where the engineer, conductor and brakeman would each grab their orders with slightly crooked outstretched arms. A minute later a bell would ring, indicating that train number 123, heading west was on the "block" or station's approach approximately three miles and three minutes out. I had dispatched many trains in many stations, and I had seen old agents perform the tasks that I saw Jacob complete, but I had never seen anyone dance his way through a complex and delicate set of tasks.

I "broke in" at the Stafford station for a couple of days before Jacob took off in his 1956 Ford Crown-Victoria. He waved with an almost, "So long suckers," attitude, but I knew that he was going home and that anything would justify his "freedom Adios."

I took over my two-to-eleven o'clock assignment immediately after my break-in period and I actually enjoyed working with the people there. I saw a number of college students come and go by train to the university at Manhattan, Kansas. I often got a twinge of wishful thinking when I spoke with some of them, especially when their response to my question.

"How do you like going to college?"

"There is nothing like it. All the chicks in the world. Party!" and the often,

"The only game in town, if you want to be anybody in this world."

After having visited St. Michael's College in Santa Fe and seeing these kids from Kansas State at Manhattan, I was more and more leaning to a possible future as a student at some university.

During my coverage of Jacob's job assignment, I got to meet many of his friends. There was Bernard Shilling and there was Amanda McConkle. Bernard came to visit the very day that Jacob was leaving. He was a tall lanky young man of about twenty years of age. He did not have a job and didn't seem to mind. I invited him out to lunch one day and again several times later. I always paid, and I guessed that perhaps Jacob had been doing this for a while too. He had an old Chevy Pickup and he drove me all around the area. I often offered to gas up the Chevy and we went "joy riding," as he called it. One day, as we approached a vacant wheat field, he brought the pickup to a screeching halt. He groped under the seat and pulled out a 22 cal. rifle. Without saying anything he set himself up on the hood of the pickup, took aim and fired. He let out a wild yell and signaled for me to follow. Bernie (he said that his friends called him that) had expertly shot a beautiful multi-colored Chinese pheasant. I followed him a ways and met him as he retrieved his prey.

"You want it?"

"I have no place to cook him. I'm at the hotel, remember?" He laughed a wild laugh.

"I just hope there's no dad-burn game wardens out today." And we headed into town. Bernie drove to a house trailer where he said that his uncle Jimmy lived. When we got there, they received us both, rather coldly.

"What you want, Bernard Shillings?" his uncle asked.

In spite of the cold reception, I couldn't help but think back to the time that I was growing up when Margie would yell, "Buddy Gatlin, you get in here this minute." And I thought, *Why do they use the first and last name of the person they're talking to?*

Bernie was not fazed by his uncle's question.

"Hey, I got me a pheasant, you want it?"

"No way! You got that there bird off season, and I don't need any trouble with that dad-burn game warden."

"Ah, Jimmy, Ain't nobody gonna find you with this stupid bird, ask aunt Francis if she want it." Before his uncle could answer, a lady walked out of the trailer smoking a big cigarette.

"What's the trouble young Bernie?"

"I just want to give you guys a pheasant for supper."

"Hey, we'll take it, won't we Jimmy?"

I turned on the radio of the pickup to avoid the conversation. Bernie took the dead bird from the bed of the truck, handed it to Jimmy and before I could wave good-by we were spinning out of the driveway. It was incidents like these that made me uneasy with Bernie's behavior. Soon, and little by little I started making excuses for not going "joy riding" with Bernie Shilling.

Another one of Jacob's friends was a young girl who introduced herself as Amanda McConkle. She was a pretty girl and very personable. She started to visit the depot during my shift. She hung around rather late and often offered to drive me to the hotel. I was thankful for her conversations and enjoyed the obvious attention she was paying me. She hinted that she'd had a bad experience with her ex-boyfriend and all she wanted now was to forget this bad relationship. During the times she drove me to my hotel, she would often stop the motor of the car and offered to talk. Her conversations started to become more intimate as our meetings progressed. I told her about my girlfriend back home and explained to her that I really just wanted to be, like Jacob, her friend. She persisted, and now she was visiting me daily. I was beginning to feel pressured and one day the day-operator, a fellow by the name of Ralph Woody asked:

"Hey, Herrera, you married?"

"Nah," I answered.

"Well," he continued, "Amanda McConkle is a married woman. Her husband is serving time at Leavenworth."

"Gee, that's a kick in the pants. I never knew that. But I'll tell you Ralph, Mrs. McConkle isn't going to come calling here anymore." *Hell, that's all I need* I thought to myself. *Why do I attract these 'troubled souls?*

That night when Amanda McConkle came to visit I firmly told her that what she was doing would get me and herself in a lot of trouble and that I didn't want her friendship anymore.

"Who told you I's married, that Ralph Woody?" and simply walked out of the station never to be seen by me again. I felt like a heel, but that night I went back to that question I'd asked myself, *Why do I attract these 'troubled souls?* I quickly realized that it was because I was one of them.

Jacob came back from his vacation, refreshed and ready for another year of whatever the job threw at him. Meanwhile, Ralph Woody had already argued his case for time off, saying that Herrera had done a good job during the second shift and didn't know why he couldn't continue a three-week time off for him, doing the day shift. He was granted his leave request and I got committed to three more weeks in Stafford. I was content enough working there, having become acquainted with the office, the traffic, the personnel and even the visitors. Something was to happen during that last week there that brought Ralph back a week early and would send me off into the wide open spaces of central Kansas, it was a tremendous snow storm in early February. It was, what the guys at the office called, a "doozy."

The snow started one afternoon and three days later it was still snowing. I had never seen so much snow fall at one time. The effects of the regional storm were soon beginning to be felt. On the western border of Kansas, all trains were snowbound and could not move in either direction. Train traffic was halted in the entire area from Topeka to the Colorado border. The most serious effect of the storm was that power lines, telephone and telegraph lines were all down. Dispatchers had to rely on help from short wave radio operators in order to know what was going on at both ends of the train traffic holdups and to initiate the movement of those stranded trains. This was the third day of a complete stoppage. At Stafford, where we had local company telephone service, all furloughs were cancelled and Ralph Woody's vacation was cut short. I, on the other hand, received orders to vacate my assignment and was reassigned to a railroad depot away from the main lines and northwest to a town I couldn't even locate on the road map.

The station was in Nekoma, Kansas, approximately one hundred miles west of Great Bend, KS. My orders were to open that station and assist in the receiving and delivering of "freight" destined for the telephone and electric companies in that area. Our own maintenance department would also be included on those recipient lists, I later found out.

A couple of days after receiving my orders and after Ralph Woody's return, I boarded a train west to Kinsely on the main line and was scheduled to board another one there, north to Great Bend and yet another west from there to Rush Center and Nekoma. I took my suitcase and the clothes on my back and started this unexpected journey at eight in the morning. The trip to Kinsley was short, less than fifty miles from Stafford. I had a one and a half hour wait at Kinsely and then about eleven o'clock I was on my way toward Great Bend, the great bend on the Arkansas River. I reflected on what I knew about this river and I was anticipating meeting an old friend here in the middle of Kansas.

The Arkansas is, after a fashion, a home river. It is born in the bosom of the Rocky Mountains in Colorado from seeps and rivulets just south of Leadville. It drains off the Aspen and Vale watersheds. Just after leaving Leadville, the Arkansas grows quickly. It drops fast as it loses altitude, crosses the town of Buena Vista, where the majority of the population of people can only see the flowing river from behind storm fences and barbed wire, for here is located the Buena Vista State Penitentiary. The river rushes downhill through Salida, takes an acute turn east and heads into and through a gorge, called the Royal Gorge. The river heads east, past Fountain and when it reaches the western fringes of the plains in Pueblo it is already a formidable river. It is here, with its respectable steel-girded bridges that the Arkansas gets the first infusion of industrial waste into its pristine waters; it is the poisoned waters and smoke from the steel mills that give the city the dubious title of "The Pittsburgh of The West."

The Arkansas continues its long journey east and fills the aquifers of the farming communities of Fowler, Rocky Ford and La Junta, where luscious watermelons and cantaloupe are grown. The river then runs towards the Kansas border on its way to the Mississippi. Today, I anticipated meeting my old friend again.

I traveled northeast in whiteness. We passed the town of Larned and I suddenly remembered a young man that I had met in Pueblo, at telegraphy school. His name was Joel Garcia. He was a mild mannered guy, whose voice was soft and his demeanor was almost servile. When my roommates and I visited his apartment we noticed a large picture of a beautiful girl. Joel said it was a picture of his girlfriend. Written on the corner of the picture was, "To Joel, With Love and Kisses" It was signed "Ramona." The boys with me started teasing Joel and suggested that while he was at school in Pueblo that the football players back home would take his girl away. I had thought of my own situation and did not participate in the teasing. As the weeks wore on at school my friends continued to tease Joel and one day, without explanation or without saying good-bye, Joel left school and returned home. I thought of Joel as I rode on the train through his hometown and wondered what had really happened.

Had he come back to his girl and married her? Had the football players beat him to her? Stupid speculation, I thought and vowed to look Joel up if I ever came back out here.

I arrived at Great Bend about one o'clock that day and was welcomed by the station agent whose name was Craig Mathias. He invited me to lunch after he cleared the train that would continue on to points east. We got into a 1941 Chevrolet sedan with a "For Sale" sign on it. We ate lunch and I asked him about the price that he was asking for his car. He said he wanted two hundred dollars. I offered to take it off his hands for one hundred and fifty dollars. Before our lunch was over we had made a deal. I did not have that kind of money with me, but I told him that I would call my bank in La Villa and see if they could wire me the money. Agent Mathias was a shrewd operator and he said that he would wait but meanwhile, he could take me to the local hotel since no trains would be heading west to Nekoma on that day. He said that he would not relinquish the car until he got paid.

I asked him about the Arkansas.

"There is no river this time of the year, it's frozen over, and this year, especially, and it is also covered with snow."

I was put off for the moment but vowed to return to see the mighty river some other time. I knew however, that the Arkansas was still flowing under the ice, undeterred on its way to its final destination.

Next day, around noon, Agent Mathias received a telegram authorizing one hundred and fifty dollar be given to me. I signed over my moneygram to C. Mathias, he gave me a title to the 1941 black Chevy and I was ready to head west to Rush County and Nekoma.

By the time that I made ready to drive west, I learned that the storm had devastated the region on the west-central part of Kansas. The reports that C. Mathias had shared with me included downed telephone poles in a radius of fifty miles, wires strewn throughout the company's right-of-way and people without power and telephones. C. Mathias also told me that my job would be at a recently-closed depot and that I would have the "honor" of reopening it to receive the tons of poles, electric transformers and other equipment. With that information in mind, I stopped at a large grocery store, bought a few cans of food, a sauce pan and a water jug. I was on my way.

I left the relatively well cleared streets of Great Bend and immediately entered a snow-packed two-lane highway. The snow had been blown by removal equipment to either side, creating a huge tunnel that was higher than my car. It was eerie driving without being able to see anything on either side for miles. I traveled about twenty miles when I began to see some of the devastation of the late winter storm. There were huge poles that were broken in half, some hanging from the stump in the ground. Wire was hanging like spaghetti from the cross arms of the poles and the whole scene looked as if a giant hand had simply slapped the row of poles, all falling in one direction. *What a mess,* I thought, *and what's it going to take to rebuild it?*

I had learned from Mathias that these freaks of nature caused ice storms in addition to the snow. He said that thick ice forms around the wires and the weight of this ice just pulls down the wires, breaks the poles and lays waste to power and communication lines, including our telegraph lines.

At points, along the way, I could see beyond the tunneled snow but there wasn't much to see except a snow that was higher than the fences and except for the tree breaks that would interrupt the view, I saw snow as far as my squinting eyes could see.

In The Middle of ......Somewhere

I reached Rush Center about one o'clock that afternoon. It was a small town on a crossroads: To the west were Nekoma, Ness and Scott City, south to Jet and north to La Crosse and Libenthal and of course, east to Timken and Great Bend. The snow here, as in the rest of Kansas covered everything. There were two views of the world here, snow and the sky. Heavy growth of trees on the south end of town hinted at a creek, now most likely covered by snow. The most prominent buildings in these parts were wheat silos. The road from Great Bend to Rush Center followed the train tracks, and the devastation of poles.

Upon reaching the town, I looked for the train depot in order to get my bearings and to find out where I could locate the keys to the Nekoma depot, a short seven miles away. When I walked into the station I noticed that the telegraph key was silent and that the office was dark. A middle-aged, serious-looking man rose up to greet me from his desk by the signal board lever. He rose and introduced himself as Archibald Archer. I introduced myself and when I offered the information about me being the replacement operator at Nekoma he stopped me.

"I know. We got the news on the wire just before it went silent." I assessed the situation there and my thoughts wandered, as they had often done in church, to something irrelevant to the setting. I wondered why any parent would want to name his kid, *Archibald. With a name like that*, I thought, *The kid will never grow up. Imagine the ribbing at school.* I was brought back to the present when he offered to answer any question that I might have about my new assignment. He said that the keys to the depot were being held my Mrs. Miller, the postmaster at Nekoma. I asked Archibald about any motels in Nekoma. He smiled.

"There are none in Nekoma, and even if there were, nobody has electricity. Your best bet is to go north to La Crosse. They still have electricity there."

Archibald informed me that the previous operator at Nekoma, an Eddy Jones, had roomed at the Oetkens. He suggested that maybe I could do the same. I left wondering if a more appropriate name for Archibald should have been, perhaps, Malachi or Zacarias or such names as I'd seen in the Gideon Bible that I had "borrowed" from one of the many hotels that I'd frequented. *A person's name should match his personality*, I thought.

I left the Rush Center depot and took the short ride to Nekoma, only to find a truly rural place there. There was a store which doubled as the post office, one grain silo, several homes scattered in small ranches and, I learned later, an old-folks nursing home. There was one large building near the post office, with a sign: "Bank of Nekoma, J.J. Morgan, President."

I went to the post office and introduced myself and picked up the keys to the lonely depot. The postmaster was a friendly, good looking, middle-aged gray-haired woman who commented on how young she thought I was, "To be a telegraph operator," she'd said. I left and drove to the depot and went inside. It was a vacant depot, with no telephones or telegraph key.

This is a depot that has been closed down I told myself, *And I hope that it will be closed again soon so that I can go on home or at least to a working station.*

I left to La Crosse to find a motel and promised myself to return early the following day.

I found a nice, clean and comfortable room at the "Prairies Motel" in La Crosse and paid for one week's stay. I went to Nekoma the next morning and made it a point to meet the Oetkens, the family who had provided room and board for Ed Jones. When I drove up, an old man, tall but bent at the waist, was trying to shovel snow off some path leading away from the house. When he saw me he yelled, "Martha, John," and directly, a heavy set woman with glasses came out of house through a wire screened porch to greet me.

"Howdy there, are you the new operator at our depot?" she asked.

"Yes, I'm Gibo Herrera,

I hope to be working here with you folks a while."

"Well, I'm Martha Oetkens, that's Bill and in a bit, you'll meet John, our boy." Bill gave me a broad smile, I noticed that he had but one tooth but I could tell that he was a friendly man. Martha asked me to step inside and began to tell me the story of the depot, the former operator there and the fact that she didn't know why the depot had been closed and reopened again. She complained about the storm and said, almost as if she'd known me all her life:

"You know Gibo, this storm has been one hell of a mess. No electric, no phones and worst, no TV. What you think 'bout that? You had breakfast yet? You know that Eddie Jones, he used to board with us until he took up with that woman in Rush."

Just then a tall forty-some year old man walked in.

"John, this here is Gibo, what did you say your last name was?"

"I'm Gibo Herrera," and shook the man's hand. John Oetkens took off his baseball hat.

"Glad to know you Gibo."

This family and I took to each other almost instantly. We talked about a lot of things.

"What nationality are you Gibo, We're German, can't you tell by our name?" I laughed at their sincerity.

"I'm Hispanic."

That seemed to satisfy Martha's curiosity. Bill then spoke from the table where he was sitting.

"You like apple pie? Martha just made apple pie yesterday, and we's hopin you come eat some pie with us, we knew you was coming."

Without another hint, Martha got up from her seat and took out some plates from blue and white cupboards and a pie from a ledge on the window. It was as natural as my mother serving pie to her family. Martha asked, while John made small talk about the snow.

"Do you want me to heat the pie Gibo?" On that cue it was Bill's turn.

"There only two kinds of pie I like," and he waited for me to ask him what kinds these were, then he said, "It's hot pie and cold pie," and he broke out in shrill laughter.

I laughed too, and the bond between that family and me was made that afternoon, eating pie and getting to know each other. Later on, I asked Martha about the possibility of boarding with them. She was honest in her response.

"Gibo, I would be happy to have you stay but we have no electric, no running water and not fair to you. You can eat all your meals here though, I have propane stove and I cook all you and Bill and John can eat." She laughed, I did too. I thanked them for their kindness and excused myself, telling Martha to expect me for lunch the following day.

On the very first day of reopening the Nekoma Depot, I saw what was in store for me for the duration of the reconstruction of the fallen power lines and the restoration of services. I had a visit from two "big shots," head honchos from the power company. They wanted to see the space that we had for delivering poles, equipment and other materials needed for the task of repairing what mother nature had so casually knocked down. I didn't know much about the grounds myself, but proceeded to show them the siding and the railroad property that could be used to stack up their materials that came in. They made some notes on a clipboard and left, saying that their crew supervisors would be here in a few days.

I assessed my own situation there in that vacant depot and baggage room and made a big coal fire in the pot bellied stove still in the office of the depot. I did some general dusting and cleaning of widow ledges and the former passengers' waiting room. Then I made my way to the Oetkens. They received me like a member of their family. I remembered a similar way in which the Mitchells had received me in Maxwell, in spite of the fact that I was a stranger in this land and that I was being made welcome the best way these kind folks knew how.

"Before I sit down to eat your food, Martha," I said, "Lets take care of the details. Tell me how much you'll charge me for these meals that you will serve me."

"Oh, Gibo, she said, Don't worry 'bout this sort a thing, you pay me what you think is fair."

"No," I said, "What were you charging Eddy Jones when he ate here?"

"I charge him two dollars for breakfast and three dollars for lunch and supper. That sound fair to you?"

"More than fair," I said, not imagining the culinary treats that I was in for with this German family. I paid for one week in advance knowing that she probably needed to buy groceries for the extra guest that they now had to feed.

From the first time that I ate at the Oetkens, it was an adventure in good eating. Martha, I soon established, was the best cook in all of the state of Kansas. She made roasts, sausage and sour potatoes casseroles, wursts of different kinds and the best pies and strudel cakes, of which I had never before tasted. I knew that the meats were expensive, so I got into the habit of asking when she and John would be going to La Crosse to do some shopping. When this day came I always threw in an extra twenty dollars.

"So you can buy us some of that good German sausage that I love," I would say. I think that Martha was very happy that I appreciated her cooking and she out-did herself all the time.

One day her mother, Grandma Brock from Hutchinson, came to visit and stay a few weeks. The eighty-year-old grandma was wonderful, inquisitive and talkative.

"Gibo, come here, sat down by me. I want tell you my story." She said to me when I first met her.

"I was born in Russia. We were very poor and we work in the field, picking potatoes everyday. Someday we be so hungry we eat the potatoes raw from the field, other times we take one, two potatoes in our pockets, and make goot potato soup dat night. Gibo, but the day my mother get paid for our work, she go to the local market and buy the best black bread and cheese you ever ate." And she pursed her lips and kissed the tips of her bunched-up fingers.

"Vary goot, vary goot," she would say.

"What kind of black bread did you eat, Grandma

Brock?"

"I show you one day."

The trains started to come about a week after I got there: flat cars full of creosote-coated telephone poles, box cars with huge electric transformers, rolls of cable, boxes full of clamps, bolts, nuts, rivets, and open gondolas with riprap (gravel). Everything industrial seemed to be arriving at the Nekoma Depot. My job was to receive the material, inventory the individual freight, help store the many boxes in the baggage room and begin to deliver the materials called for by the different crew bosses and supervisors.

It was an avalanche of material and the snowy grounds around the depot were soon covered with hundreds of poles. The daily traffic of trucks and loaders used to haul away the materials trampled the snow and soon it was crushed and melted. There was more commotion in Nekoma than I imagined had ever happened in this small rural town. Suddenly the depot became the center of attention and the small store was doing a lot of business with the crews buying sodas, cakes, canned meats, milk and whatever the hungry men needed. I became a sort of folk hero because the town folk saw me walking around the yard, taking stock of the huge amounts of material and saw the bosses accede to my orders in dumping materials in key spots on the property. One of the several visitors that I had was a Mr. Jones, who identified himself as Eddy's father. He claimed that this was really Eddy's job but that he had taken a job outside Nekoma while the depot reopened. The reactions were funny. Some people wondered if the depot would be reopened permanently and whether or not full passenger service would be restored to the area. I discussed these matters with them but essentially said that I had no answers to their concerns.

The most interesting visitors that I had, however, were a couple of kids who, like the Oetkens were destined to be my friends. The two, a brother and sister came to the passengers' room window one afternoon and introduced themselves as Karl and Ellie Lunden. He was fifteen and she was fourteen years old. They were both dressed in Levi bib overalls. They were inquisitive and extremely friendly. On my off-time at the depot we would talk about everything and about nothing. Ellie was the more aggressive of the two and soon started asking personal questions. I liked the pair and soon invited them to ride with me to a hotdog stand in Rush Center called "The Dog's Tail." I enjoyed their company because it was totally without conditions. We'd sit in the car, sometimes for hours, listening to music. I'd accompany the singer in some of the songs I knew and they would mimic my actions. Once, when the radio came on with Sam Cook's

"You Send Me," I revved up the volume, got out of the car and started to dance by myself. For a minute I was dancing on the porch at Belica's and I was mimicking her dance steps and her movement. My reverie did not last because as soon as Ellie saw me dancing she got out of the car and began to dance, facing me but tracing my dance steps with arms opened wide. The strains of the song pulled at my heart but I feigned that I was simply in a state of bliss in my dancing. Ellie's dance was strained and a bit awkward. She was skinny and taller than me and she reminded me of the graceful sandhill cranes that I had seen in the Bosque del Apache, a game reserve in Belen, New Mexico. The song by Sammy Cook ended and we all laughed, but Karl had not joined us in the dance. The two siblings enjoyed the new kid, although I was a full six years older than Karl. I too, enjoyed these naive, unsophisticated, genuine human beings. We made fun together. One day, on our way back from another trip to The Dog's Tail, the heater was humming its warm air and the radio was playing. Suddenly Karl, who was on the back seat at the time, tapped me on the shoulder feverishly and said, more than once, "Stop the car Gibo, stop the car." I looked back to see if he was in some kind of trouble and I drove the car on to the shoulder of the road. A song on the radio was on almost full volume, it was "Poison Ivy," a fast, peppy song and it was Karl's turn to dance. He got out of the car, left the right rear door open and began to dance to the lively song. It was a hilarious dance: Karl was a wooden doll, he was stiff and all that moved were his feet which he stomped as if crushing grapes. Ellie and I laughed until we thought we would burst, but Karl persisted. When the music was over he came back with a big grin on his face.

"How'd I do guys?" Ellie answered as any sister would.

"You danced like a puppet, you looked like Pinocchio, but it was a funny dance," she said, laughing.

"What did you think Gibo?" he asked me, ignoring his sister's remarks."

"Hey Karl, You were smooth as ice. Don't let anyone tell you different."

Ellie and I looked at each other and Karl sat back, relaxed and complete. He too, had danced to the snow, to the stars and the wind.

Weeks rolled into months and the feverish activity around the depot began to diminish. Half the poles were gone, electricity was restored, and the terrible days of the storm were slowly becoming less than a memory. I had quit my room at the Prairie Motel in La Crosse and had chosen to sleep in a folding cot in the depot. I had become acquainted with the personnel at the Rest Home and would shower there three times a week. I continued to frequent the libraries in Rush Center and La Cross and to enjoy the company of the Lunden brother and sister. I had spoken to Karl about the fishing that my brother and I used to do back home in the mountains and one day he showed up with four large catfish, an animal that I had never seen before. He said that his father had caught them the day before and I was shocked to find them still breathing.

"When catfish are wrapped in a wet gunny sack, they can survive for as much as three days."

I found this amazing. Trout would survive fifteen minutes out of the water. I asked Karl to help me skin the big cats (whiskers and all) and I drove over to the Oetkens to present them with Karl's gift. Next day we had eggs and catfish steaks for breakfast.

February seemed to vanish in the time it took to feel the breezes of March. One evening, a giant, orange and splendored moon arose on the eastern horizon. I had never noticed a moonrise like this one. It was a bigger moon than I had ever seen and it looked like some primeval, red-orange planet as it sat suspended in the flat horizon. My moons had always been small silver rings by the time they'd climbed the mountains, but this one lay large, heavy and out-of-this world. Ellie and Karl were with me and they marveled at my ignorance of such a sight.

"Wait till it gets to the other side," Karl commented.

"What happens then?"

"It looks just exactly like that one," he said and he laughed as if talking to a child.

The moon rose, Karl and Ellie went home and I saw the giant orange pumpkin turn into a perfect silver orb, smaller, like the moon I knew but in that wide, pristine Kansas air, I thought that I could touch it.

My mind raced home and I remembered the silver moon peering through the branches of the cherry trees under which Belica and I walked one April night. My heart filled with sadness and homesickness. I missed my land, my family and I longed for Belica with a hunger that I knew could lead to lunacy. During the whole time that I had been here and so far from home, I had anesthetized my deep love for Belica. I had to do this to survive and to keep me from one day bolting and quitting my commitment to myself and my family. This moon was so provoking that I knew I had to get away from its spell. I got in the car and drove nowhere in particular. I listened to music and even here, my thoughts of Belica would not leave me. I began to make some definite plans that included my return home. I had found a home away from home in the kindness of the Oetkens and the camaraderie of Karl and Ellie, but the mountains and my Belica beckoned.

After that moon-lit night, things continued on a rapid change. The sun transformed, in a magical moment, the landscape of central Kansas. Where there had been a world of white, now green appeared everywhere. The snow of the winter had caused the prairie earth to erupt in grasses and in fence rows and corners, flowers of all colors seemed to sprout out of nowhere. The earth had come to life again and I was glad to have seen the transformation. On a budding elm, outside my depot window, I was greeted by the musical lyrics of a meadowlark. In the woods that followed the Walnut Creek I could hear the calls of the ubiquitous ravens and high above the clear prairie sky, goshawks circled their deadly intents. Spring had come to Nekoma and now I knew why these folks had chosen to call this place home. I realized then, that I had come to the middle of nowhere, and found it was the middle of somewhere special.

I had been in Nekoma for what seemed, just two short months. I had seen the devastation of weather on things human and I had done my part, if unwittingly, to help overcome the problem. By the end of March I had completed my task, including getting the track maintenance crews to clean up the debris left over from the tremendous amounts of materials that had come and gone through the Nekoma Depot. I readied the place, as one does when vacating one's home, to close it down again. I was awaiting instructions by mail for reassignment when Archibald drove up to the depot and announced that he had convinced the dispatcher to allow me to remain and protect the Rush Center Depot while he took a much needed vacation. I closed down the Nekoma Depot but I still slept there during the time that I worked at Rush Center. Martha and John had gone to Hays, Kansas purportedly to bring back a surprise for the family. Bill could not keep a secret and revealed to me on the morning of John and Martha's trip to Hays that they had gone to a German meat market.

"To see a man from Libenthal, a German town," Bill said, "to get some special ingredients for a going away meal for you."

Sure enough, on the following day I guessed at the preparations being made.

"Gibo, don't make no plans for Saturday, I cook that day for you, like Grama Brock say, 'vary goot,' you see!"

On Saturday I was there early and John and I went out to throw a few pitches, using a couple of leather baseball gloves that he said were used by him and Bill, until Bill got too old to pitch.

"Why does your family tease you with Loretta Morgan, the banker's daughter?"

"Gibo, my family just teases me. If I really had a girlfriend, they probably wouldn't agree with my choice.

Loretta, like me," he said, "is just one of those human beings that doesn't seem to have been born to get married. Wouldn't it be something if I married money?" he asked. "It would, for just a boy," he said laughing.

I remembered the often spoken phrase, "For just a boy," used to describe John by his mom and dad.

"John just fixed the door to the shed," Martha would say, and Bill would say,

"That's good, for just a boy."

Why 'Archibald,' why, 'for just a boy?

Martha yelled, as she stuck her head out the window.

"You guys, food is ready, come on in and get it!"

The layout was even greater than any meal Martha had served before.

"Gibo, this is your going away present, it's special, I hope you like it. Look, kidney pie, German cheese and Russian black bread."

Grandma Brock sat passively at the table and smiled and Bill had on his toothless grin. I felt like bawling. We sat down, and for the first time at that table Grandma Brock said a prayer of thanks, then said, "I tol you Gibo, I bring you Russian black bread."

"Thank you Grandma Brock, Martha, John and my friend Bill. I will never forget you. I will tell my parents about the wonderful folks I found here in Nekoma."

The kidney pie was a baked-kidneys casserole. It was out of this world; with sour potatoes, a hard white cheese which smelled a bit like wet boots, but tasted like pumpkin cake and a black rye bread that was the aromatic equal to percolating coffee. The meal was wonderful, the company was unparalleled and the conversation was of reminiscence.

Grandma Brock was the first to open this line of conversation.

"When I first saw Gibo I thought he was Japanese. He cute, but his eyes are Japanese. Martha tell me, 'He say he Mexican American' I tell Martha, No, Gibo not Mexican, He Japanese."

We all laughed. Bill recalled the day when Martha and John had gone off to La Crosse and he had to make breakfast for both of us.

"I burned the eggs," he said, "Gibo looked funny but he don't say anything, next time John and Martha go away, he bring a can of spam from Helen Miller store and he make breakfast for both of us. Remember Gibo?" and we all laughed again.

I asked, "Why do you guys say to John, not bad, for just a boy?" They roared with laughter, and Martha said, with tears in her eyes from so much laughing,

"Because, John himself used to say that about himself. When he did anything around the house and I say thank

you John, he would say, 'not bad, hey, for just a boy'."

John piped in and said, "Yes, but that's when I was just a kid. I'm forty one years old now and you'all still say, "not bad for just a boy, a forty-some year old boy." And everybody guffawed!

I then said, "I'll never forget the day I met Martha and Bill and Bill said that he liked only two kinds of pie, I thought he'd say, apple, peach or something like that but instead he said, hot pie and cold pie." The kitchen was in a regular hysteria until it was time to go.

I had a week left before I would leave. I had received my work orders to report to the Garden City Depot, a station on the main line again and I was excited about leaving to another site. On the next morning of the day at the Oetkens I went to the Post Office and found a letter from Belica. She and I had written to each other at least once a week and I thought it strange that I had just recently received a letter, which in fact I hadn't yet answered. I opened the letter and it was brief and to the point. She wrote:

"*Gibo,*

I feel very bad about having to write you this letter but you have to know from me, and no one else, that I am dating a guy from Conejos, Colorado. We are going to his Prom this weekend and he is talking a lot about marriage. Sorry to do you like this, but I'm being honest. I do want to see you when you return.

Love, Belica."

Kick in the ass, I thought, grabbing the back of my head, *I can't believe this.*

Suddenly I looked up at the cloudless sky, but the sun was gone. I stumbled to my car and just sat there for a long while, someone passed and honked their horn and waved but my mood was dark and my soul was slowing spiraling down to the depths of hell. Purple shadows enveloped me. I started the car and drove away. I traveled north after reaching Rush Center, past La Crosse, Libenthal and into Hays. I got into a bar near the university campus and got drunk.

I drove back as far as La Crosse that night and stayed at the Prairies Motel, for old times' sake. Next day I called in sick to the office of the Dispatcher and tried to think of any other day that I might have reported in sick, but I couldn't remember one. I needed time to think. I needed time to heal. On top of my emotional knockout, my head was a throbbing mess. I had to think but the message in that Dear Gibo letter kept going round and round in my head. Yesterday I was happy and eager to return to work on the main line and eventually go home. Today, all I wanted was to heal from the hurt that I felt. I even welcomed my throbbing headache to avoid thinking about her.

I had one more thing to take care of before I left Nekoma and Rush Center. I had to see my two little friends, Ellie and Karl. A couple of days after my traumatic encounter with fate, I picked up the Lundens at their home and offered to buy them some hotdogs and a couple of shakes. They eagerly agreed and Ellie was the first to notice.

"Hey Gibo, are you sick? You look like something the cat dragged into the house."

"That bad?" I asked.

"Nah," said Karl, "It just looks like you're just hung over, like my uncle Pete, he's always hung over and he looks like you."

I laughed and said, "I'm glad you guys are my friends, otherwise I would think you're putting me down."

They both laughed. We went into the Dog's Tail and ordered hot dogs. Karl ordered two, plus milk shakes. I asked the clerk if he had any sour kraut.

"All the time," he said, trying to be hip and pointed to a five-gallon jar with sour kraut.

I must be stupid, I said to myself, *I'm in the middle of Germany, how could they not have sour kraut?*

We ate and talked.

"I'm going to miss you Gibo. Why don't you just stay and go to college at Hays, you know they have a big college there," Ellie said,

I had shared with them my desire to return to college at the end of my stint with the railroad. Just then a song came on the jukebox, it was: "My Baby, Does the Hanky-Panky." I laughed at the irony there somewhere and I laughed out loud. I got up from our booth and pulled Ellie to the middle of the floor and started to dance. She seemed gorgeous in her long flowery skirt and white silk blouse. I noticed she was beginning to bud and her adult attributes were beginning to show. She also danced graciously.

She must have practiced her dancing, I thought. But we danced. Ellie's innocence combined with the magic of our dance made me want to float away into a dream. When the song was over, I asked her to remain on the floor while I punched the song again and we continued to dance. Meanwhile, Karl got up and joined us in the middle of the floor and we cut a crazy threesome as we danced.

"We look like three Greek dancers," I said. We laughed and enjoyed each other's company that night, but I needed to dance to break the spell that was holding me. That night, I took my friends home, I said we'd see each other before I left, but we never did. I missed them when I left, but I really wanted to end our visit with thoughts of that last night together; dancing at the Dog's Tail Café.

The Long Trek Home

I left Rush Center early one morning and headed south. Garden City was a good one hundred seventy five miles away and just past Dodge City, the Division Headquarters. I was in a sedated mood from the highs and lows of the previous three or four days, I didn't exactly remember which, but my emotions were now at an even keel.

As I traveled south the sun was strong through my left car window and I had to squint to see. The sun was still at the flat horizon of the Kansas plains and it would be a while before it rose high enough for the shade to work. The countryside lay before me like a tabletop. Green covered the world and the sunflowers waved good-bye. I thought about Bill and Martha as well as John and Grandma Brock. I knew, somehow, that I would never see some of them again. In my vulnerability of the last few days, I felt that I was losing them too and my eyes welled up with tears. I cried for Bill, and Grandma Brock,

I cried for Martha and John and I cried for me.

I shut the radio off the rest of the way to Garden City. At approximately twenty miles from Rush Center I came upon a flooded highway. The entire area was covered with about six inches of water, but because the road had not been closed by the highway department, I continued to drive over the miles of flooded road. I felt sorry for the flowers that must have been inundated by a rain that both blessed and cursed. For some strange reason my thoughts turned to the darker side and my mind was cued, perhaps by the flood, to a poem I'd once read.

Some say the World will end in Fire, Others in Ice.
From What I've known of Desire, I hold with those that favor Fire.
But I know enough of Hate (and loss),
To know That Ice will suffice.

I reached the one gas station town of Jet and stopped to get a coke. I had traveled about fifteen miles on a flooded highway, but now at Jet I could see the flowers look back at me. They waved in a gentle breeze and the winter wheat, now a good two feet high, undulated in the wind. I thought of *golden waves of grain*, and I thought of my own weathervane emotions that just had to be restrained.

I arrived in Dodge close to noon and vowed to return to visit boot hill, the saloons that made history of the west and to see if I could find a restaurant that served Mexican food. I was hungry for love, I was hungry for soul food and I was starving for the peace I'd enjoyed just two weeks ago. From Dodge I drove to Garden City where I visited my job site for the following three weeks. I heard the busy telegraph key again, I saw the commotion of the operator getting ready to receive a train, this time train number 22, El Capitan, that had so long ago carried my girl and her cousins to California.

I was glad for the assignment to Garden City. This was a busy place and I had little time to mope or think outside the heavy duty schedule that was afforded me on the two-to-eleven o'clock shift. I slept late and started early with little time to wander around. My time outside the depot had been curtailed by this odd schedule. I rented a hotel room in Garden City and frequented essentially two restaurants while there. I didn't find any restaurants with Mexican food and I didn't try too hard to find one. I stayed in Garden City three weeks and was assigned another two in a town called, Gillette, a few miles down the road that mimicked the Santa Fe Trail, on the Cimmaron Branch.

It was late May when I experienced a meteorological event there that reminded me of home in the summers.

It was a lightning storm. It was a lightning storm, unlike any that I had ever seen. It was one without thunder. It rode on heavy water-laden clouds and it was hanging there, it seemed, just a few hundred feet overhead. The storm was strange to me because it seemed to be within the clouds themselves, zapping through the clouds and lightning the bowels of these sheets of mist. The clouds were nothing like the cumulus cotton clouds of the mountains nor even the angry behemoth cumulus nimbus that rained down the bolts of lightning that killed horses, or men and which could split a giant yellow pine from tip to root. No, these silent, horizontal waves of light just emitted a zapping noise as they lit up the clouds and the horizon. It then occurred to me that it was lightning like this that I would see flicker as a pale rosy red light on the eastern fringe of the mountains surrounding my valley. Now I had traveled to the other side of the world and seen the source of those wistful silent flashes of red light that came from "somewhere" beyond the mountains.

On the first week while living in Garden City, I took time to write three letters that would determine my future. One I wrote to my employer, the A.T.& S.F. Railroad Company at its Las Vegas Division Headquarters. It was my resignation letter effective the end of the summer just a few months away. The second letter was directed to the Dean of St. Michael's College in Santa Fe, New Mexico.

The letter was simply my intentions to enroll at that college in the Fall of that year, just a few months hence. The last one was sent to my brother Vivian, asking him simply to go to Arroyo del Hongo, visit with Belica and ask her to return my class ring that I had given her in what seemed eons ago. This last letter was intended not so much to recoup a ring, as to see what was happening with her. I had agonized over our break-up but I yearned to know what was going on with her, what she was thinking; what she was doing. I was sure that the aggressive, inquisitive brother of mine would find out for me just how things were.

In due time I heard from the College. They had welcomed my inquiry and had sent me application papers and a kind, hand written note from Brother Simon Coulier, the Dean, recalling my visit to the college approximately a year ago. He warmly extended me a welcome to St. Michael's.

The response to my letter of resignation was in the form of a personal telephone call at the station and coming from the Las Vegas Dispatcher, indicating his regrets for my leaving the railroad and encouraging me to stay. He intimated a permanent assignment somewhere in New Mexico. I responded with a grateful thanks for the employment and the opportunity of having some wonderful experiences while in the railroad, but that it was a personal issue and I wanted to return to school and to be as close to home as possible. He said that he understood and asked if I could stay till the end of August. I agreed and we ended our conversation.

From Gillette I was assigned to a station farther west called Satana. It was here that on the first week I made a rash decision. I looked at the map and realized I was less than four hundred miles from home. I made up my mind that on Friday after work I would drive my 1941 Chevy home. At the end of my shift on Friday I started home, a place that I hadn't seen in six months. I called no one, I wrote no one about my intentions, I simply notified my local dispatcher that I would be gone on Monday but that I would be at work on the next day. I read the map, ate a quick lunch and started my long trek home.

I traveled all night, from the Kansas border, through the Oklahoma Panhandle, through Boise City, Oklahoma across the New Mexico line, past Clovis, Springer and a meager seven miles south of Maxwell. On an early morning I made the eastern side of the Sangre De Cristo Mountains. I felt I was home. The smell of the air was mountains, the look of the sky was mountains, the ions at these heights were mountains and my heart was pounding mountains; a mountain man was coming home. I arrived home as the sun topped the eastern peaks and flooded Embargo with yellow light.

I knocked on the door to my parents' bedroom and I first heard some whispering and then my mother looked out the window and she yelled.

"It's Gibo, it's my hijito (little son) Gibo." She rushed to the door and hugged me hard, combing the back of my head with her hand and saying,

"You never said you were coming, why?"

My father then came out of the house and shook my hand.

"Sure is good to see you, *mi hijo*."

It wasn't long before the whole household was milling around me. My brother Van stood straight, with eyes pleading to be recognized. Flo, now a beautiful woman, simply said.

"Welcome home Gibo, I've got to talk to you." Cleve at six years of age still clung to my mother's side. Eve just smiled a tough love kind of smile and said nothing. Jo, a young girl of sixteen was looking pretty, even with her long uncombed hair that early in the day. Vivian was the last to show. He spoke in his usual indolent manner.

"Well, now we know who the favored one really is, otherwise, why all the fuss? I'm just kidding," He said, "You have a lot of unfinished business in these parts, I'm glad you're home."

"What unfinished business?"

"Well, there is the cleaning of the ditches, which I

had to do since you were gone, the harvesting of wood for the winter…"

"You never lose an argument, and I'm not going there with you, little brother." We both laughed. We had a hearty breakfast and we joined each other in idle chatter. It was heaven to my ears and a warm soothing medicine for my home-sick heart. I told them about my plans to leave the railroad and enroll in school.

When there was a lull in the conversation, Flo called me aside.

"I have something important to tell you, do you remember Beto Artiaga, Belica's brother?"

"Yes. I met him once when he came on furlough from the service."

And my heart seemed to explode at the sound of her name but I kept my composure.

"Well, he and I have been dating for about three months now. He is back from the service and we…" she shrugged her shoulders, "…have been dating, I really like him. And what about you, *tontito* (silly boy) why haven't you written to Belica and why did you ask Vivian to go get your ring?"

"She still loves you man." This time it was Vivian who had come up behind us. "She's still beautiful."

"And you," I said, "some kind of brother you are, I send you on an errand and you don't have the courtesy to write me back about anything."

"I don't know what game you're playing man. She says you have been returning her letters and that she doesn't even know where you are."

"Did she tell you about a boyfriend that she has in Colorado?" My voice betraying my pent-up anger.

"Whoa man. There is no more boyfriend. She still has feelings for you man. I'm telling you, but the ball is in your court. Now you know what I know."

And he walked away. Flo wanted to talk some more but I feigned that I had forgotten something in the car and left her sitting there. I went to the trunk of the car and brought out a paper bag full of goodies: candy, cakes, peanuts, lollipops and juicy-fruit gum, all junk food that I had bought at the different gas stations where I had stopped to gas up. I said this in passing and Van wanted to know where I had stopped, at what time I had stopped and what did I say to the clerk when I stopped at his station. Van was like an encyclopedia and this was his way of filling his hungry need to know. On one of the days I was there, I asked him,

"Have you seen the red flicker on the edges of the mountains this Spring?"

"Yes, on April the 22nd, on April 23 and again on May 10th and 11th."

"Are you for real?" I asked, knowing that these dates

seemed to coincide, in my mind, with lightning storms that I had witnessed on the other side of the mountain.

I enjoyed my family on the short three days I was there. One evening when I was talking with my parents about taking my forty-nine Mercury back to Kansas and leaving the 1941 Chevy behind, Flo, beautifully dressed, walked in and leaving the door open, motioned to someone to come in. It was Beto Artiaga. He was a handsome young guy about my age but, unlike me, he seemed in top physical health; he'd just returned from a three-year stint in the army.

"Hi Gibo, remember me?"

"Hi Beto, welcome home, I hear you are now a free man."

"I guess so," he said in a very soft spoken voice.

I don't really know him, I thought, and my heart was racing as I contemplated the fact that he was Belica's brother.

"You going to Arroyo before you leave?" he asked. "Flo tells me you're here just for the weekend."

"Yes. This is my first time in six months since I've seen my family," I said, evading his question. But he persisted.

"Belica is waiting to see you, why don't you go see her tonight? She's home."

"I might do that, or maybe tomorrow, I don't want

to impose."

"Ok," he said as he and a beaming Flo walked out the door. I walked to the door with them. He looked over his shoulder and said,

"She is waiting for you, *Cuñado* (brother-in-law)." I felt aglow with happiness, but my pride and my hurt did not let me go to Arroyo del Hongo this time around. I left back to Satana on the evening of the next day.

My return to Kansas was simply a visit. I remained at Satana two more weeks and then it was time to return to New Mexico and home. I did not get involved much in Satana, and what I can remember of that little town now is that on Friday and Saturday nights, between midnight and one o'clock in the morning, it was the custom of the teenagers in the community to race around town, blasting their car horns and yelling at the top of their lungs. This happened every weekend that I was there and I thought: *Why do the people here tolerate such behavior? One cop car with sirens blaring would bring a quick halt to these proceedings.* Life here was so quiet, so lay back that it made Embargo look like an all day parade.

No, I ventured, *the people here tolerate this weekend madness to remind them that they are alive.* Again, far fetched speculation, something I was prone to do.

The time came to bid "*Au revoir*" to Kansas and I drove west, south west around noon, past the Kansas border and into the Oklahoma Panhandle. I went through long stretches of earth mounds or sand dunes. I noticed half buried fences, old abandoned machinery and decrepit old barns. I saw that this was a place where few flowers grew and where, if not for some juvenile Russian Thistle and milkweed, the countryside would be bare.

And then it came to me; I was seeing the legacy of the much-recorded dust bowl days. I was, I surmised, in the heart of dust bowl country. I reflected on the impossible living conditions on humans, plants and animals during this terrible time in the settlement of the Panhandle. Little did I know that just a few hours later, I would experience, in living color, the nature of the nightmare scenario these people lived.

I had traveled about four hours in the heart of the Panhandle. It was around four o'clock in the afternoon and I had long passed the land abandoned by desperate families and I was a short twenty miles from Boise City, close to the New Mexico border, when it happened. Out of the western sky I could see a clouded horizon. It was a brownish colored curtain that seemed to grow, even at the distance when I first saw it. The outside air was perfectly still and only the wind that was created by my car's speed made any noise. The cloud seemed to grow higher as I approached it. There were occasional cars traveling in either direction and soon I noticed tail lights lit up and cars stopped alongside the highway. The huge cloud of brown approached rapidly and I drove right into it as it enveloped my car in a silent blanket of brown dust.

My mind rapidly recalled an afternoon in a La Crosse restaurant when at two in the afternoon the world had turned dark brown. When I saw cars on the street with their headlights on, I really took notice, even though the waitresses seemed not to mind. This was the same thing. It was a dust storm. This one, however was *humongous*. The cloud quickly enveloped my car and several cars now parked on the highway shoulder. It got darker and soon I couldn't even see the tail lights of cars just yards ahead of me. I kept my motor running, turned on my lights, to avoid some car rear-ending me and I awaited the dark from hell.

For a moment I thought of those poor souls who had experienced this death shroud for weeks on end. A few minutes after entering this gargantuan dirt maelstrom, the wind that drove the dust now hit us. It was a ferocious wind. It rocked my large car like a bouncing ball and I feared that it would topple us. There was no escape for anyone. I could not drive forward, I couldn't turn and run, I could not hide anywhere in this flatland and I, like those in the cars ahead and behind me, simply endured. We must have remained there at the mercy of the storm, which must have extended for thirty miles in either direction, for about thirty minutes. It seemed an eternity. The wind drove the dust ahead towards Kansas and then it started to rain. The windshield ran chocolate. The raindrops, permeated with dust, fell on the car and slid off with the increased rain. The air cleared, it continued to rain and the strong wind persisted. And a thought came to me.

Lest we forget who rules these flatlands, the master, the wind, soon let me know.

I drove west, past Boise City and into the Land of Enchantment, even though there isn't much enchantment in this part of the long emptiness. I arrived home late that night and a day later reported to the Santa Fe Freight Depot, my assignment for the next two weeks. I resisted calling Belica when I was home and even though I was only one hundred miles from Arroyo and Embargo, I never attempted to communicate with her. My mind had adjusted to the deception, my heart had been quieted and my instinct told me to beware. I worked at Lamy for another two weeks, following my stint in Santa Fe. During this time I made several trips to St Michael's to complete my application and to begin my long awaited experience in a college or university. Brother S. Coulier gave me a complimentary library card to the college library and I acted as if I was already attending classes while working in the area.

On Separate Roads

My last work experience took me to the El Paso Freight Depot located on Santa Fe Street, five blocks from the Mexico/American bridge. It was early August and I was simply letting the clock run out. The depot in El Paso was a modern affair. It communicated by teletype senders and receivers and was a precursor to the end of the telegraph key. I knew that perhaps my decision to leave the railroad was quite timely. I envisioned automatic train signals guiding the trains and radio, making the telegraph operator a relic of history. I rented a room at the El Cortez Hotel, another relic of history. I met my co-workers who would work with me for the rest of the month and I was glad to find an Herrera among them. They were all a jovial lot. A couple of days into the job, one of them teasingly made a comment.

"Hey Gibo, it's time for your initiation. Tonight after work we all go for Carta Blancas across the border."

"Yah," another said. "There's a new girl at the Club

San Luis and she looks ready for the picking." They all laughed and I walked right into their game, with my feigned look of someone who had just fallen off the turnip truck. I agreed.

At eleven that night, three of us piled up into an old Chevy and rode across the bridge and into Mexico. We parked right outside the club San Luis. An older man with an old beige army cap ushered us into a good parking spot. My friend Herrera handed him a dollar and we walked into the noisy interior of the club. We were met at the door by some three or four young women who led us to a table on the far wall of the place. A couple of them knew the guys and feigned to have missed them, not having seen them during the past twenty four hours.

I took my place on the table indicated, while the two guys introduced me.

"*Que guapo*," (He's handsome) one of them said, and she rubbed my cheek with the back of her fingers. Herrera then whispered in her ear and the girl walked away from our table and quietly chatted with a pretty girl, about my age, who served behind the bar. The young girl, in a bright red skirt and a low cut, white cotton blouse smiled broadly and came toward our table from behind the bar. She was brazen as she approached our table.

"Jus who iss this guapo Gringo Pochito that jus arrive?"

The guys pointed at me. No one had ever called me

a Gringo Pochito (Mexican, born in the U.S.).

"Hola," I said.

"Hola, mi amor," she said, pulling a chair and sitting next to me. The guys thought that she was appropriately intimidating me, and they laughed.

"What is my Pochito's name?" she asked me, as if we were talking about someone else.

"*Soy Gibo Herrera, y tu nombre?*"

"Gabo, thas a nice name."

"It's Gibo."

"What you gonna drink tonight Gabo?" she teased.

"Una Carta Blanca would be fine."

"So wha bring you so far to heaven and so close to the Gabachos?" (slang for Americans) she asked, with an almost hostile air. The guys roared.

"Don't be afraid of her," said Herrera, "She's just trying to set the ground rules, which are that they control the agenda here."

"Fine. Now that you know my name, what's yours?"

"*Yo soy Guadalupe Miranda Cuevas, but my frens, they call me Lupe, jus Lupe.*"

I took the initiative.

"I don't want to drink with just these pochos. What do you want to drink Lupe? I'm buying."

"*Asi hablan los hombres,* (that is the way men should

talk)" she said.

She returned with our drinks while her two friends sat around the table flirting with my friends. They each winked their eyes at me and let Lupe take care of me.

Lupe was wise beyond her years. She was witty, pretty and sometimes an overpoweringly attractive girl. I had trouble keeping up with her dialect and her double meanings. But we started getting along fine. Just as we clicked our bottles of beer to a wish of "salud," (good health) a group of five musicians in mariachi garb walked in. They headed straight to our table and started to play. The first song must have been a favorite of the girls, because they joined in on the singing.

"You like this kin o' music Gabo?"

"Me gusta."

The second and third songs were local, regional songs and then Lupe asked for her choice, it was called, "*Yo Te Perdi*" (I lost your love). The strains were so melancholy and the words developed the theme of lost love:

"*Yo te perdi, como pierde, un buen perdedor, cuyas cartas la fortuna les dio, una suerte fatal.*

(I lost your love, like a loser whose hand has been dealt a fatal turn by fortune's game of chance).

After my second beer and a shot of tequila, ordered for me by my pal Herrera, I was beginning to get morose.

"Whas the matter, my Gabo?"

"You thinking of someone?"

I confirmed her suspicions when I asked the mariachi to play the song again. She leaned over and whispered in my ear.

"Don't let your frens know that you are hurtin, they don't understan, they just laugh at you Gibo. Let's dance."

I got up to dance with Lupe and the guys and the women with them, yelled and clapped their hands. Lupe was a fine dancer and I hadn't danced that close to a woman since I had danced with Belica, almost a year ago. Lupe electrified me. She was gentle and soothing.

"Les sit over ther, I wan you to tell me who made you so melancholic," she said.

I ordered a couple of margaritas and we talked and danced and I admitted to her that I hadn't felt so comfortable with someone in a long time, as I did with her.

"You don worry, my little injure bird, I have the cure for your melancholy."

The mariachi came to our table one more time and I wanted them to play the song again, but Lupe pleaded with me to let her order a song this time. I knew she was trying to prevent my rapid decline into a maudlin mood.

"No body die of love, my pajarito, they jus go on

livin or they become shrivel like a chicharron (pork skin)," she assured me.

She laughed and invited me to laugh with her. I was slowly getting bewitched by Lupe and the power of the liquid spirits I had imbibed hurried the process.

I started to tell Lupe about Belica but she stopped me with her finger to my lips.

"Not now. Tomorrow night you and I talk. I have a lot to confess too. We are the two halves of an orange, I love when you smile. Lets join the others."

"We are goin to get marry," she announced to everybody at the table, and the group, now plenty drunk, all laughed till they seemed to want to cry. Everybody was having a good time and when the two-o'clock hour came around, Herrera, my namesake got up and said that it was time to go.

"We'll see you gorgeous women, *mañana por la noche, bueno?"* he said.

"I see you tomorrow Gibo. You and I have a lots to talk about," and she kissed me on the mouth.

The following day, I thought of the night before and wondered if the guys would want to cross the bridge again tonight. Herrera beat me to it.

"My wife got on my case last night. I told her that a new guy had started to work at the depot and that we had taken him out for a couple of beers," he said.

"You guys ready to go over for a while again tonight?"

"I'm game," I said and before long he had spread the word that I was inviting to drinks at El San Luis tonight.

A couple of girls met us at the door of the club again and Lupe smiled broadly from behind the bar. After she'd cleaned up the bar, where a couple who had been drinking, left, she came to our table.

"Carta Blanca?" she asked, and she tussled my hair as she left to get our order.

"Say, this is working quicker, than I thought," said one of the guys.

"Gibo is not the shy one we thought he was," said the other.

We raised our bottles to a *salud*, and the girls took chairs around the table and ordered beers from Lupe. It was understood that the guests always sprang for the girls' drinks, this was part of the fee for "entertaining" the guests. I gave Lupe a ten dollar tip, together with the cost of the drinks but she put the ten into my shirt pocket.

"Get yourself a drink, Lupe," I yelled after her, she just smiled. Lupe walked over to a jukebox at the end of the bar and punched some dance music. She invited me to dance and she held me tight.

"I thought of you last night," she said. "Why Gibo,

am I falling for a gringo pocho who I just met yesterday?" she asked, not looking for an answer.

"I thought about you all day today," I said.

"Before you drink too much tonight, tell me about the girl that broke your heart, my injure bird." She teased. "I want to know who my competition iss," and she laughed.

I tried to evade the question because my mind was not yet emotionally primed to talk about Belica, not just yet.

"I'll tell you, maybe more than you want to know, but first tell me about you. Are you from here? Where do you live? What did you want to tell me last night?"

I bombarded her with questions. We danced and Lupe began to talk about herself. She seemed to detach herself from the place.

"I'm from a town called Jalapa, in the state of Vera Cruz. My father works in a distillery of Agua Ardiente (tequila) and my mother take care of my litol brothers and sisters. I'm the older girl of a large family and I go to school until the end of *Primaria* (sixth grade). I go to work for a rich family in Jalapa when I was fifteen and I live with them because I was too far from home. I cook, I clean and I do all the laundry. I even take care of the garden and feed the birds in the cages. I work hard Gibo but I soon had a problem. The owners had a son by name Gabriel. He was three years older than me and he was very friendly to me. He went to town one day and brought me a white silk blouse and a pretty "*medalla*" made of gold, with a picture of *Nuestra Senora de Guadalupe*, my patron saint. The boy was always good to me and I was falling in love with him, I think he was fallin in love with me. *Que crees* (what do you think)? One day when his family go to the Puerto of Vera Cruz he did not go. That night I heard some noise outside of my room and when I yelled, who it was, I was scare, he whispered, 'It's me, Gabriel' and he came into my room. We talk for a while, he touch me and we make love. He was still in my bed with me when the rooster in the garden crow and the sun peek through the window the next morning. Gibo, I have never love anyone else. I told him I hop I don't get pregnant and he said that no matter what, that he would take care of me. I thought about my love for this boy and I knew that maybe it was a prohibit love but I don't care. He told me he love me too."

Lupe and I sat down as we had done before, on a separate table from the rest. She asked one of the girls, now at the bar, to get us a couple of margaritas, and she continued to talk.

"Gibo, Gabriel and I make love for many nights that summer. When his parents went to the big city we slept in his room. The moon would come into the house and lighten up the whole room and his huge bed. We were always naked like Adam and Eve. He called me his Bird of Paradise and I call him my *toro de seda* (my silken bull). One day, at the end of the summer, his parents came home a day early and found us in bed together. The father smile and walked out, but his mother didn't talk to me for two days. I was afraid of what would happen to me. Gabriel was in a mood all the time and I didn't see him for about a week. That seemed like forever. I thought about how foolish I was, that maybe he didn't really love me, that we lived in two different worlds, that we would always walk in separate roads that diverged away from each other, never to meet again. I hoped, most of all, that I wouldn't be pregnant, then I would have to deal with my parents as well as Gabriel's.

Then, what I was so afraid of, happen. Gabriel met me in the garden one night, when the slice of the moon was going down the Sierra Gorda. He kissed me and said he needed me and I let him get under my blouse. I stop him and asked him what his parents had told him. He told me, 'Ah, they're crazy, they want to send me to Europe to finish my school.' Are you going, I asked him, I knew, Gibo the answer to that question already. 'Just for one year,' he said, and I started to cry and that night, in bed I cry till I fall asleep. That night I dream that I had a baby and someone was trying to take him away from me. I dream of the *albularia* (herb healer) in my village who pulled out worms from the belly of sick people with her magic. I have a nightmare.

Gabriel and I met secretly one night in a palapa guest house at the end of the property and we made a desperate love that I will always remember. I yearned for his body and he said he never forget me. A week later, he left to Europe. I was so sad, life did not have any importance for me. A week after Gabriel left, his mother came into my room one morning and said, 'get ready Lupe, I driving you to your parents house, you don't work for me anymore.' I knew that this is the price I had to pay for my forbidden love with her son."

"The rains came to the Sierra Gorda and Jalapa and my love fever for Gabriel never wanted to leave me. I started working in sidewalk restaurants but could never make enough money to live on. I did not want to be on my family's way, they had too many other children. I had to leave. It was a year after Gabriel left and I moved to another city. I work for some people there but I was not happy unless I was traveling, I guess, looking for something that I could never find. I never fall in love again, Gibo," she said.

I was so taken by her story that I wanted to cry. It must have showed because she said,

"Don't worry for me Gibo, I left my heart in Jalapa

and don't expect it to come here. Now tell me about your Gabriella."

Lupe's story was sad and tragic. *What can life be worth if you lose hope*, I thought. I saw Lupe eager to hear my story and I told her everything. I told her that I had been Belica's boyfriend for three years, I told her my feelings when I first met her, I told her about my longing for her and I told her about her deception.

"You still in love with her?" she pondered. "Do you think she still love you or are you the proud macho who think she is soiled because she go out with another boy?"

Lupe was astute beyond her age, which I had learned, was one year younger than me.

"You tell me she ask for you and want to see you but you afraid of being hurt again, huh? Well, my guapo little pocho, for you there is hope and you have love on your side. What you waiting for? You wait and she really find another, what, a pendejo? I wish that destiny would have been so kind to me. Vete (go) and claim her again. If you have to, take her like you take a filly horse, mount her and dig in your spurs, show her you are the man."

I was surprised by Lupe's comments, I think that she was showing her impatience with my apparent cowardice and passivity.

"Gibo, you got all the instruments that God gave

you, I know, I feel your manliness when we dance. You a handsome man, you have money, you still have a chance, Vete! Go, before destiny looks away from you and you end up "*llorando cimeras*."

"What exactly is that?"

"You will spend your life crying for things that might have been."

I was taken aback by Lupe's candor and advise. She rose from the table and pulled me to the dance floor. I knew that she worked at the behest of the man behind the bar, who had been patient with her attentions to me, so I said, almost trying to save myself from the dressing down I got.

"Take this twenty, no thirty bucks, and tell your boss to order drinks for everyone in the house."

She winked her eye at me and said,

"She is a lucky girl Gibo, this Belica. She got a good man. If I didn't understand the things about the heart, I do everything to keep you here. But I tell you something and I give you my word, crossing herself, that if she turn you away after you try to *reconciliar* with her, I wait for you. I'm not stupid, I know a good man when I see one, Gibo you a good man," she said, adding, "but with a broken wing."

She laughed and we danced the rest of what remained of the night.

Lupe's words burned inside my head. I was ready to bolt and rush north to see Belica and try to make up for all the time that I'd been without her, but I got a surprise next afternoon when I showed up to work. It was my brother Vivian, who had followed me to El Paso in his 1941 black Chevrolet, that looked, strangely familiar with its Kansas plates.

"Hey, Carnal, what are you doing here?" I asked him.

"Somebody's got to take care of a softie like my brother," he said.

It was good to see my brother again. That evening we took in a late dinner at an all-night diner and I told the guys to say hi to Lupe for me if they went across that night. Next day was my day off and I invited my brother to go across the border with me. We arrived in front of the San Luis around two in the afternoon. I ordered a couple of beers and asked the girls about Lupe.

"Oh, she'll be showing up in a couple of hours," they said.

Vivian and I talked and ordered another round of beers. I was hoping to wait until Lupe came in. I wanted to introduce her to my brother. Then my brother said he was going to the bathroom. I noticed a man come in from the street. He walked in with a shoe-shine box by his side, he too, went into the bathroom.

Suddenly, I heard a commotion and I could make out my brother's yelling and cursing. I rushed to the bathroom and I saw the shoe-shine man sprawled on the floor and his shine box way over on the far end of the bathroom. My brother was in an angry mood and pointed to the fallen man and said, this *pinche* surprised me while I was taking a leak.

"What did he do?" I asked.

"He came in and knelt down, hugged my right leg and wanted to brush my right shoe, I turned and hooked my left, right on his s.o.b. forehead."

The man was just now beginning to recover from the blow and he was groping around for his shoe shine box. I went over to him and said,

"Hey *vato, lo siento* (I'm sorry) but here's for your box, *por tu caja,* and gave him three dollars and change. He limped out of the bar. By then the owner came in and looked at my brother suspiciously. I handed him a five and told him, "*lo siento.* This is for someone to clean up after this mess."

We sat down at the bar momentarily and the girls smiled at me with tortured smiles. I told Vivian to finish his beer that we'd better go. He balked.

"Why should we go, that pinche had it coming."

"This is not Kansas, Dorothy," I said. "They'll have us for supper if you don't watch it."

We exited the place and drove back over the bridge, to the place of relative safety.

"You still like to get into trouble, don't you brother?"

"Nobody screws around with Roy Rogers."

We both laughed at an old standing joke between us. My brother returned home after staying with me some three days and I felt comfortable in going back to El San Luis a few days after that.

Meanwhile, my decision was slowly but surely taking form. I had decided to resign my assignment two weeks early and do what Lupe had admonished me to do, that is to find Belica and see what the future had in store for us. I danced and drank with Lupe a couple of more nights and we both knew that there were unresolved issues with me.

On the last night there, she confided on me that "a friend" was coming from the Capitol to visit her.

"Who is your friend?"

"He is my protector. He is the one that pays the rent and comes to see me now and then. *Es un delegado* (he is a delegate to the congress). I met him here in Cd. Juarez about six months ago, we became friends and he rented a very nice two room apartment for me."

"So how are you going to wait for me if my girlfriend doesn't like me?" I teased.

"You serious my Gibo and I be your girl forever, remember that."

I knew then that Lupe would always be victimized and like Patricia of long ago, I felt real pain for their luck.

The Rose

On the last day at work I thanked the guys at the depot for having been "cool" with me and thanked them for having introduced me to Lupe. They knew that I was cutting my assignment by two weeks and that I had other things on my mind. They knew that I would be going to college right after Labor Day.

"Don't forget us just because you don't work for the RR anymore. Stop and visit when you're in El Paso," Herrera said.

I rode out of El Paso on the following day. I could not help but think that I was in a particularly historical site. It had been here that the early settlers with Juan de Oñate had crossed the river and christened the site, *El Paso del Norte*. It was here that the settlers held their first Penitente Mass in the new province and here is where they started the trek north in 1598.

These were the settlers whose descendents would settle the far north, including my mountain valley of

Embargo. As I traveled north I couldn't help but recount my own journey, one that had taken me close to three years to complete and I counted the railroad towns in which I had worked: *twenty-some*, I figured. I was now on the King's Highway, the Chihuahua Trail; the primitive road to settlements and new lives for the earliest non-Indian peoples in a new land.

I thought of Belica and my determination to mend an old love and to meld a new future. I began to compose a poem in my head but I could not mold it until I had a chance to write it down.

I passed Las Cruces and reached Rincon, where the steel road took off north and north east into the high desert wilderness and away from the river lowlands. This is exactly what the old settlers had done. And just as the railroad through Kansas and Oklahoma had followed the route of the old Santa Fe trail, both had followed earlier human foot paths. I didn't know the reason why the railroad had followed the old *Jornada del Muerto* route, a waterless, rocky difficult way north but I knew the settlers' reason for their detour. It was because the clumsy wooden wheels of the carts were getting bogged down on the soft soil of the river causeway and the threat from native tribes accosting them at every turn.

I remembered Rincon with pleasant thoughts. Here, I had seen the Aurora Borealis in the early morning darkness. It was here, that I had ventured into a living desert, and it was here, that I had met an old train-yard custodian and train engines tender and heard his stories of the spirits that haunted the mesquite and ocotillo gullies; spirits of the desert-dwelling Indians that had lived there before any white European had even dreamed of walking there.

I drove the monotonous road north, past the big reservoir and the town of Truth or Consequences and a couple of hours later, reached Socorro, named after the plea for help, for succor, that the caravan of settlers made after their trek through the barren Jornada. I stopped to eat at the old Valverde Hotel's restaurant, a place where I had stayed during my assignment at Socorro a while back. While I waited, I wrote down on a napkin, the words that had been mulling inside my head while I thought of seeing Belica again. I titled it, *The Rose.*

The Rose

It's Time to smell the Rose Again

Mi Rosa de Castilla

The ember's glo, the love that grows

Mi amor del dia

The years have passed, So many paths

That we have walked together

Those different roads have marigolds

But it's the Rose that matters

I felt pretty good about being able to put my napkin poem together and I felt that I would share it with Belica someday after we had gotten back together. Meanwhile, I had my lunch in this first of the New Mexico towns, where the inhabitants most resembled the rest of those in northern New Mexico. The language with its archaic forms, the food, which was more Rio Grande Indian cooking and their traditions all made this for a historical boundary between the old settlers and the rest of southern New Mexico. I had just had an authentic chile verde enchilada and buñuelos as my bread.

I passed Belen, with its cross-road role for the railroad coming from Vaughn and Texas to the east, and which headed west to the coastlines of California. It also ushered through, the southerly El Paso route which headed west at Rincon, to join the Southern Pacific at Silver City. I went through Albuquerque (and the yards) and passed the "faceless" Bernalillo. I thought of Frank Lucero in Domingo and wondered whether or not he had succumbed to his terrible illness, or whether his loneliness had done him in. *Either way*, I thought, *Frank had dedicated his life to the company and now he was facing his reward.* I had to leave these thoughts because they were not helping me as I entered a large rainstorm where giant bolts of lightening rained down on the countryside with deafening claps of thunder. I was exhausted by the time I got to Santa Fe. I gassed up and after a coke at an A&W stand on Cerrillos Road, I continued my journey north. I was just a short one hundred miles from La Villa and just a short distance to Arroyo del Hongo. I was practically home. I reached La Villa when long shadows had covered the land just above that chasm that is called The Rio Grande gorge. I felt too tired, or simply not ready to stop to see Belica that night. I drove on to Embargo.

Something bothered me when I thought of seeing Belica again. I really couldn't put my finger on just what it was but I guessed that it had to do with residual feelings I had, following my shocking disappointment caused by her "Dear Gibo" letter. I then thought that it was a sort of resentment, anger, I didn't know what. It took me two more days before I saw Belica, and this came about simply by chance encounter.

On the third day back home, with my brother Vivian prodding me to go see her, we drove to La Villa on banking business. I had just come out of the bank and was just sitting down on the driver's seat. I reached to close the door when someone stopped me. It was Belica. I was truly surprised to see her.

"Hi Gibo, it's nice seeing you." She reached and touched my arm and kept her hand there. A surge of love, hate and love again came over me. I looked at her and she was looking directly into my eyes, while mine pulled away, like those of a hurt child.

"I have been waiting for you but you never came to see me, why?" I couldn't help my cruel sarcasm.

"I thought you were married by now."

Her face turned red but she evaded my comment. "How long are you going to be here?"

She asked, more to keep the conversation going. My brother Vivian pretended to look out his window and Belica's friends backed off a few steps.

"Nice seeing you Gibo. Belica, we'll wait for you at the car."

Vivian too, got out of the car and walked away, not wanting any part of a boyfriend, girlfriend dispute. Belica tried again,

"You know that I've really missed you."

"Oh yea, what about your new boyfriend? I insisted. She now moved her hand from my arm to my hand, forcing me to open it and she held it tightly.

"The only boyfriend that I have ever had is you. I sent you letters telling you that and apologizing for my stupid letter but all my letters were returned. Why?"

Then she got in one of her own.

"Maybe it's that girlfriend your brother told me you have in Maxwell. Is that why you are so cold with me? Did you even plan to see me now that you were here?" she asked almost in desperation.

"Are you going to be home tonight?" I asked, as if no discussion at all had happened.

"Yes, will you come and see me tonight?" she effused.

"Yes." I said, and in a moment of weakness I said, "Could even see you this afternoon or early this evening."

"Yes, Let me get back to Valdez with my cousins and you can come to the house around three today."

She came close to me, I could smell her "rose" perfume and I wanted to eat her with kisses.

God in Heaven, how I love this girl, I thought, but I feigned seriousness and did not reveal my feelings. She tried to give me a kiss, but I turned slightly away and all she did was rub my cheek with her lips. My heart was still pounding when we waved goodbye and my brother and I drove back to Embargo.

That afternoon as I drove south to Arroyo I was determined to reconcile with Belica and to begin our relationship again. I had no strategies, no preconceived notions about getting together with her, but as fate would have it, two things happened in quick succession that promised to wreck even mine and her intentions.

I got to her house just before three o'clock and she had still not arrived. Some fifteen minutes later she and her mother showed up and they were surprised to see me there so early. I greeted her mother and said I was happy to see her.

"Hello Gibo, It seems a long time since we've seen you. Are you here to stay?" Belica tells me that Flo told her that you're going to start college at St. Michael's," she said.

"Yes, I'm tired of playing the hobo." We laughed and Belica invited me into the living room.

We sat. I was much more animated than I had been when we met at La Villa and I had promised myself that I wouldn't revert to that spoiled, injured role that I had played a few hours before. Belica sat by me on the couch and I touched her hand.

"I've missed you," I said.

She held me tight.

"Let me see if mother is around. I want to kiss you but I don't want her to surprise us."

She got up and said, going into the kitchen and partly for the benefit of her mother's ears.

"Do you want a coke or a water, Gibo?" I didn't answer. She really didn't want an answer. I stood up and walked the old familiar living room, slowly filling the void of my memories that I had held for so long.

Then it happened: I spotted a young man's photograph close to my high school picture. I took it and saw a writing that simply stated,

"To Belica, a Wonderful Girl from Arroyo."

/s/ Harry V.

My atavistic instincts took over. My hair seemed to stand on end and my heart started to palpitate. Just then she came in, oblivious to me holding the picture.

"I see that you haven't cleaned your room in a long time, or maybe you didn't want to clean it completely."

She put down a couple of cokes she had in her hands and she saw me holding the photograph. "Oh," she said, really nervous and not looking me in the eyes.

"That's Harry, the guy I wrote you about, he means nothing to me."

"Is that why you invited me here today, to rub this idiot's picture in my stupid face?"

"No, Gibo." She was incoherent. "I..., I was going to send his picture back. He wrote me and asked me to send it."

"Does that mean you don't want it anymore?" I asked demandingly.

"No." she simply said.

"Well, I'm glad I came here just in time. I'll help you with your problem," I said sarcastically. She continued to look down and kept saying

"I'm sorry, Gibo, oh, I'm so stupid, I've ruined it all." Just then, I took off the back from the picture frame and slid out the photograph.

"You sure you don't want it anymore?" I teased. She said nothing. "Ok," I answered myself.

"So that this picture doesn't clutter this room this is what I'll do."

Like an angry juvenile I began to tear the photo in long strips, slowly, pretending that I was merely performing a task allocated to me. She looked up for a minute and looked at me straight into my eyes. I evaded her look and continued to tear the picture.

"Just in case you change your mind and want to do a puzzle, I'll take this middle part and cut it this way," cutting the picture in half from left to right. I pretended to look for a waste paper basket and when I found one I tossed the photo into it with aplomb.

"I feel like the most stupid girl in the whole world." she said.

"And I feel like the biggest fool in the world."

"I love you Gibo," she muttered.

"You have a hell of a way of showing it."

"What do you want me to say, what do you want me to do?"

"*Que te pasa* (what is the matter with you)?" I asked, frustrated. "Why hadn't you gotten rid of that *pinche* photograph before I came here? Heaven knows, I gave you plenty of time."

"I'm sorry," was all she would say and she sat with her hands on her lap.

I felt like roaring like an animal with all the rage inside me. I recouped my composure for a minute and said.

"You know what Belica, let's just consider tonight a loss and I'll see you tomorrow sometime."

I started walking out.

"No," she said, I want you to give me a chance to explain."

"Explain what?" I asked, "that you were either too stupid to hide a shit photo or that you're still in love with the guy? Spare me," and started to walk away to my car.

She followed me all the way to the car and begged me again and again.

"Listen, tonight is ruined, at least for me, let's see each other tomorrow, we'll talk then."

"I'll wait for you in the morning," she said and she let me go. As I drove out, I could see her standing just where she'd been by the car. I went home confused, angry and blaming myself for being such an idiot. I figured, this is probably it, *aqui se acabo* (this is over).

My father asked me, when I got home so early, "I thought you were going to visit your girl in Arroyo."

"Oh, I'll see her tomorrow," I said and went into my room. I forced myself not to think about what had happened tonight and in a childish way, felt pretty good that I had at least killed the s.o.b.'s picture.

What a kick in the pants, I thought and went to sleep early. I had a troubled sleep that night.

The next day came quicker than I had expected. I was up early. I took a walk down to the river and the rocky river path leading to the log bridge that led to my Uncle Tone's. The log bridge would go up every summer, be wiped out by the spring floods and be replaced again.

I recalled the old scary stories about "*La Viejita del Punche*" (The old Tobacco Lady) who would jump on any kid's back who tried to cross the wooden bridge across the swollen river. She purportedly lay in wait, and when a kid, by himself, approached the river, she would hurl herself, reeking with tobacco breath, and despite her huge hunchback, jump on the back of the child. She was a scary figure and the story did what it was supposed to do; it kept kids from crossing the log bridge without someone watching. Of course, for me now these were simply tales, told to make the kids scared enough not to do what was unsafe.

I returned to the house around ten and had a late breakfast. I had showered and shaved for no apparent reason since I had not planned to go back to see Belica that day or perhaps any day. I was now looking to enter the college and I surmised that I would have my hands full with my studies.

Around eleven o'clock a car drove up to the yard and my father went out to greet the people in it. He returned quickly.

"This one's for you, Gibo, It's your girl and some of her friends, they're asking for you."

I went out and Belica got out of the car. I waved at the girls inside, they waved back and the car started driving away.

"Your friends are going to leave you behind," I said, anticipating some kind of confrontation if she stayed.

"I told them to leave. I came to see you. You're not going to get away from me that easy, Gibo Herrera. You made me fall in love with you and now you're stuck with me."

She smiled, trying to diminish my seriousness.

"Get in the car. Let me get the keys, I'll take you home."

She sat close to me, something she had never done before. I continued my sarcasm.

"Did you learn to sit close to him, you never did with me."

"Gibo, I don't want to fight. I want to tell you, if you want to listen, what has happened since you left me to go roam the world, where ever that was."

"Ok, I'll listen to what you have to say and then I'll

tell you my side of the story."

If she tells me that she liked the guy in the slightest I will tell her about Patricia and Lupe and any other girl that I can invent. But she didn't.

She must have practiced a script that night because she was lucid and focused. She told me about the chance meeting with this guy from Colorado and dating him three or four times. She told me that he was always annoyed with her because she kept talking about me.

"We went to his prom," she said "but we went on a double date with my friend Gina and a friend of his. My mother had made him promise to bring me back that night, he did. I told Gina that I had a funny feeling about this guy, that he took me to his prom just to show me off to some old girlfriend of his. I even teased him about this possibility. When he didn't give me a straight answer, I was really happy that I didn't have to pretend with him anymore, and that perhaps I would be seeing you soon. I wrote you and all my letters came back. There were at least five of them. If you want, I'll show them to you. They're still sealed. I told you in these letters the same thing that I'm telling you now."

We rode up the canyon past the huge open-pit mine that was destroying one whole mountain and would probably start on another soon. We drove up to the tourist town of Retriever and into a road north and west of that town, one that was well graveled and which, after going over the mountains, led back to La Cueva.

We rode into the mountains for half an hour and the road seemed to go nowhere, although I had driven it before and knew that we would end up back home.

We came to a beautiful meadow and a brook meandering through it. It was called the Midnight Meadows. I stopped and parked the car near the stream. I rolled my window down and I could hear the water gurgling over its rocky bottom. There was a quiet that spoke only of an occasional insect flying and making winged noises. I could not help but notice the fluttering leaves of the quaking aspens. I had serious misgivings about being face to face with Belica. I was afraid of my own emotions and I realized I needed to control them by talking frankly to her. I faced Belica.

"What about the part where you and he were talking about getting married?"

She muttered something but I wanted to press an issue that was bothering me, even if answers turned to tragic results. I did not even hear her answer to the question. I thought of Lupe's suggestion that I mount her and show her who the man was, but I stayed my impulses to do that.

"I'm going to confess to you," I said, "that after seeing you yesterday I was willing to forgive and forget but then you pulled that stunt with the picture last night which has confused me all over again. Answer my question. What was that thing about marriage? Do you still have feelings for him? If you have been intimate with him, I do not want a part of you, even if it kills me. After all, I had nothing to do with that relationship. It was between the two of you. When I got your letter it almost destroyed me but I vowed to let you go, just to see you happy. Give me an answer to my question. I need to know and I promise that I will simply leave. I'll never see you again, I promise you," I said.

Belica lowered her head, big tears fell out of her eyes and she said nothing for a moment or two, but I waited. She started to speak, even though her voice was breaking.

"I have dreamed of your return and instead it has turned into a nightmare. I didn't even sleep last night. I was afraid that I had already lost you. I knew, this morning, that if I didn't come to see you that you would never come back to my house, I know you. That is why I showed up at your house this morning. I'm going to tell you something, Gibo, and you can believe me or not, but I swear by my church and God that I have never loved anyone but you. When you were gone for such long periods of time, I was so lonely that I asked God not to let me love you so much, but he didn't listen to me. Gibo, my girlfriends like you, but they tell me that you are a charmer, and that maybe you have girls in every town where you work. I ask them, do you mean a charmer like the one who charms snakes, like I've read about? They laugh at my stupid questions, but what they say makes me think, and you know what, I get jealous too, Gibo. I'm sorry for the letter, I'm sorry for the stupid picture, I'm sorry about making you angry and hurt. But let me tell you that I love you, that I have never been with a man and No, to all of your questions. My words about marriage, was a stupid girl's way of telling you that I missed you terribly and that you should come home. If I haven't been intimate with you, and it is you that I love, why would I be intimate with someone I just barely knew?"

I heard what my heart wanted to hear.

"Belica, when you touched my arm yesterday at the bank, you filled my heart with a joy that made me want to cry. Your touch brought me back to life, as if I had been dead and you woke me up to life again. When I die, it will be your face that I last see as I close my eyes. I love you Belica. Thank you for being honest with me. I'm sorry I stayed away so long. Let me go to school and I promise you that soon, real soon, I'm going to ask you to be my wife and the mother of my children."

She started to cry again, and this time I kissed her in

that desperate love that Lupe had talked about. I drank of her love and I wanted to kill her with my kisses. We sat there near that meadow for hours and promised each other that this was the start of a new love affair that would last us for a lifetime. I believed every word we said to each other that day and I kept seeing Belica every day until she went back to high school and I started my college classes.

The Golden Apples Of The Sun

.…and pluck til time
and times are done
  The silver apples of the moon
The Golden Apples of the sun
W.B. Yeats

Late August is a time of gathering in the valleys of northern New Mexico: The wood cutters, the piñon pickers, the alfalfa balers and the apple pluckers of Agua del Lobo up on the foothills of the San Cristobals. The honeybees had gathered their honey pollen and I had recovered my love. Life was good, it was purposeful and it was magical. Belica and I had re-ignited a relationship that had floundered and had almost been lost because of neglect and distance. I had come close to becoming the man that had gained a fortune and lost his soul, where all he had left were the tears of an old man.

I started my first year of college at St. Michael's in Santa Fe in September and Belica started on her senior year at La Villa High School. I made friends soon after starting there, I even met up with Hernan Gallegos, my colleague at Rowe. And because I wanted to finish the college requirements as soon as possible, I maximized my academic load. I enrolled for twenty one and twenty two hours, when the maximum allowable was eighteen hours. The college advisor cautioned me against this practice, but I assured him that entering college at my age, I must make haste. Belica and I saw each other every weekend, beginning on Friday night and ending on Sunday night. I focused totally on my studies during the remaining time at the college; the library was my home away from home. To relax, I exercised and either read the rich store of Spanish language books in the Spanish Library or visited the college chapel. This became my routine with the reward of being with my girl on the weekends.

The first full year at the college went without a glitch. I even managed to make the Dean's List during that time. Belica completed her high school diploma and we celebrated this event by attending a dance and having hamburgers at The Pig Stand. I thought back to my friends in Rush Center and The Dog's Tail. I told Belica about Ellie and Karl and she said she wanted to meet them some day. Belica's and my love seemed to grow stronger as we saw each other, as we grew older and as we completed one task (like her graduation) after another.

That summer she took a job at the courthouse and I stayed in school during the summer session. In August of that year, a full year after I had returned, I surprised her with a ring. It was time to begin to close the circle that had for so long eluded us. I vowed to make her happy and I was going to do whatever it took to keep her.

One Friday night, I got to her house a bit later than I usually did. I had held a wedding ring set on a lay-away at Gordon's Jewelry in Santa Fe and that day I took out the engagement ring and I brought the "promise" with me in a small ring box. We went out to La Villa for a while, went to a movie at the drive-in and when we got home that night while the lights were still on at her house I offered her the ring.

"Belica I got you a small gift, I hope that you accept it," I pulled the small box from the glove compartment and gave it to her. She opened it and she began to cry.

"I'm so happy, Gibo. I was beginning to wonder when this would happen," all the while looking at her ring. She kissed me three times rapidly and got out of the car.

"Come with me," she said as she came around to my side of the car. "I want to show my ring to my parents."

I was a bit uneasy but she was so exuberant that I relaxed.

"Look, Mom, Dad, look at my pretty ring. Gibo and I are engaged!"

I felt that I had to say something to break the silence.

"Belica and I have gone together for several years now. We love each other and it would be an honor for us to receive your blessings."

Her father's eyes watered and I knew that this event, for better or for worse, had struck a cord. Her mother simply said,

"That's a beautiful ring."

A month after our engagement, Flo and Beto announced that they planned a November wedding. This took everyone by surprise, but I was happy for my sister and I was getting into this family in more ways than one. Flo married Beto in November and they left to Santa Fe to work at the State Capitol. I visited with them once in a while but nothing would deter my trip north to see my betrothed. Flo and Beto's wedding was a simple affair. The reception took place in Embargo and relatives from both sides attended. Belica and I held on to each other as if the commotion would threaten our own closeness.

November rolled into Christmas. I took Belica to Santa Fe on Christmas Eve. I invited her to Midnight mass at the college chapel. This mass was a spiritual affair: The Christian Brothers sang the Mass in Gregorian

Chants, and the nativity scene had special significance in this place. The chapel, an old army barrack, was of a bare, high ceiling construction supported by dozens of four by six inch roof rafters. These gave the chapel a look of a manger or simply that of a barn. The effects of the lights, decorations, medieval chants, prayers and Belica by my side turned this into heaven on earth. As we left, around one o'clock in the morning I asked her to marry me.

"When?" she asked almost matter of fact. "

Let's get married in February, just before I return to school."

"Yes, yes Gibo, maybe we can get married here. This is such a lovely place." Belica spent the night at Beto and Flo's and I stayed at the college dorm, which was mostly empty for the holidays.

When Belica broke the news to her family, her mother objected to having the wedding outside her parish. I saw no problem to this and on February 4th, Belica Artiaga became Mrs. Gibo Herrera and I became her happy husband. We celebrated our wedding, much like Beto and Flo, but this time it was held at Belica's home in Arroyo del Hongo. Several of my friends from the college attended as well as a couple of my high school buddies. The Langes, from my childhood and John Wallace were there.

I had called the Dean at the college to tell him of my plans to marry during one of the first days of opening classes. He said,

"Mr. Herrera, the college usually grants our students one week off from classes for their wedding."

We took advantage of this and Belica and I went off to our honeymoon on the evening of our wedding. She was now my wife and my partner for life.

She was the goddess that I had always known that she would be. She was virtuous, if a bit awkward and we knew that we had the rest of our lives to get it right.

For a couple of days we visited my old railroad haunts. I told her of the feelings that I had left behind in each of these places: my thoughts about her, fears, and the yearning to return to her and to our home in the north. We treated ourselves to some of the nice places in the big city and we returned to Santa Fe and to an apartment in the same building as Beto and Flo's. This was the beginning of the rest of our lives together.

Time passed. I graduated from St Michael's College at the end of my third year there. We had now been married for a full year and a half. *Time had passed like the fleeting mists of spring, like the writings of the wind on a canvas of clouds.*

Where The Heart Is

After graduating from St. Michael's, I got a scholarship to pursue post-graduate studies at Arizona State University in Tempe. After a year there we moved to California to pursue my work. We had returned to a place that my wife had always liked and where she had spent a few years of her very young life. I was happy to be anywhere with her even if we both missed our families in northern New Mexico, a place we were able to visit only during our summer vacation.

Today, I am sitting in my study at home and I hear my two children playing and quarreling outside in the yard where their mother is knitting a pair of baby shoes. She calls to me from her chair,

"Gibo Honey, give me a hand with these kids, they keep fighting over some toys. Malo is acting like Malo today, he's making Berta upset again. I need for you to talk to him."

I walk out to where all my family is occupied with

one thing or another and she tells me,

"Babe, I'm getting so big, I've got to see the doctor on Monday. It will be April in three days, what if the baby is born on April the first, on April Fools Day?" She laughed.

"Well, then I'll name her Embel," I said, "She'll be my April Angel."

Printed in the United States
147839LV00001B/4/P

9 781438 925813